A SHADOW OF DOUBT

The sight of Jim's body had darkened Rita's mood even more than it already was. The autopsy apparently had had the same effect on Charlie. Outside the morgue, Rita noticed that he had a strange look on his face. He mumbled, "Paul did this on purpose, you know."

"I know," Rita answered.

"He played this big game like someone needed to be present for the autopsy, like there might be some hint of a homicide, and the only reason he really wanted us in there was because he knew we wouldn't believe it was suicide until we saw it with our own eyes. He could have sent someone else."

She didn't say anything. She could see Paul approaching. She thought he had probably heard what they had been talking about, at least the tail end of it.

Paul came right to the point. "I'm sorry. Yes, I sent you in there on purpose because I knew you'd be like me—unless you saw it for yourself, you wouldn't believe it. I'm sorry." That's all he said.

WITH EVIL INTENT

C. N. Bean

AN ONYX BOOK

ONYX
Published by the Penguin Group
Penguin Putnam Inc., 375 Hudson Street,
New York, New York 10014, U.S.A.
Penguin Books Ltd, 27 Wrights Lane,
London W8 5TZ, England
Penguin Books Australia Ltd, Ringwood,
Victoria, Australia
Penguin Books Canada Ltd, 10 Alcorn Avenue,
Toronto, Ontario, Canada M4V 3B2
Penguin Books (N.Z.) Ltd, 182–190 Wairau Road,
Auckland 10, New Zealand

Penguin Books Ltd, Registered Offices:
Harmondsworth, Middlesex, England

First published by Onyx, an imprint of Dutton NAL,
a member of Penguin Putnam Inc.

First Printing, February, 1999
10 9 8 7 6 5 4 3 2 1

PUBLISHER'S NOTE
This is a work of fiction. Names, characters, places, and incidents either are the product of the author's imagination or are used fictitiously, and any resemblance to actual persons, living or dead, events, or locales is entirely coincidental.

Dedicated to fsh

and three
angels

M.J.
Jessica Marie
Sarah Elizabeth

ACKNOWLEDGMENTS

Audrey LaFehr, as always, bless you.

I thank the Vermont Studio Center for a generous fellowship that made work on this project possible.

—Johnson, Vermont
1997

He lusts with lust all day long . . .
the sacrifice of the wicked is
hateful; how much more when
he brings it with evil intent.

—Proverbs
The Hebrew Bible

1

On a well-lighted wall were five rows of eight-by-ten photos. Captain Rita Trible of Wisconsin's Criminal Investigation Division (CID) was examing one in particular—Brittny Neuland, a ten-year-old Brookfield girl who had disappeared while walking to a friend's house. There had been a rash of missing children lately, which had her worried. One group in particular had their own row: Cassidy Schuck, M. J. Dunn, Michael Alderson, Jennifer Ladden, Beth Tuma, and Gemini Gold, all of Milwaukee. They were listed as too young to fit the usual profile. Something wasn't right . . .

The telephone rang, and Rita woke up. Despite looking around for it, she could not find the telephone. Someone handed it to her.

"Hello." Her mouth was dry. Her tongue tasted like stale alcohol; her head pounded. She had drunk too much. Deep inside her throat, she could feel the acids of heartburn churning.

The room was dark. She tried to focus her

eyes, but there was nothing to focus on except the telephone.

"Captain Trible?"

She didn't recognize the voice on the other end of the line. She raised her head to see the clock, but Mike had turned it so the light wouldn't shine in his eyes. All she could see was a red glow on the wall. "This is Rita Trible."

"This is Trooper Giles of the Wisconsin State Police at the capital. I'm sorry to bother you at this time of the night, but I'm patching through a call from Colonel Paul Clowers of the Criminal Investigation Division. Hold, please."

There were a couple of clicks, then a third click. "Rita?"

"Paul, what's wrong?" She got out of bed, carrying the portable phone, and went into the bathroom so she wouldn't wake Mike. She closed the bathroom door and turned on the light. The brightness made her shield her eyes with a hand.

"Jim Swearingen is dead."

"What?" She was instantly wide awake.

"Jim Swearingen is dead."

"Oh, God."

She could hear Mike calling from the bedroom: "Rita, that's wrong?"

In shock she opened the bathroom door and said, "Jim is dead."

Mike turned on the bedside lamp as he sat up in bed. "Swearingen?"

Paul told her, "Rita, I know this is coming as

a shock—it's a shock to all of us—but we have
to keep our heads together."

What was he talking about, "keep our heads
together"?

"It could get messy before it's all over. I need
you in Madison."

"What's going on?"

"I'm out at Lake Mendota. That's where they
found Jim. Two ice fishermen found his body."

She waited for what seemed an eternity while
her mind passed from shock to a bitter realization that what she was hearing was real. Jim
was dead. "Paul, what's going on?" she insisted.

"Two ice fishermen went to their shack on the
lake about two this morning"—Rita snapped her
fingers and pointed at the clock. Mike turned
it so she could see: 3:48—"and found a fishing
stringer secured to the wall of the shack. They
thought someone had been trespassing and had
been run off before he had had a chance to pull
up his stringer of fish."

Rita took a deep breath. She didn't want to
hear any more. Jim had been tortured, then
dumped in the lake. What kind of case had he
been working on? The last time she had talked
to him, she had asked him to help with the
Brittny Neuland investigation. That was nothing, a few routine inquiries. He hadn't mentioned any important investigation when she
had talked to him. He would have told her had
he been working on something major.

"When they pulled up the stringer, up came

his hands, wired to the stringer." Rita could hear Paul let out a breath. "That's when they noticed Jim's coat, folded, and his boots and socks near the door. There were also wire cutters with Jim's prints on them and a bundle of wire in a pocket of the coat. I hate to say this, but it looks like suicide."

Rita could feel a sickness welling deep inside, only this time the sickness was not from alcohol—she had sobered to the point that even the alcohol taste in her mouth was gone. "You don't really believe that, Paul," she said. "Jim would never do anything like that."

"He's been depressed, Rita. He's been seeing the police psychiatrist, you know."

No, she hadn't known. "I talked to him a couple of weeks ago." She tried to remember if there had been anything out of the ordinary then. "He was fine."

"Trust me, he was depressed." Then, "Rita, things like this happen, especially in our line of work. We're all under a lot of pressure."

She didn't know what to say. She still didn't believe Paul.

"Rita, I could use your help."

There was no hesitation. "I'll be there at five-thirty or so."

"They've scheduled the autopsy for seven. You'll be there for it, won't you?"

"Paul, I said I'd be there."

"You know Jim and I were always close. The

autopsy is something I can't face, but someone has to be there. It'd be better if it was one of us."

She sighed. "Paul, I'll be there."

She clicked off the portable phone and leaned on the edge of the sink, unable to move. Not even in her wildest imagination could she see Jim killing himself. It couldn't be true.

"Rita, are you all right?" Mike asked. He didn't ask what had happened, didn't pry, just asked if she was all right. She was glad that was all he asked. She didn't think he had heard enough to guess that suicide had been mentioned. If he hadn't guessed, she didn't want to tell him, didn't want anyone to think such a thing.

Mike hadn't known Jim all that long, but had taken to him from the first time they had met. It was a typical reaction with Jim. People liked him. That's how it had always been. She didn't want Mike to have any negative thoughts.

She brought out a travel bag and stopped long enough to kiss Mike. "That's nice of you to be so understanding," she told him. She tried to swallow the emotion inside her and be as calm as possible.

"Are you all right?" he asked again, putting on his glasses. He was growing a beard again; there was a lot of gray and white in it.

"Can you put on some coffee?" she said, not wanting to talk about how she felt at that moment. "What time did everybody leave last night? I was so exhausted, I fell right asleep."

"After midnight."

Maybe Jim had died while she was enjoying herself at the office Christmas party. She had invited everyone to the house, including members of the newly established child-abuse task force unit in Milwaukee. Paul had asked her to add the unit to her office after the Wisconsin legislature had passed a family-violence law, and she had had no alternative but to say yes. The task force was made up of social workers, medical personnel, sheriff's detectives, local and state police. So far there were twenty-six photographs of children on a lighted wall in the central briefing room at her Wisconsin Avenue office in downtown Milwaukee. It was more than she had bargained for. "What time did you come to bed? I don't remember you crawling in."

"After I cleaned up the mess. No, I don't think you would have remembered." He forced a smile. "Not in the condition you were in."

She glanced at him. Had she really been that bad? Her headache, dry mouth, and heartburn told her she had, but she wondered if it had been obvious to others. "You cleaned up?" She felt weak, as if she were trembling. She needed coffee.

"Take your shower."

She raised a hand to his tangled gray-brown hair. It was thick and didn't go back down after her hand came out. "I'll be done in a few minutes."

He put on a robe and slippers and left the room. She could hear his slippers on the hardwood floor in the hall.

She dialed Charlie Dalton's number and told him what had happened. He sounded as shocked as she had been. In a hushed tone she also told him what Paul had told her—it could be suicide.

He asked if he could go to Madison with her. He said he didn't believe for a moment it was suicide.

He was right. It would be better if she was with someone. She told him, yes, she could use his help. They agreed to meet at Shoney's in Delafield. They frequently had coffee there together. It's where she had met Mike.

She called Vince, her assistant at the office, as well. Jim and he had been partners in the early days. Vince took it hard, she could tell. She did what Paul had done to her—put a burden on him. She asked if he would run the office while she was away.

It was the least he could do, he told her. He seemed relieved to be offered a way to contribute. Friends were like that. They supported each other, no matter what. That's why she didn't believe Jim had committed suicide. He wouldn't burden his friends that way.

In the shower, she wept. Then she dried, dressed in blue jeans, a blouse, and a sport coat. She always wore jeans now. The children liked jeans. She combed the tangles out of her auburn hair, still damp. There was more gray in it with each passing day.

Mike was waiting with coffee for her. She looked around. Everything in the kitchen was spotless. He was that way. He didn't like anything to be out of place. "Can we sit by the tree for a few minutes?" she asked, taking a sip of the coffee. It was strong, not necessarily the way she wanted it, but probably the way she needed it.

They went into the living room, where she plugged in the Christmas tree. Red, yellow, green, blue, and orange miniature lights came on, throwing reflections on the shiny bulbs. She sat in her favorite rocker and tried to put on her socks and lace up her suede boots, but the rocker kept moving on her, making her dizzy, so she had to shift to the sofa. Her eyes kept coming back to the packages under the tree. There weren't many. She hadn't had time, and they couldn't afford a big Christmas anyway.

Mike's consolation was simple: "I'm sorry."

"Can you cut a grapefruit for Greg this morning?" She hated to ask him. Normally she got Greg set up for breakfast. Otherwise he wouldn't eat, and he had bad enough eating habits as it was. Now that he had turned fourteen, he ate a lot of junk food and skipped all kinds of meals. "That's why I don't like to have people over on a weeknight. I never get anything done. They shouldn't have stayed so late."

"Don't worry, I'll take care of it."

"That's all you have to do. He can make the rest of his breakfast himself."

"Okay." He yawned. "Nothing else?"

"There's hamburger in the refrigerator. I took it out of the freezer to thaw last night, so by the time you get home from work, it should be ready to cook. There's a can of Manwich in the cabinet. You can make sloppy joes. There's chips and buns in the pantry."

"I might take Greg out for supper."

She shook her head. "Mike, we can't afford that. We're minus four hundred dollars in our checking account right now. I'm only hoping we have that many secret dollars to cover the checks I've already written."

"Okay. I think I can figure out how to make supper. Remember, I had a life before you came along. Not much of one, but I had one."

She tried to smile, but it didn't feel right. "I don't know if I'll be able to make rehearsal tonight." She and he had volunteered to direct the Christmas play for their church, and since Mike had written the play, she knew how much it meant to him.

"Don't worry. We'll take care of things on this end."

"I'm pretty sure I'll be there for tomorrow's rehearsal. What time is it? Six-thirty to eight-thirty?"

"Why are you worrying about everything?"

She wasn't sure. The funeral arrangements. She didn't know when the funeral was. "I was thinking about what you told the children—how in order for something like this to work, everyone had to carry his or her own share."

"I think we can make an exception in this case."

"For sure, I'll be back for the Saturday afternoon practice." Jim would be buried by then. "And I wouldn't miss the performance on Saturday night for anything."

"Rita."

It was ten days before Christmas, and she was behind in everything. She hadn't even finished the Christmas shopping, though she didn't know where she was going to get the money they needed to have the kind of Christmas she wanted.

"Listen, I'll handle everything on this end. Don't you worry about a thing."

She stood. On the belt to her jeans she attached a holster that held her service weapon, a 9mm. She removed its ammo clip to make sure it was loaded. Into the inside pocket of her tweed blazer, she slipped her credentials. "I better kiss Greg good-bye." She knew she no longer kissed Greg before she left in the morning—these days Greg hated any kind of affection like that—but right now a kiss felt imperative.

She paused at Greg's door. She imagined Jim, neatly dressed, his salt-and-pepper mustache trimmed, a smile on his face. That was the Jim she remembered. She opened Greg's door, letting light into the room. A sour odor met her.

She saw its source. Greg's gym shoes, tied together, were hanging over the post of his bed. She thought of Jim's hands bound together.

There was an especially strong odor of perspiration in the room. Though she often emphasized to Greg that he was getting older and needed to wear deodorant, invariably he came home from basketball practice reeking of old sweat. She stared at him. He was growing up quickly, too quickly.

She gave him a peck on his warm forehead. He never stirred. He was taller than she was now and on the chunky side. She found tears slipping down her face. God, how am I going to get through this day? she wondered, wiping away the tears. She wanted to wake Greg up and hold him.

From behind her, Mike took her shoulders in his hands. He turned her gently, and she found her face in his chest. He pulled her into the hall, drawing Greg's door shut at the same time.

Through silent tears, she said, "Why did he have to die? And by drowning. He was so terrified of water."

Mike said, "When I was a kid, the man who lived in the house behind ours filled his bathtub with water, climbed in, and shot himself. Tom Walters was his name."

So Mike had heard enough to guess that suicide had been mentioned. "Jim would never kill himself."

He shrugged. "I've wondered all my life why

it happened and have never come up with a satisfactory answer."

She pulled herself away from Mike and went into the bathroom, where she got some tissues to blow her nose.

Mike stood in the bathroom doorway. "I'm sure Paul would understand if you told him this was too much."

"I'll be okay," she said, using the tissue to blot the moisture from around her eyes. She looked in the mirror to make sure her eyes didn't look like she had been crying. From a drawer, she brought out a bottle of eyedrops and put one drop in each cinnamon eye. She blinked several times and blotted her eyes again. She looked at Mike. "Does it look like I've been crying?" she asked.

"There's nothing wrong with crying when a friend dies."

She looked back at the mirror. "I've got to go." She gave him a hug, squeezed him tightly. It was the type of affectionate hug she'd given Jim back in the old days. And now she'd have to go view him laid out on a table. Dead.

2

From the passenger seat of her state sedan, Rita caught glimpses of the snow-covered lake through the trees. She flipped a page in her notebook and studied the notes she had made during the trip from Milwaukee. The lake was approximately six miles east to west and almost five miles north to south.

She opened a map of Madison. On the south shore of Lake Mendota was the University of Wisconsin campus. She made a small X where Jim lived. Her eyes passed along the edge of the lake in a counterclockwise fashion. On the east shore was the governor's mansion. North of it was the Mendota Mental Health Institute. On the west side was Governor Nelson State Park, near which she placed an X to mark the spot where Jim's body had been recovered. Strangely enough, his body had been found on state property. The ice fishermen had their shack within the bounds of the park.

When Charlie turned into the snow-blanketed park, Rita experienced both a numbness and a hollow feeling. The snow was pristine. She should have been drawn to its beauty, but the whole setting reminded her of Matthew Hammond, Laurence Cassell, and Kyle Wishause, the three boys whose mutilated bodies had been found in state parks in the Milwaukee area. That investigation would forever haunt her. It especially troubled her when she thought about Greg, who had almost become the fourth victim. Looking out the window, she experienced the full horror of the past once again. A little voice inside told her to be careful. The case, involving an insanely vindictive ex-husband, had intentionally targeted state parks too—to become dumping grounds for his victims in order to make sure she would have jurisdiction in the investigation.

She noticed that Charlie's black fingers were pounding the dash.

She wondered if he was bothered by the same feelings that were troubling her. He wasn't a nervous man, and yet he was tapping the dash incessantly. She didn't think he realized it.

"Charlie, do you mind?"

He looked over, then realized what he was talking about. His fingers came to the steering wheel. Then there was only the sound of the traffic on the police radio.

Charlie didn't look at her as he said, "I know you're going to think this is strange for a grown man, but when we get to the lake, you think I might be able to search along the shore while you go out on the ice?"

She didn't say anything right away, perhaps because his comment had caught her so off guard. She had expected him to be thinking the same thing she was thinking—about their previous experiences with murders at state parks.

In the parking lot were various police vehicles. Uniformed officers were milling about, drinking coffee and talking. She could tell the officers were cold because they kept their feet moving. Two or three of the officers were even stomping their feet. Near the parking lot, yellow tape stretched along the beach of the park. Out on the frozen lake was a wood shack. A well-worn path stretched from the beach to the shack.

She said, "Talk to me, Charlie. What's the problem?"

He stopped the car. Still not looking at her, he confessed, "I don't like water."

She looked out the window. It was a bleak December morning. Not a day for a friend to be pulled from an iced-over lake. "You don't know how to swim, do you?" She loved to swim and could tell when someone was afraid of water.

"No."

"Jim didn't know how either." She could feel Charlie looking at her.

He told her that neither he nor Claudia, his wife, had ever learned. "Keisha's getting lessons. She can swim like a fish, but the two of us can't." Then, "Jim couldn't swim?"

"No."

"That's what I mean. This isn't any suicide."

She ignored the comment. "Okay, you search along the shore of the lake."

He released his foot from the brake. The car began moving again to a parking spot. "Thanks."

"Walk a half mile or so in each direction. Look for anything out of the ordinary—shoe impressions, anything that might have been discarded, any evidence to suggest that someone might have been keeping an eye on the shack. There must be something. Jim was out here for some reason." She nodded toward the shack. "I'll go out and look around, though I doubt I'll find much now that everyone's trampled all over the place."

Just then Paul Clowers opened the back door and got in the car, bringing in a rush of cold. He slammed the door.

Rita turned the heater fan on high, filling the car with warm air again.

Paul said, "I might as well come right to the point. As I explained on the phone, this has the potential to turn messy. Rita, I already asked you, but I might as well ask you too, Charlie. I know you both have your own assignments and caseloads, but I need someone to ride shotgun on this incident so it doesn't blow up in our faces."

What did he mean, "blow up in our faces"? she wondered. He kept talking in riddles.

"You might as well know—you're going to find out sooner or later anyway—the state attorney general has been investigating Jim."

The car was silent except for the noise of the heater running and the police radio. She turned both off, then the silence closed in on her.

"I'm sorry to have to tell you two this, but Jim had a mess on his hands."

She glanced at Charlie. He looked like someone had knocked the breath out of him.

"I don't have a lot of details," Paul continued, "because the attorney general's office has been hush-hush about it all, but I do know it has something to do with Jim's ex-wife, Diane. She's Diane Hoeveler now, you know."

Jim had been with a lot of women in the years Rita had known him, but Diane was the only one he had ever married. They had stayed married for only six months. Jim was that way—couldn't live with anyone. Rita thought it had something to do with Vietnam. The war had messed him up in certain ways.

"It's really too bad because I always thought Diane was a nice woman, but she got herself hooked up with the wrong man, Al Hoeveler, a Milwaukee contractor. Bad news. In and out of jail. I always thought she could do better. Anyway, he's involved in local organized crime over in Milwaukee and was supposedly tied in to a murder the feds were investigating down in

Chicago. I don't know the story from there. Either Jim tampered with some evidence, or he destroyed some evidence in order to protect Diane from becoming implicated. Anyway, he really pissed off the FBI and U.S. attorney over there. The state attorney general has been collecting evidence to take to a secret grand jury." Paul looked at her. "I'm not surprised you haven't heard any of this because I'm only just now learning about it myself."

Charlie admitted he had heard some rumors about some kind of rift between federal officials and local authorities in Milwaukee, but would have never guessed it had any negative ties to Jim.

"That's the case I'm talking about," Paul commented. "They were going to put pressure on Al Hoeveler and get him to talk, but Jim stepped in and screwed up the investigation the feds had going."

"I guess I got a slightly different version from the one you got," Charlie told him.

"What version did you get?" Rita asked him. "Am I the only one who hasn't heard any version at all?"

Charlie said, "I've been on the streets. With that new children's unit, you've been tied up quite a bit."

"What do you know, Charlie?" she asked.

He didn't respond right away.

"You do know something, something that involves Jim, don't you?"

"Nothing negative, like I said. I heard Jim was trying to help out an old friend of his, the civil rights activist, J. D. Grove."

She knew that Jim and J.D. had been in 'Nam together, but she had never understood why Jim had maintained ties with J.D. after that. J.D. had a reputation for being a hothead. Most recently, he had been arrested for burning a stack of automobile tires in the backyard of his Milwaukee home in order to defy city ordinances that prohibited the burning of refuse. He had done it to call attention to all the local companies whose smokestacks routinely polluted the atmosphere.

Charlie said, "I admit J.D. gets carried away at times, but he says some sensible things too, and he's built a pretty good following."

She asked, "How was Jim trying to help J.D.?"

"It had something to do with all the hell J.D.'s been raising about that new hospital NationsCare of America wants to build down in his neighborhood."

She knew something of that battle, at least. NCA was a chain of hospitals that was quickly becoming the largest and most powerful private chain in the United States, taking the place of the embattled Columbia chain.

"It's a 'super' hospital being billed as one of the premier heart centers and transplant centers in the world."

Rita said, "Charlie, we all know about the hospital. What does this have to do with Jim?"

"You may have heard some of this, but what you haven't heard is that NCA's big cheese, Chad Whitaker, says he won't build in Milwaukee unless he gets full cooperation from the city. He has the city council running this way and that because council members are afraid they're going to scare him off if they're not careful."

Charlie glanced over at her. "This isn't really public information yet, but blacks who live in the area where Whitaker wants to build know what's happening and are trying to stir up opposition to the project. A lot of rumors are flying. Whitaker himself says all he's trying to do is clean up the neighborhood because it's the only way a major hospital complex can take off in that particular district of the city."

Rica said, "And J.D. Grove is leading the fight against the project."

Charlie nodded. "You got it," he replied. "J.D. is positioning himself for a fight, and I guess that's causing quite a stir. The feds have moved in to get him, but some of the local police are giving him protection." He glanced at her. "He's got friends, you know. I heard Jim was one of the people looking out for J.D."

Rita scribbled notes in her notebook. "Which means the feds would be out to compromise Jim for just about anything."

Paul said, "That only confirms what I already suspected. This thing has the potential to turn into a major scandal, and we need to keep a lid on it."

Charlie did a drumroll with his fingers on the dash in front of him. She knew he wasn't someone who liked to sit around for too long. "Let's take a look at where they found Jim's body," she said. She and Charlie each took a portable radio from a battery charger plugged into the cigarette lighter.

Paul said he was going back to the office. "I'll see you after the autopsy."

Once she had put on the old fishing jacket that had belonged to her father—she barely got it on over her winter coat—she and Charlie went their separate ways.

She walked through the icy cold to where the police officers were milling about. She passed under the yellow police tape that stretched across the perimeter of the crime scene. Feet had tromped a number of paths out onto the lake. She passed the uniformed officers. They watched her, but no one said anything.

The temperature was probably in the teens, but with the wind blowing, the windchill was closer to zero. She could tell by the way her lungs felt. Wind whipped ice crystals up off of the snow, which was more of a hard shell than a soft blanket. It crunched as she walked across it, out to the shack.

A uniformed officer guarding the shack handed her a battery-operated lantern. With it lighted, she went into the shack, which smelled of the bales of hay lining the inside walls. The hay kept the wind from sweeping underneath the walls.

The physical evidence had been packaged and taken away. She hoped good crime-scene procedure had been followed, especially that the scene had been photographed before anyone had touched anything. She also hoped someone had drawn sketches. If everyone had assumed the death was a suicide and not a possible homicide, they might not have followed careful procedure.

She closed the shack door and turned off the lantern. From a pocket in her fishing jacket, she brought out a small light that had an ultraviolet bulb. With it lit, she examined the interior of the shack for any trace evidence that might have been missed during the previous searches. She found nothing out of the ordinary, nothing to suggest foul play.

As she stepped back out in the cold again, her handset crackled. "Rita—"

She pressed the button on the side of the handset. "Yeah, Charlie—" Her eyes scanned the shore, looking for him.

"Look to your left—at the embankment."

There he was, waving. "I see you," she said. He was standing at some trees whose naked branches were crusted with snow. The embankment hid him from the waist down.

"I think you better get over here."

She returned to shore and found him.

Near where he stood was an area of packed snow. She put on her bifocals and brought out a camera from one of the pockets of her fishing jacket. The snow appeared to have been packed down by a single pair of boots.

While she took photographs, he held a tape measure to mark the length and width of one of the most distinct impressions. He commented, "These are relatively recent—at least since the last snow."

Using her radio, she called for a forensic team. She also requested that the radio dispatcher get in touch with the local weather service. "I want to know the weather conditions for the past ten days, the snowfall, temperatures, et cetera."

She was encouraged by the find. Why would someone walk out this way? It was too far from the lake for fishing, and the way the snow had been packed down by a single set of shoe impressions left little doubt that someone had spent a significant amount of time here.

She headed for the road to show the forensic team the way in. When she came out of the trees, the wind lashed her face. She could feel the tops of her ears getting cold. She took off the black leather glove of one hand and cupped her hand over her ear. Then she turned her head and cupped the same hand over her other ear. Was it Jim? Had he been watching the shack? Why? What had been going on out there?

At the road, she stomped her boots, knocking

off the snow and ice. Her toes were cold. It wouldn't take long to get frostbitten, she knew.

Charlie joined her. "It was Jim," he told her. "He was watching someone, and whoever it was found out. Someone killed him and dumped him in the water."

If that were the case, there would be other evidence. "Paul wants me to handle the autopsy," she mentioned. "You want to tag along?"

"Fine. We'll do the autopsy, then we'll talk to those fishermen who found him. If you ask me, we're on to something. Come on, two fisherman go out in the middle of the night and pull up a dead body? What's the chances of that happening? There's something going on here."

A single forensic specialist arrived, which got Charlie upset. "They only sent you? Where's everyone else?"

The specialist shrugged. "I was the only one they left at the scene. I've been sitting here for the last several hours waiting for permission to go back to the lab."

Charlie told him what he had found and pointed out the area the specialist was to process for evidence. The specialist didn't seem enthusiastic. A drowning that looked like a suicide was not an exciting case, he said.

"Come on," Rita said. "Let's see if the autopsy will tell us anything."

3

In all the years that had passed, Mike was the only person she had ever told about the time she had seen Jim Swearingen almost drown. She, Paul Clowers, Jim, and a young woman named Patti had been at a law enforcement convention down in Tennessee, and all of them had gone out to a lake to swim. It was during July, hot and humid. On the path to the lake, Patti made a comment about Jim's smoking. That was after he had come back from Vietnam; he smoked a lot then. She asked him if there was ever a time when he didn't have a cigarette in his mouth. Jim chuckled. Patti said, "I bet you have a cigarette in your mouth even when you make love." He laughed at that too and said, no, he had never tried making love and smoking a cigarette at the same time. He asked her if she was volunteering to give it a try with him. Patti said, "No, thank you," and asked if that was all he ever thought about—sex and cigarettes. No, he told her, laughing, he thought about booze too.

At the rocks overlooking the lake, Rita watched Jim watch Patti take off the towel she had wrapped around her waist. Patti had large breasts that were contained by the one-piece white suit she wore, and Rita could tell by Jim's eyes that he liked the rest of Patti's tanned body as well.

In bare feet, after stripping, they all walked gingerly down to the dock. The gray wood was hot. Without testing the water, Patti asked Jim if he wanted to race to the raft. The raft was out a hundred yards or so, floating lopsided on barrels. No, Jim said, he wanted to finish his cigarette first. Patti asked Paul if he wanted to race.

The two of them dove into the lake and began swimming. They swam hard. Their voices were loud. They were yelling and laughing as they swam. Their voices echoed across the lake.

Rita dove in herself. Treading water, she looked back at Jim. He was pale, standing on the dock, wearing only his tight red jockey shorts—he hadn't brought a suit—with a cigarette in his mouth. "Come on in," she called back. "The water's great. You won't believe how nice it is."

"Go ahead. I'll catch up with you."

Rita swam toward the raft. She was in no hurry, not like Patti and Paul. She looked back to see Jim dive off the dock. It wasn't a graceful dive, but it wasn't a bad one either. Next thing she knew, his arms were flailing. His body, which looked like he was trying to stand, sank. Then all she could see were his arms and hands. They were thrashing the water. She started back. She swam fast, but by the time she got there, one of his hands—his head was still underwater—caught the ladder of the dock. In an instant Jim pulled himself out of the lake, water gushing off of him, grabbed a cigarette, lit it, and hurried into the woods.

"Did Paul see?" Charlie asked now that Rita was telling him the story also.

"He was too busy racing Patti," Rita told him.

"So Jim couldn't swim. Why in the hell did he dive in if he couldn't swim?"

Rita and Charlie were waiting for the medical examiner to open the autopsy room. She said, "The only thing I could figure was that he thought the water was shallow, and all he had to do was stand up once he dove in."

Charlie shook his head. "Um, um, um."

"I bet it was twenty feet deep right at the dock." She took a deep breath. "It's scary it should end like this." She looked down at the polished floor.

The door to the autopsy room opened from the inside. Dr. Clyde Jenkins, the medical examiner, said, "Morning." He looked like he had just gotten out of the shower. His thinning gray hair was slicked back, and his mustache was neatly trimmed and combed. Rita had worked with him a few times over the years, but never had she thought she'd have to watch him perform an autopsy on one of her friends. Clyde introduced his assistant, a graduate student in biology at the University of Wisconsin.

Jim lay on a stainless-steel table. His empty eyes were slightly open and filled with the dry, drugged look of death. His hands were bound loosely in front with wire, as were his feet, at the ankles. A foamy mass protruded from his mouth and nostrils, a classic sign of drowning. ". . . forty-three-year-old white male, pulled from Lake Mendota . . ." Clyde had wasted no time in beginning to dictate his report.

Rita stared at Jim's face. The foam of edema and mucus that bulged from his nostrils and mouth looked like thick suds in a drain after too much detergent had been used to wash dishes. Yes, the foam might have been the result of strangulation, she knew. Victims of strangulation often foamed at the nose and mouth as they struggled to get oxygen. But there were no signs of strangulation. No marks on the neck. And there was every sign Jim had been alive when he had gone into the icy water. His skin still had gooseflesh, the kind of gooseflesh that clings to a person who has drowned in cold water. And his face, neck, and chest were bright pink from exposure, at least to where the collar of his soggy shirt was open.

Jim had drowned, no doubt about it. In her

more than twenty years with the state police, she had seen enough drowned bodies to know what one looked like. She had also seen enough suicides to recognize one. She looked around at the morgue, feeling sick to her stomach. She had hoped to see some obvious sign of foul play. The hands and feet were crudely wired. He could have done that himself.

The morgue was in the basement of the state health department complex in Madison. The walls were of large green hospital tile, and the polished floors were granite. The tan floors, shiny under the fluorescent lights, didn't match the green of the wall tiles, but it wasn't the kind of place one would have expected to find coordinated colors.

Off to one side of the large room was an X-ray table, and a shield for the medical examiner to stand behind when he or she X-rayed a body. Not much else except a tray of medical instruments and the central table upon which Jim lay, still dressed except for boots and socks. No suicide note, the examiner was saying, but purposeful actions, such as the coat, boots, and socks that had been neatly left near where the body had been retrieved. The wire in the coat pocket.

Oddly enough, despite the foam bulging from his nostrils and mouth, there was an otherwise calm expression on Jim's face. One of the curious idiosyncrasies of drowning. She had read cases of near-death drowning experiences. Although there was no concensus, there was some evidence to suggest that at some point the drowning victim relinquished any thought of being rescued and stopped struggling. Still alive, the victim no longer experienced the physical distress of drowning, and escaped into the pure thoughts of past experiences, not resigned to death but apathetic toward the inevitable.

Rita listened to Clyde tell his assistant, ". . . it's usually not much of a challenge to say whether someone was alive or dead at the time of submersion. This person was alive. The difficult task is saying whether the drowning was suicide, accidental, or homicide." Clyde's eyes studied Jim.

Had he seen something she hadn't seen? she wondered, suddenly interested again. What did he mean, "accidental or homicide"?

"Take Jim, for example"—Clyde pointed at the wrists and ankles that had been bound with wire—"It's not unheard of for someone who wants to commit suicide to bind his or her wrists and feet, even to tie a weight on to hold himself or herself underwater. Most people who really want to commit suicide know there's going to be a last-minute struggle for survival, and those who are serious about dying don't want to survive at the last moment, or at least want to know it's hopeless to struggle.

"The odd thing in this case, though, is the wire. I'd say that's highly irregular. But I suppose Jim would have known that wire was a restraint he wouldn't be able to break or work out of."

She and Charlie began to do what they were accustomed to doing. They collected physical evidence. She took fingernail scrapings and clippings, he took fingerprints from Jim's sodden, wrinkled hands, and she took hair samples. They worked meticulously. It didn't help. She kept thinking about what had happened. The wire bothered her. Despite what Clyde had said, the wire didn't make sense. Why not handcuffs? Jim was a cop. He would have known that no amount of struggle could have broken a pair of handcuffs.

Clyde continued to talk to his assistant: "Of course, the majority of drowning deaths are accidental. Next, I would say suicide is the second most common type. Last is homicide. I mean, think how hard it would be to drown a grown man. And in this case Jim is a trained law enforcement officer. It wouldn't be easy to hold him underwater." Glancing at her, he smiled. "I've played tennis with Jim. He was a tough little bastard. Never wore down."

Rita's eyes went back to the wire wrappings on Jim's wrists. It was true, the Jim she had known wouldn't have gone easily. In her notebook she began to sketch the wrappings. They were crude. That kept bothering her. Jim could have easily done them himself.

A police photographer arrived. Rita had him take numerous photographs of the ligature and marks. Then she took her own photographs. She had always said that film in a death investigation was the cheapest investment an investigator could make. After all, there was no way to bring back the body, and a photograph was a good way to preserve a lost moment.

Charlie commented, "Doesn't it strike anyone as being odd that whoever wrapped the ligature was an amateur, not a professional?"

Rita thought it was a good point. She said, "If you look closely, there is some evidence of struggle." Up close, the ligature marks were deeper than they appeared from the distance. The skin had actually been torn by the wire. Not a violent struggle, but nevertheless, a struggle. Cutting distally from any binds, she removed the ligature on his wrists and packaged it as evidence. All the while she wished there really was something no one could see, some rational explanation for what had happened, such as that Jim really had been drugged. She kept telling herself that the Jim she knew would never commit suicide, and he certainly wouldn't have done it by drowning himself. Jumping into an icy lake would have been the last option he would have chosen as a way of dying.

Clyde, talking while he cut, shook his head. "No," he said, "I've seen cases in which parents have drowned children in bathtubs. I've even had a case in which a parent held a baby under a running faucet, drowning her, but unfortunately this isn't that kind of thing." He looked at her, then at Charlie. "I don't want to face this any more than either of you do. Everyone around here liked Jim."

In a precise, methodical process—sketching what she saw, having the photographer take photographs, taking her own photographs, writing notes, and packaging the evidence—she removed the ankle ligatures.

Then together she and Charlie undressed Jim, removing his clothing piece by piece, carefully moving the body this way and that, so that the clothing remained in tact.

Jim's penis was semi-erect.

Clyde said, "Whoa, he's still alive!" and laughed.

Charlie laughed too. "Wild man!"

The men roared with laughter.

She commented, "It must be a guy thing." It was the kind of thing she was accustomed to hearing during an autopsy. An autopsy often became an occasion for anecdotes, jokes, and a lot of bantering. It was a way of escaping the ugliness. She searched the pockets of Jim's clothes. "Where are the personal effects?" she asked.

Clyde shrugged. "I didn't take them. As far as I know, no one did. A uniformed officer rode with the body."

"No wallet, car keys, or anything?"

Clyde's face brightened. "Yes, there was a set of keys. Tucked inside the boots. Probably his house and car keys. As far as I know, that was the only personal effect there was—a set of keys."

Jim did a lot of jogging and hiking. The park was thirty minutes from where he lived. He could have been out for a walk. Possible, but not likely, she thought.

Clyde seemed impatient to begin his work. His job wasn't cars, or keys, or personal effects. Rubbing his hands together as if they were cold, he commented to his assistant, "Actually, it's not unusual for a man to have an erection or at least a partial erection when he drowns."

Rita marked bags of evidence, still a bit perplexed about the absence of a wallet and other items one routinely kept in one's pockets. She thought of Greg, her son. Whenever she washed his laundry, she invariably found gum wrappers, loose change, and notes in his pockets. Even on a walk, it was odd Jim hadn't been carrying any personal effects other than his keys. What about his police credentials? Not even a wallet?

Clyde began to take physical measurements. At the same time he studied the body externally, from head to foot. He was thorough. She knew that was his reputation. After opening the body, he lifted each organ and turned it this way and that. "I'll be checking for drugs and poisons," he said, then held the stomach over a stainless-steel bowl, where he punctured it. Greenish-yellow bile gushed into the bowl. It smelled like fresh vomit.

She was relieved he did that. There had to be something, some clue.

Parts of Jim's body were piling up near Clyde. A syringe in hand, Clyde said to his assistant, "I'm withdrawing ten milliliters of blood from the right and left chambers of the heart. I want to check the sodium chloride levels. A good test to establish a drowning diagnosis. I'll check for microorganisms from the lake also. There'll be some in the stomach contents since he swallowed quite a bit of water."

She watched him work, trying to think if they were missing anything. There were different ways to cut apart a body, she knew, no set agenda. Depending on who did the cutting.

Charlie told Clyde, "When I was in the army and stationed at Fort Rucker, Alabama, there was a young soldier whom everyone thought had drowned."

Rita looked at him as if he might be trying to say that he had noticed something odd about Jim.

"Divers searched for hours for the victim's body. They eventually found it at around midnight. It was a few feet from where the soldier had dove off a dock. He had none of the usual drowning symptoms. Apparently he had hit his head on the dock when he was coming up and had reached out from something to grab on to, and his hand had caught some electrical wiring for the lights of the dock. He was electrocuted. Didn't drown at all. Simply hit his head and freaked."

"Actually, that happens quite a bit," Clyde mentioned. "Head injuries are not uncommon in drownings. And you know what else is typical?"

They looked at him.

"The victims of accidental drownings are usually adult males." He smiled. "I guess men show off more and end up doing stupid things like hitting their heads on docks, or diving into places they shouldn't dive."

She thought of the time Jim had almost drowned. She asked Clyde, "Do you know if anyone took samples of the water from which Jim was taken?"

Clyde began to remove Jim's scalp, cutting it away. "Of course someone took samples. I took them personally."

She doubted that Clyde would ever miss anything related to his work. "I figured as much, but I thought I'd ask."

As he pulled back the scalp, Clyde told his assistant he was examining it for any evidence of bruising that might be inside the scalp but not outside. Then, "I know no one wants this to be a suicide," he mentioned to no one in particular, "but it keeps pointing in that direction."

"He might have been drugged," she repeated what had been mentioned earlier.

Clyde nodded. "Which is why I took the

stomach contents and blood samples. I'm keeping the liver too. I'll keep the brain, just in case." He sawed open the skull, exposing Jim's brain. "Believe me, if there's something amiss, I'll find it. I liked Jim too, and I know you don't want it to be a suicide. No one ever wants it to be that. But do you know something? It's not that unusual for a police officer to commit suicide. They live under a lot of stress. Sometimes stress can drive a person to do things that are totally uncharacteristic for that person."

Paul had said the same thing. So had Mike.

Outside the morgue, Rita noticed that Charlie had a strange look on his face. She patted his shoulder with an open hand.

He mumbled, "Paul did this on purpose, you know."

"What do you mean?"

"He knew we wouldn't believe it looked like a suicide unless we went in there and saw it for ourselves."

She didn't say anything. She could see Paul approaching. She thought he had probably heard what Charlie had said.

There was a slight stubble growing on his gaunt face, and his black hair was going every which way. He still hadn't showered or shaved. She could also tell by the strained expression on his face that he had been crying.

Paul came right to the point. "I'm sorry. Yes,

I sent you in there on purpose because I knew you'd be like me—unless you saw it for yourselves, you wouldn't believe it. I'm sorry." That's all he said.

4

The sight of Jim's body had made Rita's mood even more somber than it already was. All she wanted was to find something that would shed light on what had happened to him. She would interview the two fishermen. Maybe they would know something. She would look around in Jim's house. Maybe there would be a clue there. Of course, the timing was awful. There would be the funeral, then there would be the Christmas play on Saturday. Then Christmas. A lot was going on.

The autopsy apparently had had the same effect on Charlie. He said he was ready to get down to work. "We should be able to find something, don't you think?" His voice didn't sound sure of itself. On their way to interview the fishermen, he finally asked what she had been waiting for him to ask, "If by some chance Jim committed suicide, and I still don't think he did, why do you think he would do it?"

She said she didn't know. If it were true, the only thing she could think of was that it had something to do with Vietnam. "We all have ghosts in our past." She had been trying to put Jim's past together all morning. "Maybe he accidently killed a civilian in Vietnam, or something. Maybe a child. Or maybe he saw children killed." She didn't know why she said that. The night before, she had had a nightmare about the twenty-six photographs hanging on the wall in her offices back in Milwaukee. She shook her head. "I don't know." Driving, she glanced at Charlie. "We're beginning to sound like the others. I still don't believe Jim would kill himself."

All he said was, "Neither do I."

He said that as they parallel-parked in front of Bill's Seafood and Raw Bar near the University of Wisconsin campus. It was where one of the fishermen worked, Scott Renneker. He tended bar.

They didn't bother him right away since it was the lunch hour. The restaurant, especially the bar, was packed with customers, even at eleven-thirty.

Besides, she wanted to watch him, and as she did so, she was struck by how oblivious Scott seemed to be to the ordeal he had been through the night before. An oversize youth in his late twenties, he wore a heavily starched white shirt, navy tie, and off-white jeans that were so tight the corkscrew in his back left pocket looked like it might pop through the material at any moment.

While Scott laughed and joked with various customers at the bar, Rita and Charlie sat at the last two empty bar stools and looked at menus. Not once did Scott mention the drowned man he and his uncle had found the night before. Odd.

Pretending to read her menu, Rita caught a part of a conversation Scott was having with a man at the end of the bar, ". . . believe me, at that age they all look the same. Boy or girl, when she or he bends over it all looks the same to me."

Scott and the other man laughed.

Had he told anyone at all? she wondered.

As Scott made his way toward her and Charlie, he stopped in front of a woman who wore a blue flowered blouse and dark suit. "How about a nice red wine to go with that, Mrs. Onstad?"

She nodded, and he removed the corkscrew from his back pocket long enough to open a bottle of red wine.

For a sallow-looking man beside her, Scott made a martini on the rocks. He was very skilled at keeping everyone at the bar satisfied.

Before long he asked Rita and Charlie if they wanted anything to drink. She ordered a glass of sparkling water with a squeeze of lemon in it. Charlie ordered a Coke. They placed their food orders too. She got the smoked roast beef hoagie topped with fried oysters; he the lunch special, fish and chips.

A customer near the Coke dispenser asked Scott if he had watched *Seinfeld* the night before. Scott said, no, he hadn't watched television. He and his wife had been installing a wax seal on a toilet.

The customer commented, "I didn't know there was a wax seal on a toilet. Where?"

Scott explained that when a toilet was installed, the bowl seated on a gasket that kept the wastes and water from running out on the floor.

Someone else told Scott not to be so gross while people were eating, and several customers laughed. Scott apparently knew them all.

Mrs. Onstad called from across the bar, "Scott, we're sure happy you're working here now instead of Wayne." Several customers nodded.

It was one-thirty before the bar cleared out enough for Rita and Charlie to talk to Scott. When she showed him her credentials, he turned a pasty color. "I had no idea you two were cops," he said. He asked one of the waiters to take over the bar, then took Rita and Charlie to a booth.

Charlie started off, "I didn't know you were married, Scott."

Scott still had not gotten back his full color. He sat on the edge of his seat across the table from them. He wasn't married, he said. "It's all a persona. They expect you to be a certain way, and you learn to play the game. You have to be who they want you to be."

"Then the story about you installing a toilet last night isn't true either, is it?" she said.

"A good bartender knows how to make conversation," he told her. "No, I wasn't installing a toilet. But you already know that."

"I understand you're living with your uncle and aunt," Charlie said. "Richard and Pat Spiker. Isn't that your aunt and uncle?"

Still sitting on the edge of his seat, his back straight, Scott answered, "That's right. Pat's my mother's sister."

"How long have you been living with them?"

"A couple of months."

Rita asked, "Where did you come from?"

Scott sat back and folded his arms across his chest. "Wait a minute. Why are you asking all these questions about me? I wasn't the one who killed myself."

"Who said anything about someone killing himself?" Rita asked.

Scott smiled and said, "That's funny, it was what everyone was saying last night." He finally had his color back. "I've been keeping my mouth shut today because they said he was a cop, and I know how embarrassing that is, especially to learn that a cop, a pillar of society, couldn't handle the pressure. Everyone was saying last night it was suicide."

Something about him she didn't like. She thought it was his smugness. Or the fact that she had met too many Scotts in bars over the years. A consummate actor. Probably the kind of person who capitalized on any information he learned during the inebriated states of his customers. Those secrets became his power. Rita had seen several of the people leave ten dollars or more for tips during the lunch hour. People here liked him.

Charlie told him, "We're just trying to put a few details together, and we were hoping you might be the kind of person who'd be willing to cooperate as much as possible."

Scott sat forward, his back arched, his hands in his lap again. "Sure. Look, my uncle's an alcoholic, and I promised my aunt I'd look after him. He's a sports nut and likes to spend a lot of time doing things like hunting and fishing. Mostly I think things like fishing trips give him excuses to get out of the house and drink, but I don't let on to Aunt Pat about that. I've been going ice fishing with him after I get off work at night, and basically he sits out in his shack and drinks bourbon all night. That's what we were doing last night—the same thing we do every night.

"Of course, I was as surprised as anyone when we found the body of that cop who killed himself, but believe me, I know from experience that the world is full of people with problems. I've stood across from people who sit and drink all night, then climb in a car and end up killing someone. I've talked to wives who are cheating on their husbands, and husbands who are cheating on their wives. I've met alcoholics, drug users, thieves, robbers, prostitutes, even people who talk to me about killing themselves." He shrugged. "You name it, I've met that person. So I guess I'm not totally shocked about last night. Surprised, yes; shocked, no. But I still try to respect the guy. He was a human being, and I've been around enough people to learn to respect them. What, did you two know him personally?"

They didn't say.

He went on to describe the events of the night before. As he had told the police on the scene, his uncle Rich had invited him ice fishing and they had gone out to the lake. They had parked at the entrance because the park was closed. "Uncle Rich had a couple healthy bourbon and waters"—he used his hands to illustrate how big the glasses were—"and we talked for a while before walking into the park and out to the lake."

"You left your vehicle at the entrance to the park?" Charlie asked.

"That's right. Rich said that's where he always parked. He said the police didn't do anything because everyone knew people went in and fished at night."

Rita asked, "Were there any other cars or trucks parked there or nearby?"

Scott thought for a moment. He thought there might have been a van parked nearby, but he wasn't positive if it had been that night or another night. "I go out there all the time with him. I'm his designated driver once he gets soused."

"Did you see anyone else out on the lake or along the shore? Lights or anything?"

"There were one or two lights along the shore, but I didn't pay that much attention."

"What happened once you got out to the shack?" Charlie asked.

"We got out there, and no sooner were we getting settled than Uncle Rich pointed to his fishing stringer and mentioned that he couldn't remember leaving it in the water. He laughed and said maybe someone had been fishing in his shack and had borrowed the stringer."

"So, what happened then?" Rita asked.

"Naturally he was just joking, but when Uncle Rich pulled up the stringer—he's a husky man, like a logger—we see human hands. That's when we also noticed for the first time the shoes, coat, and so on stacked beside the door of the shack. I guess we didn't really pay any attention when we came in."

The story seemed plausible enough.

Rich Spiker, the uncle, said much the same thing. He and his wife owned a medium-sized home across from an elementary school on the west side of Madison. Rich, a rough-looking man in his late forties, said he was a carpenter, but the company he worked for was between projects. "A lot of my work is seasonal," he explained. Pat, her red hair in a bun, looked almost as rough as her husband. She was wearing a black skirt and white blouse. She said she worked part-time for a catering company and was getting ready to leave for work. She sat beside Rich while he explained what had happened the night before.

"Imagine my shock when Scott and I went out there to ice fish last night and found a stringer in the hole of the shack where I fish."

Rita said, "When you went in, you didn't really notice anything out of the ordinary?"

"Nothing at all," he said, "but I didn't really pay attention. The only reason I saw the stringer was because it was already down in the hole where I fish. I couldn't figure out why it was there." He glanced at Pat, who was scrutinizing him.

Rita thought Pat knew her husband had been using the shack as a drinking hangout.

"Who went for help, you or your nephew Scott?" Charlie asked.

"I did."

He looked like the kind of man who was basically a coward when the chips were down. "So Scott stayed at the lake while you went to call the police?" Rita asked. She glanced at his wife. Their eyes barely met. Rita thought she understood what was going on. They were hiding something. "We know you were drinking last night," she mentioned.

An angry expression came over Pat's face, and she glared at Rich. "I knew it," she said.

Charlie repeated his question, "So you went to call the police, and Scott stayed with the body?"

Pat was still glaring. "You better start telling the truth, Rich, or so help me—"

Rich wasn't saying anything.

Pat told him, "I'm not going to let that boy drag you into worse trouble."

Rita asked, "What's going on?"

Rich said, "Now, Pat, it's not that big of a deal, I already told you."

Pat interrupted him, saying, "Scott wasn't there when Rich got out to the lake last night. Rich went out alone, then Scott came out moments before the police arrived. He asked Rich to tell the police the two of them had been there together the whole time."

Charlie asked, "Why would Scott want you to do that?"

Rich answered before his wife could say anything. "He was worried."

Pat said, "He'd been in some trouble where he had just moved from is why he was worried, and he didn't want the police asking questions about him because he didn't want anyone to find out about his past."

"It's no big deal." Rich insisted.

Rita waited until Rich's eyes came to her. "What did Scott do in the past?"

Rich said, "I guess he's got a bench warrant

out for some old traffic tickets he hasn't paid in Colorado."

Rita motioned to Charlie, who got up and left the house. Cold came into the house from the glassed-in front porch.

Pat said, "I've told Rich all along that I didn't like that boy here. I told him he was trouble."

"For Christ's sake, Pat, he's your sister's son. And he hasn't been any trouble since he's been here—"

"At least not that we know about," Pat said.

"The only reason he wanted me to say he was with me last night is because if he hadn't been with me, the police might have started asking questions about where he had been, and when he couldn't account for every single second, then they'd start checking into his past, and they'd end up arresting him for the outstanding bench warrant, something that had nothing to do with the man we found dead. I know how police operate.

"And since he's trying to get on his feet with his new job and all, he'd probably end up losing it all." To Rita he said, "I also know how it is to be trying to get on your feet and everything's going against you."

Rita wondered if Rich had firsthand experience of what he was saying, yet she let it pass. She began to ask basic questions: Where was Scott living?

In a camper behind the house.

What had he been doing during the time he had been staying at the Spiker home?

Nothing. He stayed around the house. It wasn't like he was out running around all hours of the day and night. "He's with me most of the time he isn't working, I tell you," Rich said. "He's a good boy. He works hard. Long hours."

Charlie called her outside. He told her Scott was wanted in Colorado for questioning in a murder investigation. "And not only that, but they want to talk to him in Illinois too."

5

With the arrest of Scott Renneker, the investigation took a distinct turn. Television and newspaper reporters came from everywhere. Jim Swearingen of Wisconsin's Criminal Investigation Division had committed suicide, the reporters were saying, and someone wanted in a series of murders in other states had found the body. Reporters insisted there must be a connection. They hounded every available police official in the state. They canvassed the neighborhoods where Renneker had been working and staying, and they jumped on airplanes to go in search of Renneker's past.

Rita in the meantime sent Charlie to a motel room. The onset of the flu had gotten the best of him. She went to the state police headquarters in Madison, where she began making inquiries about Renneker too.

Police officials in Colorado had dubbed Renneker the "hit-and-run" killer, she discovered.

His modus operandi: While tending bar, he remained on the lookout for high-risk women—women such as prostitutes, travelers, and runaways, or those not likely to be immediately missed if they disappeared. When he found a desirable one, he fed her potent drinks while he fished for information. Last, near closing time, he popped open a gelatin capsule of Placidyl, the "rape" drug, and poured 500 to 750 milligrams of the drug into the final drink for the night. Naturally, he would offer to take the dazed woman home. Instead, however, he would drive out to some secluded spot, rape her, strangle her, then leave her body dumped in the bushes or weeds.

"The sickest part of his M.O.," a detective from LaJunta, Colorado, told Rita during a telephone conversation, "is that according to doctors and other detectives, our man Renneker likes to wait until the Placidyl peaks and begins to wear off before he actually strangles his victim. Apparently he likes to watch them try to wake up. They fight off sleep and their killer at the same time." In other words, all the victims showed signs of struggle. Indeed, one of his victims, a young lady in Illinois, had survived. She had described to police how she had fought off Renneker.

Rita called Paul and told him she wanted to go to Rockford, Illinois, to interview the victim who had survived Renneker's attack, Tara Fay, a twenty-year-old art student at Rockford College.

Paul said that was fine with him. He asked about Charlie. She told him Charlie was sick, and she had sent him back to the motel.

Paul said, "He didn't look very good when I saw him after the autopsy."

"We all have a lot we're carrying around right now."

"It's not a good time."

"I know."

She packed her notes and set out for Mitchell Field in Milwaukee. She would have just driven to Rockford, except that she had received a call about Bianca Willis, the little girl who had fallen down a flight of stairs. Bianca had come out of her coma. She seemed scared. At least every time her mother and father got near her, she showed signs of anxiety, the task force's child psychiatrist reported. Dr. Sardas said, "I really think you should see her." Bianca was in Milwaukee, which meant it was easier to drive to Milwaukee, see Bianca, and fly out of Milwaukee, than to drive elsewhere.

Rita called to check on Charlie. He didn't answer the phone, so she left a message that she was heading for Rockford, Illinois, and would see him when she got back.

At Children's Hospital in Milwaukee, she found Bianca still in the intensive care unit.

The five-year-old girl was fully awake, and the respirator tube had been removed from her mouth, though she wasn't talking.

"Hi, sweetheart," Rita said once they were

alone together. "I'm a police officer"—she held her badge so the dark-haired girl could see it— "and I'm here to make sure everyone's taking good care of you. Dr. Sardas said she talked to you about me. Dr. Sardas works in my office. That's where we have a new program to take care of children who get hurt. Children like you. It sure is good to see you awake."

There were scratches on Bianca's face, especially around the nose and eyes—dark brown eyes that stared listlessly at Rita. She had a large bruise on her forehead.

Rita asked, "Can I push the door shut so you and I can talk in private?"

Bianca didn't say anything, only stared. She had some white gauze taped to the right of her chin. Rita had seen the gash when Bianca had first been brought into the emergency room. Rita thought she remembered ten stitches being sewn into the chin. Below the taped area, Rita could see Bianca's carotid artery rising and lowering.

Rita smiled. "You know, you're about the skinniest little girl I've ever seen. Don't they feed you at home?"

Bianca apparently became tired of staring at her; her eyes shifted to a green monitor at the head of the bed.

"Funny-looking television, isn't it?"

Bianca didn't say anything.

"Bianca—"

The eyes returned to Rita.

"I thought maybe we could talk about how you fell."

Her pupils dilated. The rise and fall of the carotid increased.

"Don't worry. There's nothing to worry about. I only thought we should talk about it so we can make sure nothing like this ever happens again."

Nothing worked. She couldn't get Bianca to talk. She glanced at the clock on the wall in the room. Time was running out. She had to get to the airport. She asked, "Bianca, do you like dogs?"

Silence.

Rita went out to the nurses' station, where she picked up a stuffed animal Dr. Sardas had left there, a brown dog with floppy ears. She took it to Bianca's bedside and held it up. She asked Bianca if she would like to have it. "You'll have to take good care of it, okay?"

No acknowledgment or response came from the staring brown eyes.

"I'll leave it with you, and you see if you two can get acquainted." Rita raised Bianca's left hand—the one with the IV line attached to it—and put the dog under the small hand so that it was beside her body and held down by her hand. "Maybe we can talk tomorrow or the next day if you feel up to it." To her relief, Rita noticed that Bianca's hand started petting one of the dog's long ears.

On her way to the airport, Rita couldn't get

her mind off the frail girl. No, the fall hadn't been accidental. She could tell by looking into Bianca's eyes.

The state police had a small plane warmed up and waiting for Rita. She got on and thought about Bianca all the way to Rockford.

At Rockford College, she found Tara Fay hanging one of her paintings for display. The painting was done in bright greens and reds. It was of a young girl with a screaming green face.

Rita introduced herself as they stood alone in the windowed-in art gallery of the college. Tara, a tall, emaciated youth, was dressed in paint-spattered, dirty-white painter's pants and was braless in an undershirt. She had a ghostly complexion and short black hair, which Rita was sure Tara had dyed. She seemed well adjusted despite the attack, even laughed about it and said that it had helped her to get more serious about her art. She pointed at the painting. "When I woke up in the hospital and they told me I had almost died, I decided I could finally make my painting work—kind of like a revelation." She had a large grin that stretched wider than the base of her square jaw. "Actually, those days in the hospital bed gave me time to think, and I started seeing how logical everything was. I remembered that in grade school it didn't seem like I had cared for art that much, but that I had been good at it, and that's how my whole life had been. I denied what I was really meant to do, not giving myself enough credit. I turned out to be a mediocre art student because I lacked self-esteem. But what I remember distinctly—remembered while I was in the hospital—was how much as a child I had liked the smell of paint and glue and art supplies." She giggled at herself. She had a child's giggle. "It was almost sexual."

Rita wondered if she was as well adjusted as she appeared to be on the surface.

The eyes suddenly became scared. "He's locked up, isn't he?"

Yes, Rita told her, Renneker was locked up. "But, Tara, we want to keep him locked up, and it's important we gather as much information as we can about him. That's how we stop people like this."

Tara recounted how she had been at the Greyhound Bus Station in Rockford, and it had been a cold night. "Late October," she said. "It wasn't snowing, but I remember ice crystals had been blowing in the air, and it was cold outside."

Where had she been heading? Rita wanted to know.

Tara gave one of those childish giggles. No place in particular, she replied. She had run away from home, and a lot of runaways hung out at places like bus stops. "I went inside the bus terminal to get warm and had just gotten kicked out because the guy who worked there said he was going to call the police if I didn't leave.

"So the moment I step outside, there is this big red Cadillac—like a boat"—she giggled—"and this big guy asks if I wanted to have supper with him. At first I say, no, thank you, but then he says he knows I'm a runaway, and he tells me that once he was a runaway."

She went on to explain how Renneker had been funny. "He knew how to make you laugh," she said. He had offered to buy her a meal and had promised there would be no strings attached.

"I finally gave in, and everything seemed to be legitimate. He drove me to this Chinese restaurant, and everyone seemed to know him there. In fact, it had to be obvious that I was under age, but no one said anything to him when he went behind the bar.

"I had tasted Canadian whiskey and 7UP once and didn't mind it, so I told him that's what I usually drank. He showed me to a table, then went back to the bar to make drinks.

"It didn't take long for him to return. All kinds of food started showing up. It was like everyone in the place was at his beck and call."

Her face took on a sad and pitiful look.

She said, "You know how it is when something bad is about to happen, everything gets, like, bigger than life." She opened her hands and examined them. There was red and green paint on her fingers. "And then time, like, really slows down."

Rita nodded. She knew exactly what Tara was

talking about. She remembered the time Jim had almost drowned. It seemed to take forever for her to swim back to him.

"That's what happened as I was sitting there eating and drinking. I remember the food wasn't very good. The rice was pasty, and the chicken I was eating had a lot of fat on it."

Her grape-juice eyes got a distant stare in them. "This older couple came in. They looked like a nice couple, but you could tell they weren't married. It was like they were on a date, and the moment I saw them I thought they looked like they had both been married before and it hadn't worked out. I found myself staring at them, forgetting that Lou was even sitting at the table with me."

"Lou?" Rita interrupted her.

"That's what he said his name was." She giggled. "Lou Grant. It seems funny now, but at the time I didn't think anything of it. I watch a lot of old shows on TV, and I should have known, but I didn't. He said he worked at a hospital. He seemed to know a lot about taking care of people, so I thought it was the truth."

To be on the safe side, Rita brought out a stack of photographs of similar-looking men.

Tara went through the photographs and picked out Renneker without hesitation.

Rita shuffled the photographs and handed them to Tara again.

Tara smiled. She said she was an artist and never forgot a face. She picked out Renneker again. She said she could pick him out anytime, anyplace. She continued her story: She had become fascinated with watching the couple that sat in the front of the restaurant, the ones up by the windows overlooking the street.

"Then the man with the woman pulled out one of these cell phones, pushed a button on it, and all these bright green lights came on.

"While he was on the phone, the woman must have dropped some sweet-and-sour sauce on her shirt—she was eating those chip things and dip—because she took her crimson red napkin, dipped it in her glass of ice water, and held her shirt out as she scrubbed it with this crimson cloth. That's when it happened." She fell silent and swallowed thickly.

"What happened?"

"I saw Lou pour something in my drink and stir it in with one of those plastic stir sticks."

"You watched him do that?"

She nodded. "I pretended I didn't notice it, like I was too busy watching this couple, but I saw the whole thing. I even drank when he told me 'drink up.' It was like he was the doctor, and I was following orders."

"Why would you do that?" Rita asked, shocked at what she was hearing.

The little girl in her giggled. "I don't know," she said. "I guess I got excited watching the young couple up in the front windows, and I wanted to see what was going to happen to me. I could tell by watching them that the couple were going to go to bed later that night, and something turned me on while Lou was stirring whatever he was stirring into my drink. It was like I had to know what was going to happen, and the only way I was going to find out was to experience it."

Strange, Rita thought. "And what happened?"

Tara said she didn't remember much once they had left the restaurant, but she did remember waking up in a small bed. "It was a child's bed," she said, a confused look on her face. "I was too big for the bed. I remember I was in my panties, and he had them pulled down to my knees, and he was touching me."

Rita could see the horror that had filled Tara's eyes. "Take your time," Rita told her, speaking softly. Something bad had happened. "We're going to make sure Renneker never sees the streets again. Just take your time."

Tara took a deep breath. Her big eyes became watery, but she didn't cry. "He choked me while I was like that," she said. "I couldn't fight. I was paralyzed, and he was choking me. As he was choking me, he said he had to kill anyone who could be a witness."

Rita thought of Jim. Had Renneker discovered Jim spying on him?

"I remember what he said distinctly. He said, 'I have to kill anyone who might become a witness.'" Tara shook her head. "It almost sounded like he was involved in some kind of religious ritual. Then everything went white, and I saw my parents' dog, Ballard, who's a black mutt, part Lab and part something else. Ballard's face was real thin and white around the eyes." She held open hands near her glasses. "I remember calling to him, 'Here, Ballard,' again and again, but he wouldn't come. Then I came to and Lou was completely naked. He had an erection. My panties were all the way off.

"I must have surprised him that I still had strength left—I don't know where I got it—but I jumped out of bed and ran out the door of the motel. It was freezing cold and I was naked, but I didn't care. He caught me in the woods behind the motel, and beat me until I passed out, but he must have gotten scared and left."

He lost control of the situation, Rita thought. So, he was an organized killer. Didn't like to be out of control.

"Next thing I know, I woke up in the hospital, and they told me I had almost died. I was scared it was Lou's hospital, but it wasn't."

"And you told all this to the police?" Rita asked.

She shrugged. "Most of it."

Rita looked at the painting of the green girl in the red chaos and thought of the lady at the Chinese restaurant who had wiped up a mess with a crimson napkin. Then there were the bright green lights of the telephone.

Tara giggled. "What do you think? Do you like it?"

Rita said she liked the painting a lot, would

even like to buy it. "Is it for sale?" She didn't have the money to buy it, but she didn't know how else to express how much she liked what she saw.

Tara studied the piece, like a child in awe of something she had done. She said she would have to think about it, though Rita knew she would never sell it. She could tell Tara was too attached to the girl in the painting.

Outside in the cold air, Rita wondered if it was possible that Renneker had murdered Jim. Perhaps Renneker had wanted to be caught. But why? For a fleeting moment while standing there, she almost thought it all meant something, that it somehow all tied together. Almost.

6

On her return flight to Milwaukee, Rita reflected on the autopsy that morning. She knew what suicide looked like, she had seen it enough times. This case looked like it, but there were too many other things going on.

In the terminal, she was met by Mike and Greg. Greg, whose hair was still wet from a recent shower, said Rita was going to kill Mike.

Mike kissed her, then stood back, trying to look casual.

"What are you two up to?" she asked, with a smile.

"You're going to kill him, Mom," Greg said, "that's what's up. He's been spending money left and right!"

Rita could feel her face become cold.

Greg guffawed. "I told you, Mike. Look at her. I told you she'd be pissed!"

Her eyes fixed on Mike, she said, "Greg, we don't talk like that, and you know it." To Mike, she said, "You haven't been charging again, have you?" There had been a period in their first days of marriage when they had charged everything. They had both thought that with their combined salaries they would live much better, but it hadn't turned out that way. All they got were maxed-out cards.

No, Mike told her, he hadn't charged anything.

"Guess what, Mom. Mike bought a six-hundred-dollar camcorder."

She couldn't help herself. That made her angry. The only thing she could think of was that he had gotten a raise at work, but that upset her because she was sure he was already out spending the money before he had even earned it. He was like that. Impulsive. She told him she hoped it wasn't that. She knew he had never been good at managing money. She had known that even before they had been married. She recalled the time when he had suddenly disappeared for an extended weekend because he had discovered he had a thousand dollars in the bank. He had gone to Key West for several days, spending all of his money, then had appeared on her doorstep with a bottle of cheap red wine.

No, he hadn't gotten a raise, Mike told her. He hadn't spent money he didn't already have.

Greg couldn't contain himself. "He won five thousand dollars!" he blurted out. Then he turned red because he realized how loudly he had said it.

Mike laughed, patted Greg on the back, and said, "Why don't you tell the whole airport?"

Other people were passing with smiles on their faces. They had obviously heard what Greg had said.

Rita, beginning to become excited, grabbed Mike by the arm and pulled him aside. "You won five thousand dollars?"

He laughed, put his arms around her, and said, "Yes!"

Laughing with him, she said, "This sure as hell better not be a joke."

Greg told her, "Mom, don't say hell, or that's where you'll end up."

She couldn't help it. She was too excited. Five thousand dollars was too good to believe.

A lottery ticket, he told her. He always bought a lottery ticket when he bought gas, as she knew—she had often told him it was a waste of money—and today he had discovered he had won five thousand dollars when he scratched off the boxes on the ticket he bought.

So it was for real. She let out a big breath and laughed. The money couldn't have come at a better time, she thought, and with Christmas so near. She hugged him, and they kissed.

Before she had flown back from Rockford, she had called him to tell him they could meet her at the airport if they wanted. She had also told him that she had to return to Madison to wrap up loose ends. Now Mike asked if she had time to have dinner with them. "I promise we won't hold you up too long," he told her. "We still have to get to play rehearsal tonight, but I thought it might give us a chance to spend a few minutes together."

They drove to John Hawk's Pub downtown, right on the Milwaukee River, where they ordered New York strip steaks. Greg bubbled with conversation. He told her how Mike had been going crazy buying Christmas gifts. Mike gave Greg twenty dollars and told him to go next door to a game room.

Once Greg had gone, Rita tried to come back down to earth. She told Mike she didn't approve of teaching Greg to throw away money. "We have bad enough habits ourselves," she said. "Let's not pass them along to him."

Mike apologized, saying, "It is the first time I've ever been rich. I still don't know what I'm supposed to do."

They laughed together. Their drinks arrived, as did an order of buffalo wings and blue-cheese dip. Rita raised her wineglass. "To five thousand dollars at a time when we really need it."

Their glasses made a dull sound when they clinked together.

Mike said, "Cheap glasses."

They laughed and drank together.

She said, "This is a chance to get our lives back together. I want to pay off some of our bills."

Taking one of her hands in his, he said, "There's plenty of time to talk about all of that later. Right now let me ask a question: How are you holding up?"

She sobered at the reference to Jim. "I'm going to make it. I just need to do a little more checking around. Things are more complicated than what I thought they were going to be."

"Is it what everyone thought?"

"Suicide?" She hated to be reminded what everyone thought. "To tell you the truth, I don't think so."

"He was a good friend, wasn't he?"

She could feel tears welling in her eyes, but she kept her eyes steady on her glass. "Yes, he was. And I want to make sure I handle this by the book." Afterward, she hoped what she had said did not sound insensitive.

What all did she still have to do? Mike wanted to know.

The personal effects needed to be disposed of, she told him, and there would be the visitation, the funeral, and the interment.

"Is there anything else you have to do for the investigation?"

"Like I said, just a few loose ends." To be truthful with herself, she didn't know.

"Then why can't someone else wrap them up?"

"I'm doing it as a favor for Paul," she lied. "It's been especially hard on him. Jim and he started out together. He'll want me to go by and look through Jim's house. You know the sort of thing. I promise, it won't be that involved." She knew otherwise, knew she wouldn't stop until she had the truth.

"Say, what's the deal with that guy they arrested?" Mike drank some of his scotch.

She could tell he had been waiting to ask that. "What do you mean?"

He shrugged. "Nothing, really. It's just that I understood it to be suicide, and the newspaper and television stations are reporting that this guy they arrested might have murdered him."

"Can we talk about something else?" From where she sat she could see the street. She looked out the window at the cars passing. Across the street were Christmas decorations in the window of a store. What if it was Jim's footprints along the side of Lake Mendota? she wondered. What if Jim had been watching Renneker, and Renneker had lashed out? She thought of Tara Fay. Renneker had told her that he didn't like witnesses. Also, what had happened to Tara proved that Renneker could, in a moment of panic, become quite careless in his crimes. In his panic, he had beat her and left her to die. But why would he ever dump Jim in a place that would lead straight to himself?

Mike dipped a wing in blue cheese and tasted it. Nodding, he said, "Yep, that is how I like it, good and spicy. Hotter, the better."

She took a bite of her wing. Odd she hadn't noticed how spicy the sauce was before. Her mind was elsewhere. Before she could wipe her lips, Mike kissed them.

Greg returned at the same time. "Why don't you two grow up and act like a married couple?"

They laughed.

Greg tried to get Mike to go to the game room with him. Rita said, "What about me?"

Mike stood to go with Greg, saying, "Do I detect a tone of jealousy in your voice?"

Rita watched Mike and Greg leave. Greg had really sprouted during the previous year. He was almost as tall as Mike. But he was putting on too much weight. She hoped he wouldn't be fat. She had had problems with weight in her own youth, and she didn't want Greg to have to go through all that.

The waiter appeared. He put down a handful of wet wipes and a bowl for the chicken bones. She ordered another red wine.

She wondered how Charlie was doing. He had a sensitive soul. It's something she had always liked about him. She knew he was upset about Jim.

The food arrived, as did a new glass of wine. Mike and Greg hadn't returned, so Rita went in search of them. They were both leaning over a video game. Greg was trying to tell Mike how to get through a level of a game. As she watched them, she thought it was good to see them get along so well together. A couple of years before, when Greg had been having such a traumatic time growing up, Mike had not understood at all. He hadn't been able to deal with him. All he could think to do whenever Greg rebelled was to punish him. Ground him to the house and take away his telephone privileges. Now they got along fine.

Rita called them back to the table, where they ate their steaks and baked potatoes.

During the course of the meal, Greg said he was sorry to hear about Jim.

Rita was both surprised and touched at the same time. "Thank you," she replied. "That's nice of you to say that." Then, "How would you like to go shopping this weekend? If things settle down a bit, maybe you and I can have a mother and son day out."

Greg said that was fine with him, but it better happen soon. "If we don't hurry, there won't be anything left to shop with."

Rita nodded and said, "Mike and I still need to talk about that."

"You still need to talk? What were you two doing when I was gone all that time playing video games? Playing kissy face?"

Mike said, "Is that so bad? I've seen you begin to get the roaming eye yourself."

Greg reddened. "What?"

"Christine Woodall. You had your eye on her during play rehearsal."

Greg raised a hand. "Busted," he said. Mike slapped the raised hand.

In that moment Rita was jealous. Now that she had taken over the child-abuse task force, she had even less free time for Greg than she had had before. In the past days, she had told Mike that if she stepped down as the supervisor of the Milwaukee office and started working overtime, she could make more money than she was making as an administrator. That would give more time for Greg. Mike, in turn, pointed out that as the supervisor she had a guaranteed income. "We need that right now," he told her. "Sure, by working overtime you might pull in a few extra dollars here and there, but overtime's not guaranteed." He could be so foolish about financial concerns, and yet so practical at the most inconvenient times.

She studied Greg. Soon he would be driving. She and Mike would have to buy him a car. Then there would be college. How could they ever get enough money together for that?

Mike was looking at the menu again. He called the waiter over. Holding up the menu, he said, "It says here that shrimp are only thirty-nine cents between four-thirty and six-thirty. Can I get six shrimp?"

The waiter told him, "That's only at the bar. If you're sitting at the bar, you can get the shrimp at that price."

Mike pointed to the bar. "I can see the bar," he said. "Are you telling me you can't even go over there and get me six shrimp?"

The waiter, unsure of himself, said, "I'll see what I can do."

Rita was troubled by how Mike was acting. She told him, "You don't need shrimp. This steak and potato is more than enough to eat. I think all that money is going to your head."

Mike told her, "This is a matter of principle. The bar's right there"—he pointed. "Don't tell me it's such a big deal for the waiter to walk over and get me six shrimp."

Greg raised a fist. "Tell him, Mike."

Rita didn't like what she was hearing, neither from Mike nor from Greg.

Not long after, the waiter returned and said there was a manager at the bar. "I couldn't get any shrimp," the waiter said. "That's a bar special, and the manager was watching me. I'm sorry, but I couldn't get the shrimp."

Mike said that was all right, but no sooner had the waiter gone away than Greg told him, "Mike, I wouldn't give him a tip if I were you."

Rita was shocked. "Greg," she said, "we don't talk like that. I can see I need to rein you two in."

Greg said, "I say if you can't get shrimp for what you pay at the bar, and the bar's right over there, I wouldn't give the waiter a tip. I could probably go over there myself and talk the manager out of six shrimp."

Mike and Greg laughed. They slapped hands together.

Greg said, "Don't give him a tip, Mike."

Rita looked at the two of them. "We don't act wild and obnoxious like this," she said flatly.

Mike held a finger to his lips, and Greg fell

silent. Mike said, "We're sorry. We know you've had a rough day."

Was it her? She had been pretending to have a good time. She closed her eyes and imagined Jim—as he'd been in the white van riding back from the lake where he had almost drowned. He was smoking a cigarette, a smile on his face. Paul asked Jim why he hadn't swum. Jim replied that he had. He'd gone in while Paul and Patti were racing to the raft, then he had gotten out.

Jim pretended he had enjoyed the water and had had a good swim. He pretended he hadn't almost drowned. Jim had been a good pretender. A lot of people were good pretenders.

7

In Madison the next morning, Rita opened an atlas on the temporary desk she had been given at CID headquarters and again telephoned the detective who had worked the Renneker investigation in LaJunta, Colorado. Neil Hakin was his name. "From the looks of it, I'd say it's sparsely populated out in your area," she told Detective Hakin, once they got to talking. "Renneker was living out there? That doesn't make much sense based upon his M.O. elsewhere. I thought he liked to work the bigger cities."

He did, Hakin told her. Renneker had been working at a bar in Pueblo, near the University of Southern Colorado.

Okay, that sounded more like the Renneker she knew.

The woman whose body police had discovered had disappeared from Pueblo, Hakin explained. "He chose to dump her body here."

Okay, that made sense too. The motel Tara

had been taken to was actually in Beloit, Wisconsin, twenty miles from where she had been
picked up. That indicated Renneker didn't like
to dump the body in the same location where
he picked up the living victim. Very methodical.
Rita said, "By any chance was her body found
in water?" She didn't know why she asked the
question. Perhaps because Jim had drowned,
and she knew there was some connection.

There was a momentary silence. "Yes, why?"

Rita's heart began to beat faster. "I don't
know. I'm putting all this together myself just
now." No, Tara's body hadn't been in the water,
but maybe Renneker had planned to dump her
in Beloit, or someplace like it. From Rockford to
Beloit would be as close as Pueblo was to
LaJunta.

Detective Hakin agreed to share his investigative notes and photographic evidence with Rita.
He said a lot of investigators had been re-
questing the same information. He told her he
would begin to fax the materials.

Off the phone with Detective Hakin, she telephoned the medical examiner and asked him to
screen Jim's blood and stomach contents for
Placidyl. To screen for an unknown substance
could take days; to screen for something specific
could be done within hours, even minutes.

By the time she had gotten herself a cup of
coffee and had made a few more telephone calls,
Charlie was standing at her desk. He looked like
hell, but he had collected incoming materials

from the fax machine and seemed like he was ready to work again.

"Are you sure you're all right?" she asked.

"I'm here." He held a lot of loose papers. "Paul's administrative assistant said these were coming in for you from different places," he said. Without saying anything more, he sat down at her desk and began to go through the reports, photographs, and notes. He held up a couple of photographs. Though the fax made it difficult to make out details, it was easy enough to discern that on the two sheets he was holding up, the victims had ligature on their hands and ankles.

"What kind of ligature?" she asked.

Charlie studied the notes. "This one says strips of a bed sheet were used." He held up the photograph with the thick white ligature. "And this one"—he studied the notes again as he held up the fax sheet—"is rope."

"No wire?"

He thumbed through the pages. "Do you want everything on a silver platter?"

She pushed back her hair with both hands and held it there.

"I know what you're thinking," he said.

She didn't say anything.

"You're thinking he used a bed sheet, rope, and maybe even wire. That would indicate an opportunistic killer, or someone who uses whatever's in his reach or in the local vicinity."

Releasing her hair, she smiled. "Okay, let's

say Renneker spots a victim and decides he's going to kill her. So far, all we know is that his victims are female. Anyway, he looks around for anything in the immediate environment that will help him achieve his end." She stood and arched her back. She had been working at the desk since four that morning. She looked out a window that was at shoulder height. The day was drab. The clouds looked heavy, like they were filled with snow and might pop at any moment. She turned to Charlie. "How common is wire in suicide?"

"Maybe Renneker caught Jim in the garage. Every garage has wire in it."

"Jim? How did he get involved?" She dropped back into her chair.

"You know damned good and well how he got involved."

"Jim's place doesn't have a garage."

"Then he keeps his shit in the kitchen, and Renneker found it." Charlie dropped into a chair on the opposite side of the desk.

"Renneker uses Placidyl as part of his M.O."

"So we don't know about that yet, but even still, who says he has to use Placidyl?" He began shuffling through the papers. He stopped at a page, which he put on top of the stack. He smiled. "And what do you make of this?" He handed the page across the desk to her.

It was from some other materials that had come in from the police department in Muncie, Indiana, where a body had been found. There on the report was a notation: "cc: J. Swearingen, Wisconsin Criminal Investigation Division."

Charlie had made his point. Jim had been after Renneker. No doubt about it. She stood again, saying, "Okay, let's talk to Renneker again. But before we put him on the hot seat, let's run by Jim's house and see what we find."

Together they went to Jim's town house, which was located in a peaceful walled community near the University of Wisconsin campus.

Since Jim hadn't lived in that particular place that long, Rita had been to his town house only a couple of times, but things looked pretty much the way she had remembered them, immaculate as ever. At some point in his life Jim had turned that way. From a wild man, he had become very serious and formal. His town house was clean and neat. Not a thing out of place.

Disposable gloves on, Charlie opened a cabinet in the living room and gave a short whistle. "Check out this CD collection." The cabinet was full of CDs.

Rita said, "He always liked music. All kinds except country. He hated country."

"So do I."

She went into the kitchen, which was adjacent to the living room. The countertops were spotless. Everything had a place, including the cappuccino machine. It was pushed under the cabinet near the sink.

From the kitchen, she passed into a solarium filled with green plants and wicker. The solarium, she knew, was one of the reasons he had bought the house. It overlooked a courtyard. She stared at it, remembering the last time she visited him. It had been September. They sat in the solarium and drank cold beer together while they snacked on cheese and crackers. It was the last time they really talked. He told her how happy he was to find such a nice place so close to the university. "Gets me close to the pulse of life," he said, his blue-gray eyes watching her. He laughed at that. He had a big face. A big smile. A large mustache. Bigger than life. "Did I tell you I always wanted to be a college professor?" he asked. "I told you that, didn't I?"

He continued to smile. "I guess it's the life and energy of the young people. It's invigorating to be so close to a university campus. You feel like you're a part of it all."

"I'd think it'd be too noisy," she observed.

He laughed.

"You think he had a housekeeper?" Charlie asked.

She looked at him. She had been so caught up in memories of the past that she hadn't even heard Charlie enter the solarium. "I think he did have someone come in now and then."

"The place is spotless," he said. "Was he always so neat and clean?"

"Not always."

"There is one thing I found interesting. Come here, you have to see this."

She followed him back into the living room,

where he stopped at a crystal sculpture of a woman's head and bust. She was naked, her breasts quite distinct.

He said, "Rita, it looks like you," and laughed.

"And when have you seen me without any clothes?" she asked him. She could feel heat in her face and knew she must be blushing.

Charlie shrugged. "I bet that thing's worth a fortune. It's beautiful. I wonder where he had it made?"

"I don't know," she commented. "I saw it years ago. He showed it to me at his other place. Back then he had it wrapped up in newspapers."

"I bet it's worth a fortune."

As she went down the hallway to the master bedroom, she thought about Jim. Yes, he had collected a lot of nice things over the years. Why had she always been so poor? Jim didn't have a family, though. That made a difference.

She passed a second bedroom. It had been converted into an office, complete with an elaborate computer system.

Behind her, Charlie said, "Yes, it never ceased to amaze me how Jim could be such a spic-and-span guy."

"What?"

"It's more than clean. It's an obsession."

She entered the master bedroom, where she found Jim's wallet on a shelf of an open armoire. Odd that he would leave it behind, she thought, opening it. Had he wanted someone to find something in it? A suicide note perhaps?

Inside the wallet were a number of credit cards and a photo section. Though he had been married once, Jim had never had any children. He kept photographs of his nieces. She knew he had been close to his sister, who lived in North Carolina. She also was divorced. He had treated his sister's daughters as if they were his own children, having never missed a birthday or a holiday for any of them. Rita wondered if he had already sent them Christmas gifts. She was sure he had.

Among the photographs she found something that struck her as being curious, a pass for the University of Wisconsin's recreational sports facilities. She wondered how he had gotten a pass there. Had he enrolled in a class?

Charlie called her into the master bathroom. He was standing near the walk-in shower. She saw immediately what had caught his attention. Thrown over one side of the glass shower door was a blue towel. Over the other side was a pair of navy swimming trunks.

His eyes met hers. "Didn't you tell me that Jim couldn't swim—that he was afraid of the water?"

She didn't know what to say. Yes, Jim had almost drowned. She had seen it with her own eyes.

Charlie said, "Let me ask you this: Doesn't it strike you as odd that there isn't a thing out of place in the whole damned house, and then we find a towel and swimming trunks thrown over the shower door?"

Yes, it was odd, she thought, though she didn't answer Charlie. She found herself looking in drawers and cabinets, not quite sure what she was looking for. Once or twice her eyes passed over her image in the mirror. She looked tired, which didn't seem right either because she was accustomed to going days with very little sleep. What was she searching for? And yet she found herself searching frantically. What else was out of place? she wondered. What else didn't make sense?

Charlie sat on the sink counter, watching her. He was so tall all he had to do was lean back and he was sitting. "You're not going to like what I'm thinking," he suddenly said.

She stopped searching. "What are you thinking?" She ran a hand through her hair. She felt out of breath.

"I'm thinking along the lines of 'what if?' I mean, all of this is too confusing. It keeps puzzling me."

"What if what?"

"What if this is a homicide, and someone who knew what he was doing made it look like suicide? The evidence is contaminated as hell, you know."

She was thinking the same thing. Someone who wanted to discredit Jim. Her pager went off.

In the kitchen she used the telephone to call the number on the pager. It was the medical examiner. Jim had tested positive for Placidyl.

Her adrenaline was pumping.

The medical examiner said that Jim had either taken the drug to suppress any last-minute urge to fight the suicide, or he had been drugged, though short of a confession from someone, distinguishing between the two possibilities might be impossible.

"What about the ligature marks?" Rita mentioned. "Don't those indicate a struggle?"

The examiner said the struggle wasn't much. "Let me put it this way," he told her, "unless there's some other compelling evidence—such as the confession of a killer, or something as drastic as that—there's nothing more to go on just yet."

"Yet."

Off the phone, she told Charlie, "Let's go see Renneker again."

They left Jim's town house and drove to the county jail, only to discover that Renneker had become a very popular guy. A half-dozen states were sending investigators to question him. Colorado and Illinois were processing extradition papers. She learned all that from Paul, who was waiting for her at the jail. She had called him during the drive from Jim's. She said, "You're fast."

"You realize that with other states wanting him, this doesn't give us much time." He walked down the hall with her and Charlie. "If we're going to get something on him, we have to do it now, or someone's going to yank him out from under us." He stopped. "I don't care what it takes, I want this Renneker. He murdered Jim, and I want him."

They stood with him.

"One other thing," Paul said. "I hate to bring this up, but your friend Susan Hall of TV Six in Milwaukee has been hounding me."

Rita hated to hear the name. Hall had been the reporter who had caused so much trouble in the state park murders.

Paul seemed to realize what she was thinking. "We don't want her asking a lot of questions," he said. "Not just yet. We want her to run the story our way."

"We're working as quickly as we can," she said. She waited for him to leave, but he told her he was going to sit in the observation room while she and Charlie interviewed Renneker.

Great, she thought, now he's going to bug the hell out of us.

Paul followed her and Charlie to the interrogation room, where Renneker showed up in pine green jail clothes. They were wrinkled, but he looked comfortable enough in them. He sat down at the wood table in the room and, with steepled hands in front of him, leaned forward, his head tilted slightly to the right.

"It seems like you've got quite a mess on your hands," she told him.

"I wouldn't call it a mess," he replied, staring at her with his cold blue eyes.

She hadn't noticed how cold they were until that moment.

"I'd say you're trying to make a mountain out of a mole hill."

"Whatever it is, it's caught up with you this time, and I can guarantee you won't be on the loose again," Charlie mentioned.

Renneker smiled at him, leaned back in his chair, stretching his feet out, and crossed his arms, his thumbs up. His head still tilted, only leaning back, he said, "To tell you the truth, I like Wisconsin. The people are nice here. There is no death penalty."

Rita thought she sensed what he was getting at. He wanted to plea bargain.

He leaned forward again. "Here's the deal. You help me, and I'll help you." His eyebrows rose arrogantly. "Well?"

She said, "Talk to us."

"First we make the deal."

"What kind of deal?"

"I know how you people operate. You get what you want out of someone, and then you throw him to the lions. You get what you want out of me, then you say, 'Okay, we're going to waive prosecution and send him to a state where he'll get the death penalty.'"

Yes, she knew what he was thinking.

A smile crossed Charlie's face. He said, "And you want us to keep your ass here."

Renneker smiled back at him. "I like your style, brother. That's exactly what I want."

Charlie said, "I'm not your damned brother, and don't ever call me that."

Renneker rolled his eyes. "Whatever," he said.

"It all depends on what you tell us," Rita said, trying to keep the interview on track.

Renneker told her, "I'll tell you what you need to hear, but you have to guarantee you won't extradite me."

"So you make up some story and confess to something you didn't do just because you think we're desperate for a confession," Rita told him.

"Believe me, I'm not making anything up."

"Okay, talk."

"Put the deal in writing first."

Paul met her in the hall. He said, "Give him what he wants."

Charlie nodded. "I agree. Jim was killed in the line of duty, and I think we should lower the boom on him for killing one of ours."

"We have him by the balls," Paul added.

She remembered the state park murders. She said, "In Indiana one of his victims was a four-teen-year-old girl. Imagine the outrage when we refuse to extradite him to stand trial there for the murder of a child. People will say he confessed to killing Jim just to avoid a serious punishment."

Charlie said, "But look at it this way. What if a confession from Renneker is the only way to establish that Jim was murdered? Otherwise people are going to say it's a suicide. Besides, with a confession we have what we need for a conviction. Even if we send him back to Indiana, what if they can't convict him? Then we have nothing. All is lost."

Paul shrugged. "I'm not going to try to tell you how to run the investigation," he said calmly, "but Charlie's right. We have him. What if we send him to Indiana and they can't get a conviction? As far as I'm concerned, a bird in the hand is worth two in the bush."

She told Paul, "I'll need you to persuade the attorney general to go along with this. He's the one who has to challenge any extradition requests. He's the one who's going to have to approve it."

Paul had a friend at the attorney general's office, an assistant attorney general. He wasted no time in contacting him. The attorney general, in turn, approved a nonextradition plan in principle. He said it depended on whether Renneker kept to his side of the bargain. Renneker would have to give a bona fide murder confession in return for no extradition.

When she returned to the interrogation room, she found Charlie and Renneker talking about the Green Bay Packers. She told Renneker about the deal with the attorney general's office. "The letter's being typed right now for signature," she explained. "If you want to wait until it gets here, we can let you go back to your cell, where you can get some lunch, then we can meet later to talk."

He sat on the edge of his chair, his hands in his lap. "I'll go ahead and start without the letter," he said. "I trust you. Besides, this is going to take a while. We can get started, and by the time we get to the real juicy stuff, the letter will be here, right?"

He disgusted her. It made her think he might have tortured Jim in some way that wasn't obvious. Renneker look like the type who knew a lot about torturing someone. "You don't mind if we videotape this interview, do you?"

"Not at all."

He signed the waiver forms, then scooted his chair back and put his left ankle on his right knee. "Since we have time, let's go back to the beginning," he said. He got a distant look in his eyes. "When I was around eight or nine, I tried to hang a girl. We were playing cowboys and Indians, and she was playing an Indian girl, so I was going to hang her. I threw a rope over a low tree branch, turned a trash can upside down, and had her stand on the can while I tied the rope around her neck. I remember wrapping the other end of the rope around my hand, then kicking the can out from under her. For a moment I felt the weight in my hand, and it was one of the most exciting times in my life." He smiled broadly. "But the rope was too far out on the branch. The branch broke and she came down." He shook his head. "I think if she had died in my hands, it would have been one of the nicest experiences I've ever had."

Yes, he was a cold-blooded killer, Rita thought.

Renneker sat as calmly as if he were talking about the weather. "What's the matter?" he asked, staring at her.

His blue eyes had the glazed look of thick ice in them. She thought of the icy water Jim had been dropped into. She didn't say anything.

"I think you don't like me." He laughed.

"How many people have you murdered?" she asked.

Staring at her, he shrugged. "You'd think I'd remember each and every one of them, but it's kind of like making love. If you do it with enough different partners, you lose track of them after a while."

She repeated her question: "How many?"

He shrugged again. "Maybe twenty. Twenty-five." He sat as stiff and erect and composed as someone interviewing for a job.

Was he telling her the truth? she wondered. "You don't even care, do you?"

"As a matter of fact, I do care." He shrugged. "It's probably just as well I got caught too, because if I wasn't sitting here, I'm sure I'd be out hunting my next victim."

His eyes were staring at her, probing her. She could feel it.

"Maybe even someone like you." He smiled. "If we were in different circumstances—I met

you in a bar—I bet I could kill you. You have
that little girl look even though you must be—
how old, forty or so?"

His steady gaze frightened her.

"Yes, I'd kill you, and you'd never suspect
what was happening until it was too late. You're
so pretty, you know it. I love that reddish hair.
Is your pussy hair red too?" Her face grew hard,
and he smiled. "What, do I shock you? I mean,
you're trying to get to know the real me, and I
need to let you know what I'm really thinking.
It's all part of the deal, you know. You look like
a mother."

He was truly sick. She felt like he might jump
over the table at any moment and latch his
hands on to her neck.

"You're my type, you know. Small, but a
fighter. You're the kind who doesn't put up with
any crap. You can hold your own. I like that in
a woman, especially one I'm going to kill. It
makes it more of a challenge. She fights at the
end, fights like hell." He smiled. "Yes, I could
kill you. You remind me of the little girl who
played cowboys and Indians with me."

"Let's get back to your confession," Charlie
said.

She had forgotten Charlie was in the room
with her, she had been so mesmerized by what
Renneker had been saying. Wow, he had power.
No wonder he had control of all the customers
at the bar where he worked. And Tara had basically told her the same thing about Renneker

when he took her to the Chinese restaurant in Rockford. He had an ability to pull people in.

Renneker sat back, thinking a few moments. "My father kept a lot of nudie magazines around the house, and I remember I liked to look at the pictures of naked women and fantasize about having control over them. I'd daydream about making them my slaves and making them do anything I told them to do." He laughed. "The funny thing is that I was too young in those days to even know what to do with a woman if I had one—except to make her walk around naked and serve me.

"Next thing I knew, I was stealing things from stores and giving the stolen items to girls in order to get them to undress for me. At twelve or thirteen, I remember baby-sitting for the neighbors, and I undressed the little girl, and I undressed, and I lay down with her."

"How old was she?"

He smiled. "Three, maybe four."

Rita felt sick to her stomach.

"Back then did you ever try to kill anyone again?" Charlie asked.

"I think I was fifteen or sixteen when I came close to killing someone again," he replied. "She was in the same grade, I believe it was tenth, and I chased her with a knife. I can remember a voice inside telling me to stick the knife in her—to stick her again and again—but I didn't."

"Did you rape her?" Charlie wanted to know.

"No. It was just fun watching her try to get away from me, terrified. I masturbated afterward."

"Didn't she report you?" Rita asked sharply.

He folded his arms across his raised knee. "Before I let her get away, I told her if she told anyone, I'd kill her mother, her father, and her sister."

"She never told on you?"

"Nope." He smiled. "People'll do anything you tell them to do if you get them scared enough."

This was all too vague, she thought, trying to keep her anger in check. "Who was the first person you killed?" she asked. She had worked cases in which someone would claim to have killed someone, only to discover the person had read about the crime in the newspaper, or had seen it on television. She wanted to hear about murders she could verify.

"A whore down at Baton Rouge," he told her. He gave the year and said he had been in the army at the time. He had been stationed at Fort Polk, and had met the prostitute in a bar. "I drove her out on a country road and turned on the overhead light. I told her to undress. She turned her back to me, and for some reason, when she had taken off her shirt, I remembered this large screwdriver I kept under my seat. I pulled out the screwdriver, and as her hands came up behind her back to unhook her bra, I rammed the screwdriver into her. It was like sticking a knife into a watermelon. At first there was resistance, but then it went in smoothly, and I yanked it out just as suddenly." His right hand jerked back, as if he were reliving the experience. "The screwdriver made a sucking noise, and she made one small scream and looked back at me as if a wasp had stung her. I could see the terror in her eyes when she saw the bloody screwdriver. She started crying, which is when I realized she was having trouble breathing." He shook his head. "The more she struggled for breath, the more turned on I got. She begged me not to hurt her. I told her all I wanted to do was have sex with her, then I was going to let her go. I made her lie on the dirt road right next to the open truck door, and I could see the light from the truck on her. Foam was bubbling out of the hole in her back. I had anal intercourse with her as I watched her struggle for breath." He took a deep breath. "I was extremely turned on"—he let out a loud breath—"I promise you. Then I strangled her from behind as she was lying facedown on the dirt road." His left knee raised from where he had positioned his left ankle on his right knee, he rested his left arm across the raised knee and suddenly said, "That's how Jesus died, you know. He basically suffocated from hanging on the tree. Couldn't get his breath. The Bible says he gave up his breath. You think he would be willing to save someone like me?"

Rita dreaded the possibility.

8

Renneker finally asked for a break. He had been talking for several hours, and his mouth was dry, he said, though he seemed to like to talk. At least he liked the attention he was getting, which reminded Rita of Father Catalpa, the priest whom she had arrested in the state park murders of young boys. That resemblance alone bothered her. Catalpa, though guilty of other crimes, had been innocent of the murders. He too had been a talker. Why was Renneker taking so long to get at the heart of his confession?

Renneker insisted he was starved. Charlie looked peaked as well, and she could tell he needed a break, as did she. She ordered Renneker his dinner. Charlie went to the rest room while Rita waited until the jailer brought a tray of food to the interrogation room. Rita and Charlie joined Paul in the observation booth. Already, Renneker had given graphic details of six murders, all women. He had drawn maps of where he had left the victims' bodies. It all seemed legitimate enough.

Paul had a slight smile on his face. "This couldn't have worked out better," he said pleasantly. "We have a major killer in our custody. Believe me, that's going to smooth everything with Jim right over. No one will even care about any corruption probe. How about if we all run out to eat dinner together?"

Rita glanced at her watch, saying, "To tell you the truth, I need to call Mike and Greg to make sure everything's all right on the home front." What she really wanted was some fresh air. All the graphic details of the previous several hours were suffocating her. She had noticed that Renneker had relished sharing the details with her in particular, as if all the while he talked he was trying to draw her into his web.

Through the observation glass, she watched him go to the door of the interrogation room and knock. A jailer came to the door. Speaking through a mouth full of sandwich, Renneker asked if he could get a Sprite or a Coke.

The crew-cut jailer smirked. "This isn't the Holiday Inn, you know."

Reacting quickly, Rita stepped into the hallway and told the jailer, "That's fine." She gave him a dollar from her pocket. "Make sure he gets what he wants. We'll reimburse you."

The jailer shrugged. "Whatever you say, ma'am."

While the jailer went off to find a soft drink, Renneker told Rita, "Thank you."

She hated to be thanked by him.

Renneker winked at her. "It's too bad," he said. "Given different circumstances, the two of us could have had something special together."

She was glad the jailer returned with a Sprite because she needed to get away from Renneker. She wanted to put him away someplace where she would never have to think about him again. Then she realized that he would probably end up serving his sentence in the same facility her ex-husband was in, the place where Jeffrey Dahmer and Jesse Anderson had been beaten to death, the maximum-security Columbia Correctional Institution in Portage. That wasn't nearly far enough away. She went out the back door of the jail to avoid the news reporters.

Outside was cold, with the windchill well below zero again. The streets near the county jail were relatively deserted at that hour of the evening. She went to a nearby pub, where she found a pay phone. She dialed her home telephone number, but the answering machine answered. She said, "Where are you? You must have gone out for dinner. So much for our budget. Remember, don't spend all that money. We need it." She sighed. "I'm just calling to make sure everything's all right. I'm still tied up with work. I won't be home until tomorrow. I hope. I love you both. I'll call you later if I can. Greg, clean your room. Hide the checkbook from

Mike." She hung up, disappointed no one had been there to talk to her.

She had taken only a few steps before she saw Charlie heading her way. What's wrong? she wondered, but he motioned toward the phone and passed her without so much as a word.

Now that she knew he was there, she waited at the bar for him. It was at least fifteen minutes before he returned. In the meantime, she ordered a cheeseburger and began eating, not even realizing that she shouldn't have been hungry, not after listening to Renneker. Nevertheless, by the time she had thought about it, the cheeseburger was gone. She wished she had a shot of Wild Turkey to chase it down.

Charlie sat down beside her. He nodded at the basket containing the remnants of a bun and some french fries. "I don't see how you can eat at a time like this."

"I can tell you still don't know me that well, then," she said. She always ate when she was upset about something.

"The dude's sick, isn't he?" he asked. He ordered a Coke and cheeseburger.

"Didn't you just say you didn't understand how anyone could eat at a time like this?"

He told her he might as well eat because he wanted to be able to hold up as long as Renneker did. He gave her one of his big smiles. "You know what, we really should call Paul and see if he wants to join us."

She smiled back. "Paul's a nice guy, but he

was the last person I wanted to have dinner with at a time like this."

"Now that he sees things are working out with Renneker, he wants to warm up to you."

"I know what he's doing. Believe me, I know. Paul's always been a fair-weather friend. When things are going well, he's there; when things are in a mess, he stays as far away as possible."

The bartender brought Charlie's food.

Charlie commented, "I don't think he's that cold-blooded. I think he really loves you and doesn't know how to express it."

She slapped the back of his head. "You think Renneker's telling the truth?" she asked once the bartender had gone.

"You know he is."

"I'm almost afraid to ask him about Jim. I don't really want to hear how it happened."

"Me either." He shook some ketchup in his basket, near the fries, and dipped in a bunch of fries.

"Don't you hate the way he's dragging all of this out?"

"Yeah."

"He knows what we want to hear, and he's taking his own sweet time about telling us."

He picked up another bunch of fries, rubbed them in the ketchup, and put them in his mouth. Chewing, he said, "You would have thought Jim would be too smart to get trapped by someone like Renneker."

"I know. That bothers me. In fact, a lot of things bother me."

"Like what else?"

"Maybe I'm just a cynic. The cynic in me wonders why in the hell Renneker murdered Jim in such a conspicuous manner. I can't get over that part of it."

"I don't think that's hard to explain at all. Jim was after him, and once Jim got after you, there was no shaking him. Renneker got careless and lashed out. Then it became like any other crime. Serial killers tend to like to keep trophies of their victims. In this case, Renneker thought he'd make Jim himself the trophy—the big fish that everyone could pull out of the water and compare to other fish."

She didn't say anything for a moment.

"Look, no matter what we discover, it's not going to bring Jim back, but at least this'll give him a decent end. Jim was putting this thing together. We have proof of that now. That's all I care about."

She smiled sadly. Charlie was right. Jim had been working the investigation, and his work had paid off. Yes, she wanted to clear Jim's name and to make sure he got credit for leading her and the others to Renneker.

As they headed back to the county jail, Rita realized she was feeling better.

In the alley behind the county jail, a crowd of reporters appeared. Leading them was Susan Hall, the investigative reporter from Milwaukee.

Her cameraman was following her as she approached with a microphone in hand. "Captain Trible," she said, excited, "can you give us any details about the serial killer you have locked up inside?"

There was a barrage of other questions.

Flashbulbs were popping here and there, and artificial lights flooded Rita and Charlie.

Susan attempted to bar the way, but she was no match for Charlie, who plowed through the crowd, creating a path for Rita.

"What about Major Jim Swearingen of Wisconsin's Criminal Investigation Division?" Susan called after Rita. "Is it true he was being investigated for corruption and had been working overtime on this case in order to divert questions about his own integrity?"

There was a moment when Rita's rage got the best of her, a moment in which had she been able to get to Susan, she might have lost control of herself. But then Charlie reached the door and pulled her through. He pushed the door shut after her. The reporters pounded on the closed door.

Where had they come from? she wondered. Where had Susan gotten her information about a scandal? She had used the word *corruption*. Paul had used that word earlier.

Rita's pager went off. She went to a private phone and dialed the number on her pager. It was the crime lab. The shoe impressions that had been found at Lake Mendota were consis-

tent with the shoes that had been found at the
crime scene. Jim had had Renneker and his
uncle under surveillance.

By that time, however, Rita's spirits had been
dampened by the ghost Susan Hall had raised,
the ghost of the scandal Jim had been embroiled
in. Rita still didn't know as much about that as
she would have liked to have known.

Ironically, Renneker was on edge too when
they got back to the interrogation room. He
seemed to be having second thoughts. He
wanted to know about the letter of agreement
that guaranteed he wouldn't be extradited.

She dialed Paul's number on her portable
phone. He said he was still waiting for the letter
to be signed. She passed the information along
to Renneker and told him they could talk about
general things until the letter arrived.

She asked him how he had ended up in Madison. She didn't really care, but it was something
to pass the time.

Renneker admitted he knew he was in trouble. "I guess I was trying to find someplace I
could lie low for a while. I had a feeling the
police in several states were on to me."

"But why Madison?" Charlie asked.

"I knew my mother's sister was here, and we
hadn't had anything to do with them for years,
so I thought they might not ask too many questions. I figured they would just accept me as
family and leave it at that."

"Where do your mother and father live,

Scott?'' Rita asked. She knew that too, but again she was making conversation. She knew the mother and father hadn't wanted to have anything to do with him for years.

"Portland, Oregon."

"Why didn't you go home to them?"

"I figured the police would be expecting me to go back there."

"And why wouldn't they be looking for you here?"

"Because my mother hasn't talked to her sister Pat in almost fifteen years. No, the police wouldn't have thought to look here."

Charlie said, "Okay, you appeared on your aunt's doorstep. What did you tell her?"

"I told her I had been in the army, and that now I was out and had been accepted as a student at the University of Wisconsin. I said it was going to take a little time to get a job, get on my feet, and get my veteran's benefits squared away, but that then I would be able to get my own place, support myself, and pay back any help she and Rich gave me. I told her I needed someplace to stay. Rich said I could stay in a camper they owned. Aunt Pat didn't seem too crazy about that, but she gave in."

Rita showed her best skeptical smile. "Come on, Scott, a smooth talker like you? You could have run a con game on just about anyone." She held open her hand. "You'd have had them eating out of the palm of your hand. You'd have

survived well without turning to your aunt
and uncle."

Charlie agreed.

"Yet you had to realize there were certain
risks by going to your aunt and uncle."

"I had to get to know the community. My
aunt and uncle's place gave me a safe place to
learn it."

Charlie said, "Your record indicates that you
were born and raised here."

The smoothness faded for a second. "Until I
was ten or eleven. That's a long time to be away
from a place. Like I said, I needed to get to
know the community again, and I needed someplace safe to do it."

Rita ran a hand through her hair. "Okay, so
you came to your aunt and uncle for help, and
they put you up. Then what happened?"

Renneker stretched out, his legs spread in
front of him. "Well, I started hanging out with
my uncle, and I learned who his contacts were
and who his friends were. One friend in particular interested me, someone I had known in the
past, so one day I borrowed my uncle's truck
and went to see him to see if I could con him
out of some money—"

There came a knock at the door. It was Paul.

Thank goodness, Rita thought, opening the
door. Paul handed her the letter. She scanned
its contents and handed it to Renneker, who
took his time reading it. Paul entered the room
and sat on the edge of the table. A puzzled ex-

pression came onto Renneker's face. He said, "What's this about Major Jim Swearingen of the Criminal Investigation Division?"

As calm and collected as she could be, Rita said, "He's the investigator you murdered."

That automatically put Renneker on the defensive. Standing, he said, "Oh, no, you're not going to do that to me. No way. Someone's playing a game here. They've been playing it all along. I knew something like this was going to happen. That's why I was trying to make up a story about being out at the fishing shack at the time. I knew you were trying to set me up. That's what this is all about, isn't it? You're trying to set me up. You've been trying to do it from the beginning."

Rita was confused. "We went through all of this trouble to get an agreement because you promised you'd shed light on Jim Swearingen's death."

"No, I didn't," he replied. "I thought you were talking about—no, no way. I should have known." He was angry, talking loudly, and as quickly as someone who had rehearsed a speech. "I know how you people work. You want someone, so you do anything to get that person. I'm not going to be set up like that."

Charlie asked, "What exactly did you think you were going to give us in return for the letter?"

"Brittny Neuland," Renneker said. "Who'd you think?"

Rita immediately thought of the first photograph on the wall in her Milwaukee conference room. She was the Brookfield girl who had disappeared while walking to a friend's house.

"You know the one I'm talking about," Renneker said to them. "Don't act like you don't."

Rita looked to Charlie, who looked at Paul.

Renneker sat down and raised his left knee abruptly to his chest. "Let me refresh your memory," he said. He was nervous, holding his knee tightly. "Brittny Neuland is the ten-year-old girl who was supposed to have been kidnapped by her father, following a divorce in which the father was denied visitation rights." He went through an elaborate account of how he had been having a few drinks over in a bar in Brookfield and had overheard a conversation between a mother and another woman at lunch one day. The mother had been upset because the father was supposed to be paying child support, only he had quit his job, stopped paying support, and disappeared. "During the lunch at the bar, the mother said she hoped he was gone from her life for good, so I thought I would bring him back to haunt her." Renneker sucked on his teeth, then scraped at them with a finger, especially his back teeth on the right side. He pulled loose what Rita guessed was a string of meat left from his sandwich and chewed it, smiling as he did so. "But it wasn't the father, was it?"

He went on to describe in detail what he had done. He had watched the mother and daughter's routine for about a week. "Brittny would walk up the hill to the neighbor's house. One time as she was walking down the hill on her way home, I drove past and told her that she was supposed to come with me—her father wanted to see her.

"She was very good," he went on to say. "She did everything I told her. I told her I wasn't going to hurt her, and she believed me. I told her her father had sent me, that I was going to take her to him for a few minutes, and then I'd bring her right back home." He smiled. "You should have seen her sitting so bright-eyed and bushy-tailed in the front seat, looking out the window as if she didn't have a care in the world." He laughed. "I drove her all the way to Madison, right up to Aunt Pat and Uncle Rich's garage, opened the garage, and drove the car in. I asked her to wait in the car while I closed the garage door. She did everything I told her. I got back in the car, pointed out her window, and said, 'There he is,' and grabbed her neck the moment she looked." He shook his head. "I didn't really get that much enjoyment out of it," he said quietly. "It was too easy. I don't like it when it's that easy. She didn't even have much fight in her." He looked as if he had eaten something rancid. "A little kid's that way—no real strength. Takes the fun out of murdering someone. In fact, part of the reason I can't ever be satisfied when I kill someone is that you can only kill that person once." He laughed. "It'd be nice if you could kill a person over and over again."

Rita stared at Renneker's hands. They were large, rough-looking hands. They looked chapped, perhaps from washing them too much.

Charlie asked, too calmly, "Where did you put her?" He looked like he wanted to get up at that very moment and go find her. Rita knew he was thinking about Keisha, his own daughter.

Renneker asked, "Don't you want to know what I did?"

Both she and Charlie sat without saying a word. Paul had gotten up and was leaning against a wall. He hadn't said a word the entire time.

"This was the first time I've ever done anything like this," he continued. "After I strangled her and had my way with her, I cut off her buttocks, took them in the house, where I fried them in olive oil, and then put them in tomato sauce to marinate. I made "veal" parmigiana out of them and served them to my aunt and uncle." He smiled serenely. "We all loved it."

Rita was nauseated. She wished he were dead, and she hated that she was capable of such a thought.

Renneker was staring at her, a smug expression on his face. He said, "Now that I think about it, I guess I didn't need that letter after all, did I? I can see by the look in your eyes that I'm not going to be going anywhere—the state of Wisconsin wouldn't think of letting me go elsewhere, would it?''

9

Numb from the grueling interview with Renneker, Rita sat on the bed in her motel room and massaged her foot as she held the phone receiver between her shoulder and ear. Her ankle looked swollen. She took off her other boot, removed the sock, and examined the other ankle. Yes, they were swollen. Nevertheless, she didn't care. She was glad she had finally caught Mike at home. He told her he and Greg had gone out to dinner after play practice. Why was he continuing to spend money? she wanted to say, but instead commented, "What are you trying to do, spend the entire five thousand dollars as quickly as you can?"

He said softly, "By the time I got home from work and through play practice, believe me, I didn't feel like cooking."

She sighed. "Just so you remember there are some things I'd like to get too," she commented, "some Christmas gifts I haven't had a chance to pick up." What she really meant was that she hadn't had any money to pick them up.

"Like I've been telling you, don't worry, there's enough to go around." Then, "How was the day? Was it terrible?"

She put both hands at the small of her back and arched her neck. "To tell you the truth, I haven't had a chance to put it all together yet." There was a moment of silence, so she filled it: "Listen, I hope you don't think I'm harping at you, but I just don't want to keep living like we've been living, check to check. Two adults shouldn't live like that."

He laughed. "Believe me, there's a lot of people who are much worse off than we are." Again he changed the subject: "Guess what, we had quite a surprise earlier this evening." He told about how when he and Greg had returned from dinner, a black shadow had jumped out of the bushes in front of the house and attacked them. "It was K," he said, laughing at himself. "The damned dog had jumped the fence and was waiting in the bushes for us."

She laughed too. That made her feel better.

"We couldn't get him back in the backyard for the life of us. Every time we'd yell at him, he'd cower on the ground and wouldn't budge. Greg finally had to carry him."

She said, "I was going to tell you that the other morning he was out in the front yard too. When I went out to get in my car, he did the same thing, sort of shot out at me."

He laughed. "I remember that. I remember you yelling his name."

"You heard? You were awake?"

"I watched from the bedroom window." He chuckled. "It was one of the funniest things I ever saw—you trying to command a dog into the backyard."

She laughed too.

"Hey, Mom," said Greg's husky voice. He had picked up the other line. He sounded grown-up.

"Hi, hon, how are you?"

"Fine. Did Mike tell you about K?"

She laughed. "Yes." She told Greg the story about how K had surprised her the same way.

Greg thought that was funny. "He's crazy. He just doesn't understand he's a big dog now. He still thinks he's a little puppy. I had to carry him into the backyard tonight."

"I heard."

"He weighs at least sixty pounds."

She asked Greg about the rehearsal. He said it had gone well.

Calling home helped keep her mind off what was going to happen first thing the next morning, yet the moment she got off, it was back, the realization that the following morning a mother was going to learn of her daughter's murder. With the first light of day, investigators were going in search of Brittny Neuland's mutilated body. Renneker had agreed to lead them to Brittny's body.

The telephone rang. It was Charlie. He asked if she wanted to go down to the motel bar and have a couple of drinks. She knew he was troubled by the same thoughts that were troubling her.

The couple of drinks, however, led to a few more. It took that much alcohol before they were both in a state of mind that they could say how they really felt about the news of Brittny Neuland.

Charlie admitted that all he could think about was, What if something like that had happened to Keisha? Now he knew how she felt the day they had gone out to Matthew Hammond's body in the Kettle Moraine State Forest. "I mean, it's one thing to be sickened by what you see, which was how I was that day, and being terrified, which was how you must have been." He shook his head. "When Renneker was describing how he murdered little Brittny, I was actually terrified. I was thinking about Keisha, and I was thinking that if anything like that ever happened to her, I would want to kill the person who had done it."

A sobering thought came to her, and she ran her hands through her hair, locking her fingers together at the back of her head. She didn't want to tell Charlie how she had wished Renneker were dead, but she didn't want to pretend it meant nothing to her.

"I knew you were thinking about Keisha. I tried not to look at you while Renneker was talking about Brittny, but I could tell you were thinking about your own daughter. You can't get her off your mind, can you?" She knew the feeling well.

"No." The word seemed to stick in his throat. "I've especially been thinking about all the freedom we give Keisha and how many opportunities that opens up for the Rennekers of the world. I mean, even when we go to a place like Wal-Mart, she wants to be able to go to the toy section by herself. She doesn't want us tagging along. What do you do?" He shrugged, then smiled. "After today, I think she's never going anywhere by herself again."

Smiling back at him, Rita found herself trying to get more bourbon out of an empty glass. She didn't want to order another one, but she wished she had more to drink. "I guess you hope and pray your children will be safe."

Charlie tried to talk her into another drink, but she put her hand over the glass. He had noticed that she was playing with the ice in her glass. She was sure of it. She felt like a dirty old alcoholic at the moment, looking out from hair hanging down in her face. She realized her face was over the glass, looking into it.

"Are you drunk?" he asked.

She looked at him. He was leaning back with his big feet in an extra chair at the table. His shoes were off.

"No," she lied. She thought she might actually be drunk, but was afraid to test herself, for fear of what she might discover. Then, "I hate the thought of tomorrow."

"Me too. I don't want to go wherever he's going to take us. I'd just as soon that body's never found."

She swallowed thickly.

"Shit, listen to us. Listen to how we're talking."

Silence.

"What's wrong?"

"You know, it's odd about Jim."

"What do you mean?"

"Renneker said he didn't kill him, and as cooperative as he was with everything else, I can't help but think he'd have confessed to this murder too—had he done it."

His face took on a wry look.

"It makes sense to me."

She looked at him.

"That's how Renneker operates. Don't you think it's too coincidental that Jim was watching him, and Jim, drowned, ended up with Placidyl in his bloodstream? Come on, be real. What are the chances of that happening? You think Renneker is a saint when it comes to telling the truth?"

She toyed with her empty glass. "I guess you're right." She closed her eyes and saw the froth protruding from Jim's mouth and nose. For a moment she even saw the decomposed body of the child they were going to find in the morning. She knew how long Brittny had been missing, knew what she would look like.

"Rita—"

Her eyes opened to him.

"You look like you're a million miles from here."

She forced a smile.

"Is it you don't think Renneker did it, or that we're not going to get a confession?"

"Why wouldn't he confess?"

"I don't know."

"Why wouldn't he be proud?"

"My God, the guy's sick. How can anyone tell what's going on in his mind? I say he's lying, no matter what he tells us, and to tell you the truth, there's nothing I'd rather do than bust up his face." Smiling, he sat forward as if he had just thought of something. "That's it. That's the reason he won't confess. He's afraid that if he confesses to killing a cop, one of us is going to pop a cap at him and claim he tried to escape. He loves himself so much he doesn't want to die. After all, he wanted to stay in a state that didn't have the death penalty."

She was confused. She had had too much to drink. She said, "He's not afraid to die."

Charlie smiled broadly. "Everyone has a threshold of fear. You want me to find his?" He made a large fist.

She stared at the fist.

"I'm telling you, I could strike some fear in him."

She didn't doubt it. "Let's call it a day," she said, standing. She was unsteady on her feet. Don't let him see it, she told herself. "I'll see you in the morning." She made her way back to her room, where she found a message from Paul on the telephone, and she called him. Only when he answered did she realize it was almost midnight. He told her the shoe impressions Charlie had found at the lake matched Jim's shoes, the ones that had been found in the fishing shack. She told him she knew.

That didn't deflate his enthusiasm. "All I can say is that because of you, things'll probably work out just fine."

"What do you mean?"

"I mean, you insisted Jim didn't commit suicide. You were right. You do good work."

She was having trouble concentrating. "Paul, I'm very tired."

"I've talked to the U.S. attorney over in Milwaukee. His office is closing its investigation against Jim. One of the reasons is that the federal government was involved in a violent-crimes task force over in Colorado, and they were looking for Renneker too. They were so happy we caught him that they've agreed not to besmirch Jim's name. In other words, if all goes well tomorrow, I think you can wrap all of this up and head back to Milwaukee well in time for Christmas."

What could possibly go well when she was going out in the morning to find the decomposed body of a young girl? "Paul, really, I need to get some sleep."

"And you deserve it."

"I'll see you tomorrow." That's the last thing she remembered until the telephone rang at five in the morning. She didn't remember making a wake-up call, but was glad she had. She got up, showered, then went down to breakfast.

Charlie was waiting. She joined him at a small table near the front windows of Sally's, a restaurant near the county building. Since he had already ordered, he continued to eat.

She ordered only a glass of orange juice and a bagel and cream cheese. She opened her napkin on her lap. She could tell something was wrong. "What is it, Charlie?"

Chewing, Charlie slid a folded newspaper across the table. He said, "You might as well have this from me as someone else."

She opened the paper to the headline: "Suicide or Serial Killer?"

From her coat pocket, she brought out her bifocals, put them on, and began to read:

"The question plaguing many in official circles here in Madison is, how has a chief criminal investigator for the state of Wisconsin ended up dead at the feet of a confessed serial killer? Is it murder or suicide?"

She was about to read more when someone sat down at their table. Rita looked up: it was Susan Hall. As usual she looked perfectly composed, not a blond hair out of place. "Good morning, Captain Trible," she said, then nodded to Charlie, "and Investigator Dalton. Do you mind if I join you for a couple of minutes?"

Charlie gave her a big smile. "You get around, Miss Hall, don't you?"

She apparently took it as a compliment because she smiled and said, "I try to."

Rita said, "Excuse me, but yes, I do mind if you sit down. We're having a private conversation here."

Susan was not to be shaken. "To tell you the truth, I thought you'd want me to join you since I'm the one who's about to blow this story wide open."

"Please leave us."

"It's going to be a story about how a corrupt cop was in so much trouble that he committed suicide in order to escape it all, and how you and others are now rushing to cover it all up and make it look like murder. Make your friend look like a hero."

"Last chance," Rita told her warningly.

"I have some very interesting information that I'd be willing to share with you in return for an exclusive interview."

As calmly as she could manage, Rita said, "Miss Hall, I'm asking politely for you to leave."

Susan put her finger on the newspaper photograph of Charlie and Rita trying to get in the back door of the jail. She said, "This kind of thing is only going to get worse."

That was enough. Rita snapped her fingers at a waitress.

The waitress appeared, carrying a small plate with a bagel and cream cheese on it and a glass of orange juice. Placing the items in front of Rita, the waitress asked, "Is everything all right?"

Rita said, "No, it isn't," and she pointed at Susan Hall. "This stranger sat down at our table, and she is harassing us. Is the manager available?"

The waitress didn't quite seem to know what to do, though Susan did. She stood and said, "Very well, let's do it the hard way." She quietly left the table.

Charlie commented, "I wanted to hear what she had to say."

Rita tried not to smile. She began to spread cream cheese on her bagel. "She's an ass."

Charlie, eating again, said, "She might be an ass, but she's going to be trouble."

Rita, staring at her bagel, said, "Let me think for a minute, do I care?" She was silent, then began to eat. "No."

10

Rita and Charlie arrived at the county jail as Renneker was finishing a breakfast of corn flakes, orange juice, and cake donuts. The sheriff's detectives used Ace bandages and splints to wrap each of his legs so his knees wouldn't bend. One of the detectives, a short, stocky man wearing a navy blazer, navy tie with a handcuff-shaped tie clip, and gray polyester slacks, said he hoped Renneker didn't try anything stupid. The detective had only a few strands of long gray hair that he combed straight back as if he had a head full of hair. He said, "My name is Detective Keith Beck, and most people who know me'll tell you that if you try anything stupid, I'll shoot first and ask questions later."

Rita watched Renneker, who didn't seem impressed by Detective Beck, though she had no doubt Beck would do what he said. Beck not only put handcuffs on Renneker, but he also attached body chains, which limited the freedom of Renneker's arms.

Renneker commented, "I don't know why you're going through all of this. I'm not going anywhere."

Detective Beck said, "That's right. You're not going anywhere. You're not going to go anywhere ever again. And you're not going to be grabbing for a pistol either."

As she and Charlie followed, the detectives led the stiff-legged Renneker down to the closed parking garage, where he was helped into an unmarked black Blazer with tinted windows. The Blazer was running and warm inside.

She sat beside Renneker in the middle seat while Charlie sat in back. The two sheriff's detectives sat in front, Detective Beck driving. Outside the garage was an army of protection. In windows and on rooftops were sharpshooters from SWAT teams. Marked and unmarked police cars provided an escort. Streets were blocked off, and no one had the slightest chance of getting near the Blazer that carried Renneker. He sat proudly, looking out at all the attention he was receiving.

The morning was overcast, and a smoky haze rested close to the ground. Freezing rain started coming down, which had a dramatic effect on the snow. It was actually melting to expose the earth in places. Not much like Christmas, Rita thought.

Detective Beck took Interstate 90/94 ten miles

north of the city before Renneker suddenly told him to take the exit ramp. It wasn't clear whether he had forgotten where he had dumped the body and remembered at the last moment, or whether he wanted to make last-minute instructions for the dramatic effect.

"Turn left at the stop sign," he said when the Blazer was at the bottom of the exit ramp.

They went under the interstate.

"There—turn right!"

"Where?" Detective Beck said, almost turning up the wrong way on the opposite exit ramp.

"No, the next right."

Not far up the winding road that ran parallel to the interstate was a gravel road on the left. Renneker told Detective Beck to take it. Renneker was calm again, almost serene.

The gravel road was in poor condition. There were a lot of potholes in it. The freezing rain wasn't helping matters.

At the top of the hill was a cemetery. Renneker laughed. He said, "Believe it or not, that's a pet cemetery, where people treat dogs and cats better than they treat human beings. Who says I'm sick?"

The pet cemetery, a small, fenced-in plot of ground that had a spruce tree overlooking it, was full of granite markers. It looked like any other cemetery Rita had seen.

"Keep following the road," Renneker directed Detective Beck.

Another half mile along the rough road was a dilapidated building.

"This used to be the old humane society," Renneker said. "Only now they've moved it closer to the city."

He obviously had some familiarity with the territory where he had discarded his victim.

"Rita, you know you remind me of a girl I once knew."

She hated to hear him call her by her first name, hated the familiarity. The Blazer stopped.

"Tammy something. It was many years ago. I can't remember her last name. It was in seventh grade. She was the class whore. Every class has one, you know." He laughed. "I remember all of us seventh-grade boys were jealous because all the high school boys were after her. In fact, I bet she had been screwed by half of the boys in high school. Pull up closer, Detective Beck."

The abandoned building looked like one of the communes from the sixties.

Detective Beck, following Renneker's directions, parked in front of the building, and they all got out. Other police cars, marked and unmarked, crowded into the limited space. A helicopter flew overhead.

Renneker seemed oblivious to the freezing rain. He took the lead, walking around back of the abandoned humane society as if he had been there many times in the past. "Anyway, Rita, as I was saying, this Tammy girl was our class whore, and while the high school boys were all plugging her, none of us seventh-graders could get up enough nerve to do it. We were still experimenting with masturbation."

Rita wished he would shut up.

In back of the house were rows of empty cages and the lingering stench of animal wastes. Renneker passed what looked like an exercise pen for the dogs. There was still a leash hanging on a fence post.

"At some point three of us boys got up enough nerve to start teasing each other about screwing Tammy, and we started daring each other. We ended up forming a pact. We decided we'd all go down to the local gas station, buy some rubbers, then go gang-bang her." His voice was distant, remembering. "She had red hair like you do, only yours is darker." He laughed. "And there was no gray in it."

They were walking through a snow-patched field, her boots sinking into the cold mud. The field, across which huge power lines ran, overlooked two valleys. In one was a two-lane road with a lot of traffic. In the other valley was a pond. Renneker said he thought it was used for cattle, though he hadn't seen any to confirm that idea. He stopped to stare at the distant pond. He said, "I think it was the first time I realized what sluts all women were. They drop their pants and can tame even the biggest, meanest man. Tammy tamed all three of us that night. One after another of us climbed on top of her, and she just smiled."

Rita tried to ignore him. She looked down at the pond and thought it would be uncanny if Brittny Neuland's body had been dumped in the water.

"I know what you're thinking," Renneker said.

She looked at him.

His ice-blue eyes were fixed on her. There was a smirk on his face. "Yes, you remind me of Tammy."

He wants me to break, she thought. Not a chance.

"No, I didn't dump her in the pond," he told her. "I gave her a proper place to rest—there under the cross." He pointed at one of the huge steel superstructures that supported power lines. It did resemble a steel cross on a wide base. "I laid her to rest at the foot of the cross." He began walking in that direction, and everyone followed.

The closer they got, the more noticeable was an odor of decay. The rain was falling heavily. Rita was soaked.

She glanced at Charlie, who hadn't said a word the entire trip, not since they had had breakfast that morning. She knew he had been preparing himself for what he was about to see. She felt sorry for him. During the past year she had grown to understand that beneath the rough, imposing exterior, he was a sensitive person. She had seen how good he was with his daughter, Keisha, who, with leukemia, had been in and out of remission.

"Rita, did I tell you where I was living then?"

"What?"

"When we gang-banged Tammy. It was in a small town in Indiana. One of the many places I've lived. My old man had his problems with the women too, so we ended up moving around a lot. In fact, when we lived in Indiana, he got one woman pregnant and was having an affair with another woman. The whole town knew it, except my mother. She didn't know. Or maybe she did know and pretended she didn't. I don't think she did, but you never can tell."

Renneker led them right to the body. Rita held a hand over her mouth and nose, the odor was so repulsive. It seemed to be everywhere. She noticed Charlie putting a handkerchief over his mouth. Detective Beck said, "God," and turned away.

Brittny's naked body had a greenish-purple face that looked up at them. The face was so puffy and deteriorated that the eyes had swollen closed. Her body was bloated and swollen, and some of her skin had sloughed off. Her left leg had been eaten to the bone by animals. As Renneker had said, it looked as if her buttocks had been peeled off.

The next thing Rita knew, Charlie's large fist shot past her and literally lifted Renneker off his feet and sent him sprawling onto the muddy ice. It took everyone available to stop Charlie from following Renneker. Even she jumped upon him. He was nearly unstoppable, throwing them left and right. She realized he was all muscle. Then, clear of everyone, he stopped. His hair was nappy from where people had jumped him. His face was ashen, and he was winded. No one moved toward him.

Rita was in such a state of shock, she didn't know what to say.

Detectives helped Renneker up—his stiff knees wouldn't allow him to get up on his own. Renneker worked his jaw this way and that. "I'm fine," he said. "He's right. That's the only way you're going to be able to stop someone like me."

"Charlie, please, could you go back to the Blazer?" Rita said.

He left without saying a word.

She followed, but didn't try to catch up with him.

Alone with him at the Blazer, all she could say was, "Charlie, what happened back there?"

Until that time he hadn't attempted to say a word. Now he said, "His hands were moving toward your weapon."

"What?"

"His hands were moving toward your weapon."

She looked away without saying anything to him, took a deep breath, and let it out. "Come on, Charlie, we both know each other better than that. He has body chains on."

"He was right beside you. His hands were moving toward your weapon."

"Charlie—"

"I don't give a damn whether you believe me or not."

The words were so forceful she didn't know what to think. Renneker had been standing on the side where her weapon was. Had Charlie seen something she hadn't seen? Her attention had been riveted on Brittny Neuland's body. Certainly his must have been too.

"You don't believe me, do you?"

She didn't want to acknowledge it, but, no, she didn't. "Charlie, this has nothing to do with whether I believe you," she said. "But right now I have to do something that's very difficult for me, and that's to follow standard procedure." She didn't even have to ask him to give her his credentials and his service weapon. He had them in hand before she could say anything. She was thankful about that. "Charlie, damn it, I'm sorry. I don't want to do this, but you know this is the policy."

"I don't give a shit about the policy," he said. "All that matters is that you don't believe me."

He was about to climb into the backseat of the Blazer when she took him by the arm and said, "Charlie, look, all of this is happening so fast. Give me a chance to sort things out."

He climbed into the Blazer, slamming the door behind him.

Back in the field, she asked around. No one

had seen anything. Everyone had been so preoccupied with the dead body that Charlie's reaction had caught them completely off guard.

Renneker himself was grinning smugly. He
didn't mention police brutality, or that he
wanted to press charges against Charlie. He simply said that he deserved everything that was
happening to him.

On the way to the Blazer, Detective Beck
pulled her aside and said, "All I want to say
is that what happened back there could have
happened to any one of us." It was what she
was afraid to hear, that everyone else was thinking the same thing she had been thinking—law
enforcement officials sometimes did things like
that and needed to stick together.

She sent in the forensic team and the coroner,
and notified Vince back at the office. She also
asked Vince to arrange for Brittny's father to be
contacted. While the investigation was officially
in the hands of the sheriff's department, Brittny's father lived in Milwaukee, and she told the
sheriff she would help with the notification
process.

They drove back to Madison in total silence.
Rita could feel a headache coming on, a major
headache.

At headquarters, she went immediately to see
Paul. She wanted to tell him what had happened
before anyone else told him.

Paul took the news well. He didn't fault Charlie. He said, "Did I ever tell you about the time

I was driving back from Cleveland with this young man who was wanted for murder? Stop me if I did."

Rita let him talk.

He leaned back in his swivel chair. He had never liked anyone to have to sit on the other side of his desk, so he had placed the desk against the wall. The extra chair in his office he put near his. That way anyone who came to visit him sat beside him.

"I was bringing this young hoodlum back from Cleveland, and he asked me if we could stop somewhere to get a drink—he was thirsty.

"I told him, no, I wasn't going to stop right then. Next thing I know, he calls me a selfish bastard and hits me upside the head with his cuffed hands. So I stopped the car and beat the hell out of him."

She smiled.

"He never said a word about it. In fact, we got along just fine after that."

"What are you saying, Paul?"

"I'm not volunteering anything. Ask me what I did."

"Did you file an incident report?"

"No."

"It doesn't sound like there were any witnesses. This morning there were witnesses."

Paul shrugged. "I can't tell you what to do, but I bet no one ever says a word." Then he smiled gently. "To tell you the truth, I imagine this will make somewhat of a legend out of

Charlie. As long as Renneker doesn't want to
file a complaint, if Charlie says he saw Renneker
going for your gun, then I think you should
leave it at that."

Before she left, she told Paul she wanted the
keys to Jim's town house one more time.

"I thought you'd been by there," he told her.
He looked troubled.

"I want to take one last look around."

He said he would call the evidence supervisor. "When are you going home? We've got
what we wanted. Rita, believe me, we couldn't
have asked for a better scenario."

"I just want to make sure I haven't missed
anything."

She went to find Charlie. She found him at
her temporary desk in the Madison headquarters building. He had apparently gone back to
the motel first because he had changed clothes.
He was wearing jeans and a bright blue tank top
shirt. She could see the curly hair of his chest.

Holding out his credentials and service
weapon, she said, "Listen, I guess seeing that
little girl's body did something to me. I couldn't
think straight. I'm sorry. I wasn't even paying
any attention to what Renneker was doing. No
one was. I'm glad you were."

He slid his service revolver into a clip holster
on his pants. He put his credentials in his back
pocket.

She told him she was going back to Jim's

house one last time, and asked if he wanted to ride along.

He put on a leather coat.

She took that to mean he was going.

They drove to Jim's town house, where she went right to the master bedroom. Plastic gloves on, she went through Jim's wallet again. In the bill section of the wallet, she found two tens, a five, and a withdrawal slip. It was from an automatic teller machine. She handed the slip to Charlie. "I want to check this out."

Puzzled, Charlie asked, "That Jim made a withdrawal from his account?"

"No, I want to see what an ATM surveillance camera caught on tape when Jim made his withdrawal. I should have done it before."

From the wallet she also removed the recreation facility card. Under it was a locker card for a locker. In another part of the wallet was a Master combination lock card with a combination.

She looked at Charlie. "I want to check this out too," she said. "I'm wondering how Jim got access to a university facility when he wasn't a student there. Somehow he got rec privileges. I want to see what was in his locker."

Smiling broadly, he said, "What, no search warrant or subpoena?"

"I'm just collecting the personal effects of a friend."

"Yeah," he said, drawing out the word and

nodding at the same time. "That's the Rita I love and care about."

They drove to the University of Wisconsin, where they found a metered parking space near the gym. At the information desk, Rita asked where they could find the swimming pool. The desk attendant told them the pool was downstairs.

They went down, passing some rowing and cycle machines. A number of young men and women were on the machines, above which was a television that the exercisers could watch while they worked out. Several young people passed wearing tae kwon do uniforms.

Rita and Charlie followed the signs to the pool area. Outside the pool locker rooms was a desk area monitored by a young black man. Near him was a stack of white towels. A young woman passed Rita and Charlie. She grabbed a towel from the stack, handed the black man a card, and disappeared into one of the locker rooms.

In the background at the desk, music played.

Rita held out the orange recreation center card, the locker card, and the Master combination card. She told the attendant, "My husband is in the hospital, and I need to pick up his things from his locker here. Is there someone who can help us?"

The young black man spoke with what Rita assumed was a Caribbean accent. He told her he didn't think he was authorized to release personal possessions. "I'm not sure I can do this," he said. He scratched deep in his Afro hair. "I've never had anyone make such a request. Maybe I better check." He picked up a telephone.

Charlie spoke up. "Who's on the tape? Is that Sade?"

"Yes, it is," the black man replied, smiling as he began to press numbers on the phone.

Charlie pushed down the DISCONNECT button. "I think I have this tape," he said. "Is this the *Stronger Than Pride* tape?"

The black man continued to smile. "Yes, it is. What are you doing?"

Charlie removed his finger from the button. "Isn't she great? I love all her songs." He began to tap his fingers on the counter. "This is 'Love Is Stronger Than Pride,' isn't it?"

The black man's eyes glistened.

"Say, my man, help us out here. We need to pick up the stuff from the locker. It's not like we're trying to break into his shit or anything. He's getting ready to go to surgery, and he asked us to come by and pick up his things. Is that a crime? I mean, you're going to call up to some administrator, and that person is going to give you some long list of things you're supposed to do, and we're going to be playing these games for a week. Come on, help us out. We have his rec card, his locker card, and his combination. I mean, what more do you want?"

The attendant thought about it for a moment, then took the locker card and combination card. In a few minutes he returned with a large beach towel, a shaving bag, a pair of navy swimming trunks—like the ones that had been hanging over Jim's shower door—and a thick brown envelope.

Rita took the items.

Charlie shook hands with the black man. "We appreciate this."

Rita and Charlie were upstairs and almost out the door when they heard a woman's voice behind them, saying, "Excuse me. Excuse me for a minute."

Rita looked back to see a young blond woman, her hair up in a bun. She was wearing a red swimming suit, a one-piece type, with a towel wrapped around her waist. There was a Red Cross patch on the suit. She was obviously a lifeguard.

"Excuse me," she said, her large breasts bulging against her suit as she talked. She had large lips as well. "Are you the ones who came to pick up Jim's things?"

Rita didn't say anything, though she was holding the items from Jim's locker.

The young woman held out a hand. "I'm Debbie Sweet," she said. "I'm a lifeguard here. I was giving Jim swimming lessons. He said he was scared of water and was determined to overcome his fear. Is he all right? My friend downstairs said he was in the hospital, about to go to surgery."

Rita didn't say anything, though she wanted to ask, "Haven't you been following the news?"

She took Debbie's hand, which she shook. Charlie shook hands too.

"I thought Jim was divorced," Debbie said. "Arthur said you told him you were Jim's wife."

"I'm Rita Trible," she said, "a friend."

Beaming with pleasure, Debbie said, "Yes, Jim mentioned you. You once had an affair with him, didn't you?"

11

Rita was speechless at first, as was Charlie, who glanced at her as if he wanted an explanation. Finally, she found some words: "That was a long time ago." She tried to keep her eyes on Debbie, who clearly had no problem with Rita being a former lover of Jim's. Debbie seemed the kind of person who hadn't lived long enough to give that much weight to such matters.

Debbie said, "I'm glad you came along because I've been worried about Jim. I haven't seen him for a while, and he hasn't returned my calls. He's in the hospital?" What had happened? she wanted to know. Was he all right? She was trying not to look worried, but it was no use.

Debbie had been Jim's lover, Rita assumed. Too young, but clearly Jim's tastes. Well endowed. They had been close too, the kind of lovers who had obviously shared intimate secrets, the kind of lovers who had been together long enough to have had their first spat. There must have been a recent cooling-off period because Debbie had not heard what had happened to Jim. Rita asked her if there was someplace private where they could talk. The entrance of the university gym hardly seemed the appropriate place to give Debbie the bad news.

Debbie said she was on duty until two o'clock. How about if they stopped by her condo at about two-thirty? She gave Rita and Charlie the address.

Rita was thankful that Charlie didn't say anything on the way to their state car. Instead they focused on the envelope that had been in Jim's locker. They silently exchanged letters and documents. From all appearances, Al Hoeveler, the husband of Jim's ex-wife, had gotten into a letter war with Chad Whitaker, the head of NationsCare of America. For some reason Jim had copies of the entire transaction, including Al's original inquiries to NCA about participating in the construction of a Milwaukee super hospital, and Whitaker's initial response:

Dear Mr. Hoeveler:
   Thank you for your recent inquiry about NCA's exciting new building plans for Milwaukee. As you know, our new $2.3 billion multiplex will be one of the largest building projects of its kind in the nation, and will bring international recognition to Milwaukee. Having been born and raised here, I am pleased to be giving back something to the city. Milwaukee will, without a doubt, become an international leader

in health care. Naturally, we appreciate that Hoeveler Contractors, Inc., desires to participate in this project.

Our initial screening process of contractors, of course, has forced us to make some tough decisions. No decision we have made should be interpreted to mean that we are being personally critical of your work or your company's reputation. Instead, we have had an overwhelming response to our announced plans. We trust that you will be sympathetic toward our dilemma. In other words, it was necessary for us to eliminate certain smaller contractors because we simply have too many names on our list and the competition is keen.

Please understand that dark clouds do often have silver linings. The silver lining here is that undoubtedly the demands of this major project will create work for your company, perhaps more work than you'll be able to keep up with. As contractors make commitments to us, they will be forced to forgo commitments elsewhere. In other words, a project like this benefits all, and we trust this includes you.

Best wishes.

Yours sincerely,

Chad Whitaker

The letter was signed "Chad."

The initial written response from Al Hoeveler was diplomatic. On company stationery, he wrote that he thought NCA was treating him and his company unfairly, and he wanted to know how he could appeal the NCA decision. "What bothers me most," Hoeveler wrote, "is that I know some of the contractors NCA has selected. You might say I run in the same circle. The kind of information I know is not something you would want to become public. All I want is fair treatment. It's not fair I'm being pushed aside because my company's small." Was there a formal appeal process, Hoeveler asked in his letter, and if so, what was it?

Apparently no one at the NCA system responded to his letter because Al wrote another letter, this one also addressed to Chad Whitaker, in which he pointed out:

As of this date, three months later, I have not received any response from you about my inquiry. Would you please give me an update about what action you have taken with my complaint and my request for an appeal of your former decision? Again, I point out the seriousness of certain information I know about how you have selected your contractors. If you do not respond to me, I will file an official complaint with outside authorities. Thank you, and I look forward to hearing from you.

The letter was signed "Al."

Still there must have been no response to the letter because the next letter of Al's threatened to take his complaint to news organizations if the NCA system didn't respond.

Rita wasn't sure how that turned out. What did strike her of interest, however, was an article in *Milwaukee Magazine*, in which an editor claimed, "Health care backer and former resident has a bold new vision for Milwaukee and national health care, and he's not letting anything or anyone get in the way of making it a reality."

Someone had put a pencil check near the passage. Rita assumed it was Jim, because when he did research on a case, he tended to mark passages he wanted to remember. She knew his pencil marks well.

Charlie said, "From the way all of this looks, our man Al turned to Jim for help." He looked at her. "All of these threats make it look like Al had something he could blackmail Whitaker with, and for the most part Whitaker wasn't too worried about an official investigation."

Rita wasn't sure how it all fit together, but what did seem to be apparent was that NationsCare had been caught off guard enough that it had broken off all written communications with Hoeveler. Among the contents of the envelope were a number of letters that Hoeveler had sent that had either received no reply or whose replies hadn't been copied for Jim. Probably NationsCare had stopped making replies, Rita thought, because Al's letters became more and more dangerous.

Rita glanced at a newspaper article: "Whitaker Knows Best for Milwaukee."

Charlie said, "Hey, take a look at this."

She took the letter he held out. It was another from Al to NCA:

Dear Mr. Whitaker:
  Over the past several months, I have expressed to you my feelings that my company, Hoeveler Contractors, Inc., has been treated unfairly by NationsCare

of America. I have even been convinced there might be some illegal or improper activity involved. Neither you nor any representative of yours has seen fit to respond to my inquiries. This troubles me greatly because it suggests your own unaccountability when it comes to scrutiny. Perhaps that is because you do not want anyone to ask too many questions at all.

Let me be more specific. I know that two contracting companies you have recently approved for your Milwaukee building project have strong ties to organized crime. I have good reason to believe you have personal knowledge about the questionable dealings of Eagle Construction Co. and Z & M Construction.

All I want on your part is a fair review. I want my company to be treated the same as any other company that has been reviewed by the NationsCare system, and at this point it seems like there have been some biases and some improper activity in the review process. If those biases and improper activities are not corrected, I again assure you I will begin to make inquiries elsewhere, and I will go out of the city to do it.

I will appreciate your kind attention to these matters.

Sincerely,
Al Hoeveler

"I would say our Mr. Hoeveler hid away something that was incriminating enough to put Whitaker in a corner," she told Charlie. "And it looks like he dragged Jim right into the middle of it."

Charlie responded, "I don't know about the Eagle company, but I've had a run-in with this Z and M company, and Al's right." He told about how the year before, he and Claudia had installed a new patio door in their house. They had contacted Z and M, which had sent out a subcontractor to do the work. "Z and M only does huge jobs, but they're such a big name in Milwaukee that I thought I'd give them a call. I was sure if they recommended someone that person would be reputable. As it turned out, they have a lot of subcontractors who do small jobs for them, and they sent out a father-son operation." He tapped his fingers on the steering wheel.

"And—"

He stopped tapping. "This father-son team used these black sheets of plastic to seal off the living room, and for several days there was all kinds of racket behind the black plastic. Then one day the father and son pulled down the plastic and said they were done. They asked for their pay." He raised his open hands as if he were holding out some invisible package to her. "Here I am looking at this eight-foot patio door that had been installed, which was fine. The patio door was in and worked, but all of the inside trim and finishing touches hadn't been done at all." He put his hands down and shook his head. "I said, 'You haven't even finished the job, and you're wanting your pay?'

"The father, some squirrelly guy, told me the job had turned out bigger than what he and his son had expected. He said they had to move on to another job. I refused to pay. A couple hours later, Z and M was on the phone. This supervisor there was making all kinds of threats, so I explained what had happened. It isn't twenty minutes later, and this silver Lincoln town car pulls up to the house." He smiled at her, his eyebrows rising. "Out of this town car climb four of the biggest white dudes I'd ever seen."

She smiled at her image of what the men must have looked like if they looked big to Charlie.

"The car rises like six inches off of the ground when they get out."

Her smile grew.

"One of these dudes says they're inspectors from Z and M."

She laughed. Charlie could be funny when he wanted.

"Now, they don't look like inspectors at all because they're dressed in these expensive suits, but I don't argue with them. They come in, look at the door, and the one who had introduced himself and the others as inspectors tells me to make out a check for half of what I had agreed to pay. I gave them half, and I was glad to see them go. I mean, it was clear that these dudes didn't mess around."

Rita, still smiling, looked out her window. The smile vanished. She could see it go out of the reflection in the glass. "Charlie, why would Jim keep this stuff in a locker at the University of Wisconsin?"

Charlie, back to shuffling through the letters, documents, and notes, replied, "Maybe he forgot it the last time he went swimming. I mean,

I could see how that swimming instructor of his could be distracting."

She looked at him. They hadn't said anything about her yet. "She is pretty, isn't she?"

Charlie's face turned a grayish color as he stared at the sheet in his hand.

"What?"

She took the light green sheet of paper that had been torn from a stenographer's pad. The top of the paper still had frayed edges where a wire coil had held it in a book. She read:

> Dear Rita,
>   You remember how you were reminded the hard way of something a lot of us forget?
>   We look at crime and think it's out there somewhere—not really a part of us. The truth is, child abusers, wife abusers, thieves, and murderers are living right next door.
>   Sometimes they're in our own homes.
> Best wishes and love always,
>   Jim.

Staring at the letter, she remembered distinctly the day when Mike Squires had proposed marriage to her during a backyard barbecue. The words in the letter were the same Jim had said when she had lamented that her own ex-husband had turned out to be the one sexually abusing and killing children in the Milwaukee area. She could feel gooseflesh running from her neck to her face. In a numb, monotone voice she told Charlie about what Jim had said at the barbecue.

"What's it mean?"

"I don't know, except it seems rather obvious that Jim thought I'd be the one who found the envelope."

"I got that impression too." He started the car. "Where to?"

She glanced at her watch. It was a couple minutes after one. "Let's run by the bank and see if we can get the videotape from the ATM. Then I want to get Paul to give us access to Jim's computer and caseload files."

He didn't answer right away. "Paul's not going to want us digging this much."

"I know."

Charlie glanced over. "Maybe he's right."

"What do you mean?"

"I didn't know Jim as well as you did, and I'm not pretending anything like that, but let me play devil's advocate for a moment."

"Go ahead."

"Paul's going to say, 'Look, the U.S. attorney has agreed to close its investigation against Jim, so drop it.' Renneker isn't going to make a confession. We won't have a case, but the longer we keep all of this open, the more the media is going to keep digging."

To her surprise, though, Paul didn't drag his feet. He said she was welcome to go through Jim's investigative files and cases. Rita and Charlie went to see him after the bank turned over the security tape from the ATM.

In fact, he assigned one of the CID computer

technicians to make a backup of the hard drive on Jim's computer. Meanwhile, she and Charlie went through the folders in Jim's filing cabinet and desk. Jim was as meticulous at work as he was at home. Everything was in careful order. The search was relatively easy. Jim had switched for the most part to the computer in recent years.

The computer materials collected, Rita and Charlie headed for Debbie Sweet's condo, a duplex near the end of a dead-end street right off the university campus. Debbie was just getting home when Rita and Charlie parked in front of the duplex.

"Looks like a pretty nice place," Charlie mentioned.

She agreed. Not what one would expect for a college student. The duplex, all on one level, was done in a modern architectural style, its exterior a natural wood, stained dark.

Debbie saw them, waved, a smile on her face, and walked out to greet them. She escorted them to the door, saying, "Looks like we couldn't have timed this better. Please, go on in."

Rita entered a living room that had a cathedral ceiling and a large stone fireplace. The room was decorated in earth tones. She walked to the center of the room, where she turned to face Debbie, who was still smiling, though the smile suddenly turned brittle.

"Is something wrong?" Debbie asked.

Speaking softly, Rita said, "Please, sit down, Debbie."

Debbie sat on the edge of the sofa, her hands held together in her lap.

"I'm afraid I do have bad news," Rita said.

Debbie's face grew pale.

"Jim is dead."

Debbie swallowed. She didn't cry, didn't scream, didn't move. She looked too shocked to do any of those things. On rare occasions Rita had encountered such a reaction—someone so devastated by bad news that that person couldn't do anything. Debbie seemed a complete shell of the person she had been a few moments before. Finally her head began to tremble. It was almost imperceptible at first, then quite pronounced. She had to hold her face with her hands to stop from trembling. "I was afraid of this," she said.

There followed a long silence.

Rita said, "You knew he was in some kind of trouble, didn't you?"

Their eyes met. Debbie's were warm with tears. She nodded. "Jim said something might happen," she said weakly.

Rita sat down.

Charlie sat on the other side of her. He said, "Debbie, you should know something about us."

Debbie looked at him with empty eyes. She was between the two of them.

"We're here because Jim was our friend. We're trying to help him."

"His ex-wife, it's her fault," Debbie suddenly said. "She was the one who got him into this mess."

"What mess?" Rita wanted to know.

Debbie shook her head. "I don't know," she said. "Diane didn't give a damn about him, but he was the first one she turned to when her husband got in trouble."

Rita reached out and touched Debbie's hand.

Debbie forced a smile. "That's the way he was," she said. "He cared about people. He'd do anything for you, anything you asked him."

Rita told her that they needed to know everything she could tell them about her and Jim's relationship. "I know a lot of it's private," she said. "But we need to know if you saw something or heard something that might be a clue to what happened to Jim."

Debbie shrugged. "We had a good relationship. We had a good thing going."

Charlie asked, "How did you two meet?"

Debbie smiled sadly. Jim liked to have coffee in the mornings at the university's alumni center, she said. A lot of people did. The place was always crowded, so it wasn't unusual for complete strangers to share the same table. She smiled. "When he first asked if he could sit at my table, I thought he was some professor at the university—he looked like it—so who was I to turn him down? Next thing I know, I look up and he's got all these articles and things spread out on the table, his glasses are on, and he's studying them."

Rita said, "Let me guess, he was reading articles and case notes."

"How did you know?"

"That's Jim Swearingen," she replied. "He was a research nut."

Debbie said, "Well, at the time I didn't know it. All I knew was that I looked up and saw this guy sitting at my table, looking at photographs of drowned people, and it scared me."

Rita felt a chill run through her. "Drowned people?" she asked.

"Yes, drowned people. He had all these articles about drowning, and a bunch of pictures of drowned people."

Rita and Charlie exchanged a look.

Debbie gave a thin smile. "Jim must have known I was grossed out because he introduced himself, showed me his badge, and told me he was doing some work."

"When was this?" Charlie asked.

"A year ago last September."

A month after Al had written his first threatening letter to NationsCare. Rita tried to remember if she had heard about any drownings about that time. Had Jim been working a drowning case on the side? There were no major drownings that she could remember.

"Did he ever talk to you about his work?" Charlie asked.

No, Debbie replied, not in any specific terms. "I saw him doing different research at different times, but he never talked about the details," though in recent days she had seen him less and less, she explained. "It was like he was really preoccupied with something. I thought maybe he was giving me the cold shoulder."

Rita knew that was how Jim operated. He warmed up to someone, then became scarce when he thought the relationship might be becoming too intimate. "He never mentioned what he was preoccupied with?" Maybe the thought of all the previous times he had found emotional attachment impossible.

Debbie shook her head. Her eyes were filled with tears again. "Except a couple weeks ago, he said if anything ever happened to him, he wanted me to know he cared deeply about me. That's when he told me about you."

Rita felt cold.

Debbie looked in the direction of a sliding-glass door where the dining-room table was. "I thought I had been pushing him too much and had scared him off, but he told me it was only work and had nothing to do with me."

Rita could see the reflection of the light in the sliding-glass door in each of Debbie's watery eyes.

Charlie said, "When you were with him, did you ever see anyone suspicious hanging around, or did you ever notice any sudden change come over Jim—like he might have noticed something that worried him?"

No, nothing. "Not until recently. Then he seemed troubled all the time."

"About what?" Charlie asked.

"I don't know," Debbie replied. "But I can tell you how I felt. It was like during my first semester of college I came here and flunked out. All along in the back of my mind I knew I was flunking, and my parents kept asking how I was doing. I kept telling them I was doing fine." She raised her hands to explain. "They basically spoil me, and I didn't want to hurt them. I guess I was in some kind of a state of denial. When midterms came out, I knew I was in trouble, but I kept thinking I could change it. Then I'd fall back into my old ways, skipping classes and not studying. The closer I got to the day final grades were issued, the more I knew the end was at hand, but I didn't do anything to stop it or get help. The feeling I had then is the kind of feeling I think Jim had during these past few weeks. It's like he knew something bad was going to happen, and he didn't or couldn't do anything to stop it." Her eyes came back to the living room. "At least I had a chance to go off to a junior college for a semester and bring my grades back up." Tears welled in her eyes. "How did he die?" she asked.

Rita said no one was sure yet. Don't lie to her, she told herself. She added, "The newspapers are reporting it as a suicide, but we're not sure yet."

Debbie shook her head adamantly. "Jim would never kill himself. No, it wasn't suicide. He was depressed now and then, but he wouldn't kill himself. He would never do that."

Charlie said, "He was depressed?"

"Now and then, a little."

"Did you talk about it?"

Debbie shook her head. "He didn't want to talk about it, but I think it had something to do with his ex-wife. I think he was worried about her. I think he thought she was in a mess or something, and he wanted to help her but didn't want to help at the same time."

Rita asked the question that had been bothering her since she had seen the swimming trunks hanging over the shower door in Jim's town house. "Debbie, how did Jim ever get interested in learning to swim? He was afraid of water."

The slightest hint of a smile appeared on her face. "Yes, he was afraid of water. So do you want the real reason why he wanted to learn to swim, or do you want the reason he gave me?"

"Both."

"The reason he gave me was that he had been terrified of water all of his life, and he was tired of being scared. He told me of a time he had almost drowned in Tennessee."

"He told you about that?"

"Yes."

"And what was the real reason for him wanting to learn to swim, do you think?" Charlie asked.

Debbie's smile began to show her even white teeth. They gleamed in the light. "He wanted to get to know me better," she said. "The swimming lessons were just an excuse."

Rita smiled. That was Jim.

At the door, she gave Debbie a business card and told her if she needed anything, or remembered anything, to call.

Only when Debbie had closed the door behind them did they hear her start to cry, building to racking sobs. Rita wanted to go back and hold her. She seemed like such a gentle, innocent young woman.

Charlie asked, "Do you think someone should be with her at a time like this?"

No, Rita told him, she thought Debbie needed to be alone. It seemed like the kind of person she was. Private, shy, embarrassed to cry in front of others. Debbie reminded her a lot of Greg. Greg never expressed his emotions outwardly either.

12

Jim's funeral, in light of the media's new scandal, was a small, private affair Thursday afternoon. Rita and Mike drove up to Baraboo together. Charlie and Claudia were there, as were a few other people who had worked with Jim over the years, including Vince, who looked like he hadn't slept well in several days. Jerry Grier, the state narcotics agent, was there also. Jerry, known to everyone as Bull, and Jim went back a long way together. Paul and his wife, Donna, were in attendance, as was Debbie Sweet, though she was the only person no one really knew. Not at the funeral was Jim's ex-wife, Diane Hoeveler, which surprised Rita.

After the funeral, a group of Jim's colleagues stopped for drinks at the Devil's Head Ski Lodge. They all sat at a table near the windows and watched skiers come down the slopes. When the first round of drinks arrived, Rita proposed a toast: "This is to Jim, may he rest in peace." They all raised their glasses and drank liberally.

Toast after toast followed, and everything became a blur. Rita vaguely remembered getting home late in the afternoon. She remembered kissing Greg, who laughed and said she stunk like a skunk. She remembered throwing a tennis ball to K. K ran to get the ball and brought it back, but then didn't want to release it. Greg laughed as she tried to chase down the running dog. Greg said he liked her like that. He wished she were that much fun more often. She promised she would try harder. That was before she passed out on the bed.

Later Rita tried to help Greg with a science project, but her head was pounding so hard she couldn't concentrate. Greg eventually said Mike was better at science than she was. That hurt her feelings. She told Greg that all she wanted to do was to understand, but Greg said that Mike taught school. "That's his job. If someone tries to kill me, I'll call you."

She drank a lot of water to wash the alcohol out of her body, and went to bed that night feeling as if by morning she would be her old self again. She and Mike made love. They were slow and patient, then, in the dark, talked, wrapped in each other's arms. Mainly they talked about how they never had time to talk.

"You remember when we were first married?" she said.

"It hasn't been that long ago."

"We used to do a lot of things together. We'd go out to dinner. We'd go out dancing. Sometimes we'd just sit on the couch and kiss. You ever think about that?

"What am I supposed to think about?"

"How good it was."

"Each period of life has its good times."

"Those times were much better than these. Back then we used to talk and do things together."

He laughed.

She could feel his chest vibrate. "What?"

"I won five thousand dollars. That's good."

She laughed too. Yes, that was good, but that's not what she was talking about. "I'm talking about spending quality time together."

He was silent for a while after that. "I don't know what you expect," he finally said. "You work long hours, I work long hours, we have Greg, there's a lot of activities going on in our lives—"

She told him he looked good in the new suit he was wearing earlier that day.

He said thank you, that he hadn't had a new suit in years. He said he thought his luck was changing, though, that the days were coming when they would have everything they wanted.

She smiled in the darkness. He had always been a dreamer. She kissed him and rolled away from him. "I love you," she said softly. It was the last thing she remembered.

She piddled around the house after Mike had

left for work the next morning and Greg had gotten on the school bus. She was in no hurry to get to the office.

She took a slow shower and took her time dressing. She even got the shoe shine kit out of Mike's closet and buffed her shoes. When she put the kit back, she tried to close his closet door, but it got caught on a throw rug that Mike kept his shoes lined up on. She jerked the door loose, but the rug came with it. As she was laying the rug back in the closet, she spotted some money hidden beneath it. It turned out to be a lot: seven hundred and fifty dollars. At first she didn't know what to think. Why would Mike keep so much money hidden under a rug in his closet? She was totally confused. Why was he hiding money from her—especially as poor as they had been in recent months? She had even been cashing in their savings bonds to keep sufficient funds in their checking account.

Suspicions rising, she searched his closet. She went through his dresser. She went through every hiding place she knew about.

When she didn't find anything else, she left the house troubled. Perhaps there was some rational explanation. It might be a part of the Christmas money. The money he had held back for her. After all, she had asked him not to spend it all.

On her way to Milwaukee, she stopped at Children's Hospital. Bianca Willis was alone, and Rita decided to take advantage of the situation. She sat on the edge of Bianca's hospital bed. The girl moved her feet so Rita would have room. Near the bed was a breakfast tray, the food on which had hardly been touched by her.

Rita said, "Don't you ever get lonely in here all by yourself?"

Bianca didn't say. Her face was blank above the blankets, which were pulled up to her chin.

"One time I had to stay all night by myself in the hospital, and I was scared. I wasn't much older than you." Rita glanced at Bianca for some response, but the little girl gave none. "I was ten. I broke my arm, and I had to go to the hospital to have my arm set. I remember looking at it all bent and thinking how ugly it was. They had to put me to sleep to set it, but they couldn't put me to sleep right away because they can't put you to sleep if you've had anything to eat, and I had. So I spent the night. I remember my mother and father went home when evening came. Mainly it was my father's idea. He said he wasn't going to stay there all night, and he wouldn't let my mother stay there. That was my father for you. He was that way. So, I was all alone in this big room. I remember how alone it made me feel. I felt like I was the only person in the entire world."

"How?" The tiny word was barely perceptible.

"What? How'd I break my arm? Is that what you're asking?"

Bianca didn't say.

"I was at school, running across a field, and I fell." Rita eyed Bianca. "No, there's more than that. We were playing chase, and someone pushed me. It was harder than just a tag. That's what you're supposed to do when you're playing chase. You're supposed to tag the other person, but this person was mad at me because I never got caught, and so when he got a chance, he pushed me hard. I fell. I put out my arm to stop myself, and my arm broke. How did you get hurt?" The moment Rita asked the question, she realized it had been too soon to ask such a question—could see it in Bianca's eyes—so she added, "That's all right. We'll have plenty of time to talk about that and other things like it." She leaned over and kissed Bianca on the forehead. "I'll stop back to see you later. And remember, you can always talk to me. You can tell me anything you want. Can I get you anything or do anything for you?"

Bianca remained silent.

On her way to the office, Rita thought one word was better than nothing. Bianca had said "How?" At least that was progress. That put her in a better mood.

At the office, she set right in to work. On the wall of children's photographs, there had been some changes. Some photographs had come down. Gemini Gold had gone back to her mother. Ryan McGann's photograph had come down—there was insufficient evidence to prosecute for abuse or neglect. Kristen Tirrell's photograph had come down—her mother had entered a plea in return for a reduced prison sentence. The case had been closed. Up on the board were six new photographs, though. They all were active investigations.

Once Rita had assigned the cases, she sent Joyce Smoot to St. Luke's Medical Center to do some research on drowning. She asked Jim O'Donnell and Charlie to examine the files of Jim's hard drive. Vince volunteered to see a friend of his at the local FBI office. He said he would make discreet inquiries about what Jim had done to upset the federal officials.

The rest of the morning she processed paperwork, the most grueling part of her job. Then Charlie returned.

The two managed to get away after lunch to see the Hoevelers. On the way, Charlie briefed her on what he and O'Donnell had discovered so far by reviewing Jim's computer files. Mostly routine cases.

"Any drowning cases?" she asked.

"No, not yet," he replied, "and we specifically looked for drowning investigations."

"What about anything involving NationsCare, or Chad Whitaker?"

"Nothing," he replied, "though there was one thing that struck me as being odd."

"What's that?"

"The Renneker investigation."

"What about it?" She glanced at him as she drove.

"Kind of a superficial investigation, if you ask me. Compared to the other cases, it was like he didn't have very much enthusiasm at all about having picked up the trail of a possible serial killer."

She glanced at Charlie again. That was odd. She knew from experience that Jim's case reports were among the most detailed she had ever read. Renneker would be a case with major potential. "Do you mind making me a hard copy of any file you find that's suspicious?"

"Done."

"Are you growing a beard?"

He rubbed the stubble on his face. "I thought I'd see how it looked. What do you think?"

She smiled. "I'll tell you in a few days. Right now it looks like shit."

"That's not very nice."

She smiled again.

"I'll tell people about that crystal statue at Jim's place. It was you, wasn't it?"

She glanced at him. It was the first time he had mentioned anything since Debbie's revelation. "Jim and I had an affair a long time ago."

He shrugged. "Hey, I'm cool."

"Charlie—"

"Yeah."

"Let me ask you a question, and I'm wondering what you would think if you were faced with a certain situation."

He didn't say anything, only waited for her to go on.

She told him about the money she had found. Then, "We're in the red constantly." She also told about the five thousand dollars Mike had won.

He seemed to know what she was getting at. "Has he ever done any gambling?"

"The lottery. That sort of thing. They have some football and baseball betting at work."

He shrugged. "I wouldn't worry," he said.

That made her feel better. She wanted to ask more questions, perhaps to have more reassurance, but they were nearing the Hoevelers' place.

The Hoevelers lived in a new house beyond the city limits to the west. Rita was sure Al had built the house himself. In any case, it looked like the house of a contractor who was doing relatively well, a large, two-story brick house that set some distance up a paved but private road, on a well-landscaped lot.

Diane answered the door. Behind her stood a large Doberman pinscher. "Rita," was all she said. She was a short woman, on the heavy side, but she looked well kept and dressed well. Her dark hair was short and stylish, and the frames of her glasses matched the color of her hair. She looked like a professional woman.

They had never been on good terms, at least not since the days when Diane had blamed Rita for causing the break-up of Jim's and her marriage. The truth was, however, that Jim had decided to file for divorce long before Rita had ever had her affair with him, though Diane had never believed that. "May we come in?" Rita asked.

"Come in?"

"To talk about Jim."

Diane moved back. To the Doberman pinscher, she pointed a finger and said sharply, "Go to your bed." The Doberman disappeared.

Rita and Charlie stepped into the house. It smelled new, and there weren't that many furnishings.

Diane closed the door. "How was the funeral?"

Rita nodded. "It was nice. A small one." She added, "I was surprised I didn't see you."

"I didn't think it'd be appropriate."

Rita didn't say anything.

"Let's sit down in the living room," Diane offered.

They went into a huge room with high ceilings and an entire wall of windows that looked down a hill. There was a lot of light in the room. A sofa and two chairs were the only furnishings. Diane commented, "We're in the process of furnishing and decorating."

"This is a very nice place," Charlie said, and he introduced himself.

Rita realized she had forgotten to do it.

"Thank you," Diane said. "My husband built everything."

From the road the position of the house had been deceptive. It didn't look like it was set on that much of a hill. Through the windows, however, was an expansive view.

"Please, sit down." Diane sat in one of the armchairs.

Rita could tell she was trying to be extra nice.

Charlie sat in the other armchair.

Rita remained standing at the window. She turned to face Diane. "When was the last time you saw Jim?"

"Oh, I don't know. I imagine I've run into him a couple of times over the past year. He stopped by here once. We were on good terms these days, you know."

So good that you didn't see fit to attend the funeral? Rita wanted to ask but didn't. Diane was cool, too cool, the kind of cool that made Rita feel uneasy. She had to be careful. She walked to the sofa and sat down. "You say he stopped by here?"

"Yes."

"Once or twice?"

"Yes."

"For social calls?" Charlie asked. He was leaning back in his chair and looked quite comfortable, his black leather coat unbuttoned but still on over his suit.

"Yes, he was in the neighborhood and stopped by to say hello."

Charlie's head nodded ever so slightly. His hands rose in a steeple, and he said, "So Jim drove up to the house, said hello, and left."

She smiled broadly at him, though none of

her teeth showed. "We visited socially for about fifteen minutes," she replied. "I think he may have even had a drink while he was here. Yes, as a matter of fact, he did have a drink."

She was cool, all right, Rita thought. "Did Jim and your current husband get along?" she asked.

"Speak of the devil," Diane said, smiling as she rose.

In walked a short, fat man in his fifties, not at all what Rita had expected. It was as though he had appeared out of nowhere. He looked rough, like someone she would expect to find sitting on a bar stool in a tavern. The fatness was from his face down, especially at his belly, which bulged like a sack of feed. "Hi," he said. His face had a lot of scars in it, and his short white hair was brushed straight forward.

Diane said, "Al, this is Rita, an old friend of Jim's. Have you met her? I'm not sure. Rita, are you married again?"

Rita didn't say whether she was married. "Rita Trible."

Al was shaking his head. "No," he replied, "I'd remember someone as pretty as she is." He had a stupid grin on his face as he held out a hand.

Rita shook it. A smoker, she thought. She could see the yellow nicotine stains on the fingers of his sandpaper hand. Such a heavy smoker that the nicotine stains were on his lips too. He reeked of smoke.

"Hi, Rita Trible."

Rita nodded.

"And this is Charles, or is it Charlie—"

"Charlie Dalton."

"Charlie Dalton."

Al shook hands with Charlie too, smiling all the while.

"Rita and Charlie were just asking about Jim." To Rita, "Rita, I never did ask you, is this a social call or a professional call?"

"Professional."

"Was Jim in some kind of trouble? I understand he committed suicide. The news is saying all kinds of things about a scandal he might have been involved in. Of course there's talk about that serial killer they've arrested too." Diane smiled. "You had a part in that, didn't you?"

Rita didn't respond.

"Are you investigating Jim for some reason? That lady with Contact Six—"

"Susan Hall," Al said, still smiling. He lit a cigarette. He watched the match burn in his fingers for a long time.

"Yes, Susan Hall seemed to think so. She was here asking questions too, you know. Sort of beat you to the punch. Honey, do you mind not smoking?"

Al shook the fire out of the match, moved to leave the room, and said, "Nice to meet you both."

The conversation was ending too quickly. Hit

home, Rita told herself. To Al: "I was under the impression that Jim might have been here recently to talk to you about your problems with NationsCare of America."

It worked. Al looked like he had been punched in the stomach. His jaw dropped and color drained from his face. His lips turned a purplish color. "No—nnnn-no," he stuttered. "Problems with NationsCare?" He forced a laugh. Cigarette ashes dropped on the carpet.

"Why would Al have problems with NationsCare?" Diane butted in. She pointed at the ashes in the carpet. "Al, look at the mess you made. I told you I didn't want you smoking in the living room."

Al left in a hurry.

"He's been awarded a big contract with NCA." She forced a smile back on her face. "What were we talking about? Oh, yes, Jim. I told you, Jim was here for a social call, but I got the impression he might have been in some kind of trouble. In fact, after Jim left, I told Al that, didn't I, Al?" she said, calling. "I told you that Jim seemed worried about something, like he might be in some kind of a mess."

Al returned without his cigarette. "Yes," he said, "that's what you told me—that Jim seemed to be in some kind of a jam."

Rita was certain they were hiding something, but the interview had gone nowhere.

Outside, on their way to the car, Charlie whispered to Rita, "They're lying big-time."

Rita mumbled, "I know." Why was another matter. She had been convinced that Al and Diane had turned to Jim to help investigate NationsCare. She had been convinced that Al had turned over copies of his private correspondence to Jim. But how had Al managed to win a contract from NationsCare when all of the correspondence indicated that it would never happen? What were they hiding?

13

On Saturday night Rita, emotionally and physically drained, attended the performance of the play Mike had written, "The Ghost of Christmas Present." The young actors and actresses were good, and when the curtain closed, the church auditorium filled with applause. Even Rita found that the play had taken her mind off of the events of the previous week.

The curtain opened again. The young actors and actresses took a bow, which brought more applause. Mike stepped out in front of the actors and actresses. The applause grew louder, and a couple of people whistled loudly. That brought laughter from the audience.

"Some of you," Mike began to say, but there was still too much noise. He waited until the applause died down.

"Some of you know how hard it is to get me to be serious about much of anything," he said. That brought more laughter. He raised his hand, signaling for silence. "But this evening I couldn't be more serious. I'm very proud of these young people." He raised a hand to the young actors and actresses. It brought a standing ovation.

When the applause had died down again, he said, "I'd also like to express my appreciation for all the support of my wife, Rita Trible. She forced me to do this."

The audience was generous with their laughter.

He pointed, and the spotlight fell on her. Sean reached over and put a brotherly arm around her shoulder. Her older brother and his wife, Julie, had always been good about being around while Greg was growing up.

"Seriously, I've always wanted to do something like this, and she's the first person who's ever encouraged me. Thank you, Rita." He blew her a kiss. "I didn't know I had it in me."

A shiver ran through her. She changed her mind about the decision she had made. She had decided to talk to Mike later that night about the money she had found. Maybe it'd be better not to say anything—to see if he volunteered to give her the money he had stashed away.

"Now, for the best part," he continued. "The young people said they wanted the proceeds of this play to go toward feeding the poor and hungry of Milwaukee, and I think that's a wonderful gesture on their part. All of you have brought food items and cash gifts tonight. The young people are going to pass collection plates and food baskets. We hope each of you will make a generous gift because your gifts will go to the poor of our area."

Singing "Carol of the Bells," the young people began to pass boxes and baskets. Over the sound of their voices, Greg, ringing a bell, called out, "Money for the poor! Food for the poor! Help feed the poor!" The boxes and baskets quickly overflowed with food items and donations.

Rita waited her turn in line to congratulate Mike. When she finally got to him, she gave him a hug, their lips met, and she whispered how proud she was of him. Mike held her and whispered that he really did appreciate all the support she had given him.

She grabbed Greg, who was passing by with a group of boys his age. When he realized it was useless to try to get away, he bent his head forward and allowed Rita to kiss the top of his head. His face turned red. Rita said, "You were great. All of you did a wonderful job." Sean and Julie agreed.

As Greg and his friends walked away, Rita heard someone say, "Hey, Greg, you're the only guy I know whose mother can still kick his butt." That brought loud laughter from the boys, and she smiled at their silliness.

Julie arched her back. "Sean, don't you think it's time we headed home?"

"Your back bothering you?" Rita asked. Actually, she was glad Julie and Sean had signaled their departure. She was tired herself, and she knew that unless someone took the initiative to leave, they all could be stuck there for a while.

"Those weren't the most comfortable chairs in the world," Julie commented, pointing at the aluminum folding chairs.

Sean began to massage her back. "I'm ready whenever you are," he said.

Mike said, "Aren't you two going to stay for refreshments?"

No, Julie said, her back was killing her, and all she wanted was to smoke a cigarette and lie down on a heating pad.

Rita commented that she didn't want to stay very late either. Mike said that since they had driven separate cars—he had arrived at the church before she had—she could head home, and he would bring Greg home later. That was fine with her.

Actually, to go home and be alone was just what Rita wanted. She needed to have the house to herself for a while. Even to do small chores like emptying the dishwasher and putting in a load of laundry felt good. The chores gave her a sense of belonging, of presence, something she had lost track of over the previous few days. She folded the clothes that were in the dryer. Among them was one of Mike's socks. Its match was on the shelf where the laundry detergent and fabric softener were.

Carrying the stack of laundry from room to

room, she distributed it. In her and Mike's bedroom, she rested the folded towels on a raised knee while she tried to open to top drawer of Mike's dresser. The drawer came out crooked. Then it wouldn't go out or come in, so she stuffed the pair of socks down in the crack of the open drawer. She put the towels in the cabinet in the bathroom. Back at Mike's dresser, she jerked around on the drawer. It finally broke loose, but wouldn't go back in. She pulled the drawer all the way out. There was a small black book near the track for the drawer. She set the drawer on the bed and opened the book. It was filled with numbers. She knew immediately what the numbers meant.

She put everything back the way it was and went to bed. It seemed a long time before Mike and Greg came home. Even then Mike didn't come to bed right away. She could hear him and Greg talking. They seemed to be moving around the house while they talked. The water in the kitchen ran, then a cabinet door slammed; a toilet flushed. Mike looked in on her, but she pretended to be asleep. She lay as still as she could, her eyes closed. She pretended until he undressed, turned off the light, and got in bed.

In a low voice she told him about the money she had found under the rug in his closet. His body seemed very far from her at that particular moment.

"I was saving some money for Christmas," he finally said.

"I checked the balance in our account earlier today," she lied. "Everything checked out there, which means the money I found wasn't part of your winnings." She knew he was lying, so she thought she would run a bluff to see what he would say.

He gave a halfhearted laugh. "I wanted to surprise you."

"About what? That you had found a large sum of money? Found a large sum of money after you had won a large sum of money? Seems like we're suddenly into a lot of large sums of money."

He turned on the bedside lamp, took a deep breath, and, in his boxer shorts, sat on the edge of the bed. He wasn't facing her. "Do you want to get your badge and gun out and interrogate me?"

The light was hurting her eyes. "I just want the truth," she said. She closed her eyes. "I don't think that's too much to ask." Yes, a headache was definitely there, and it felt like it was there to stay. She had had a lot of headaches in recent days. Don't make me tell about the black book, she kept saying to herself. Please don't let it get that far.

Before she could say more, he did something she didn't expect. He told her he had been gambling. It was nothing new, he said, he had been gambling for years. There, it was out, he said.

"Even when we met and were going together?"

He turned on the bed so that he halfway faced her, but he didn't directly look at her. "You remember that trip to Key West when we were first seeing each other?"

"Yes."

"I didn't discover a thousand dollars in my account. I won a thousand dollars."

"For some reason, it sounds like you're proud of yourself."

"No, I'm not proud. Tired of living like I have been, yes; proud, no."

"Is that where all our money's been going to? Every few days you tell me, 'I've taken twenty-five out. Mark me down.' Is that where our money's been going to?"

He didn't say anything.

"It is, isn't it?"

Silence.

"Mike, that's like stealing."

The answer wasn't very loud. "I know, and I hate it."

"Then you admit it."

"Rita, you don't understand. Even if I go into a grocery store, if there's a Lotto machine, I have to stop and buy tickets. Yesterday, I waited at the customer-service desk of a grocery store for thirty minutes so I could pick my Lotto numbers. The woman who was working at the desk didn't know how to enter my numbers, so she had to wait until one of the assistant managers could come down from the office and help. I got upset with the young woman. It wasn't even like me, but I got upset. Next thing I know, the assistant manager had the upstairs window open, and was calling down instructions to the customer-service desk."

He looked like a shell of the person she thought she knew.

"I know you're hurt," he said, breaking a long silence, "and I'm sorry."

She let out a deep breath and put on her bathrobe.

"Where are you going?" he asked.

"To get a breath of fresh air, Mike. This is very serious. I have to think it through."

She opened the front door and stepped out onto the icy air of the porch. The night sky was clear. She could see stars. Though they looked incredibly small, she felt even smaller than they looked. Had her world been crumbling about her all along, and she hadn't realized it? she wondered. Yes, she had been trapped in a fairy-tale existence, thinking her relationship with Mike really had meant something, and it was all a lie. She went back inside.

Mike was waiting. He too had put on a robe and slippers. "Can we talk?" he asked.

She tried to get past him. "Mike, to tell you the truth, I don't want to talk. We should have talked a long time ago."

"What's that mean?"

She pushed past him. "It means, I think I should visit Sean and Julie for a few days while we sort this out."

He began following her. "I tried to tell you I had problems even when we were dating."

"I thought you were joking. I never know when you're joking and when you're telling the truth." From her bedroom closet she brought out a large suitcase, unzipped it, and opened the top drawer of her dresser.

"That doesn't look like a couple of days' bag."

"I've got to get Greg's things in here too."

"Fine."

From the corner of her eye, she could see him leaving the room. "What?" For some reason, she didn't want him to leave. She had her bag out and open, but she didn't want him to leave. She didn't know why, but she thought that if she left, perhaps they could get their problems worked out and in a couple of days she could be back; but she had the feeling that if he left, there would be no reconciliation.

"It means, if you found out I had cancer, I don't think you'd be packing your bags and moving out—"

"You don't have cancer."

"If I were in an automobile accident and paralyzed for the rest of my life, would you move out?"

"This isn't like that. I hardly think this is something like that."

"What is it like, then?" he asked. His voice was raised. "What if I were an alcoholic? Would you understand then? Would that be a real problem?"

She was stung by the words. "How dare you—"

"No, fine. Put away your suitcase, I'll leave."

"No!" It was Greg. He had appeared in the doorway. "Please don't leave, Mike. Mom, why are you doing this?"

Rita didn't say anything. She was bothered by something she saw in his eyes, a look of desperation.

Mike put his arm around Greg's shoulder. Greg was no longer a little boy. He was grown up now. Mike told him, "Greg, this isn't anything your mother has done. This is me. Please, I don't want you to be thinking this has anything to do with your mother or you. We're talking about something I did wrong back before I even knew your mother and you."

Greg's solution was simple. "Then let's forget it."

Rita put away her suitcase. One thing she had learned in managing the new child-abuse prevention task force was the high rate of suicide among teenagers. She told Greg, "You go back to bed, dear, Mike and I are talking."

Before Greg left, he said, "Please don't fight." To Rita in particular he said, "Mom, this is the first person you've ever hung out with that I like."

In a gentle voice she told him to go back to bed.

Mike sat on the bed. First he buried his face in his hands, then he ran his hands up through his hair. "Used to be, life was so simple," he said.

Rita looked at the doorway to make sure Greg was gone.

"When it was just me, I didn't care. I ran up a debt, I paid it off. No one else got involved. That's why when we were dating I tried to tell you I was crazy, and you shouldn't get involved."

"Well, I did."

"At least I told you the truth when you asked me."

"I know you did. And I appreciate your being truthful with me."

He buried his face in his hands. "God, you don't know how hard I've tried to quit."

She put a hand on his shoulder. "You're right, I can't just run away when we have a problem."

"I kept thinking it would all pay off in the end, then I could get out. But when I won that five thousand dollars, I began to think my luck had changed, and I couldn't help but to win more."

"How much do you owe?"

"I don't owe anything."

"You've paid all your debts?"

"Everything."

"You swear?"

"I swear."

"Then we'll get you help, and we'll get out of this mess."

He was silent.

"Okay?"

He didn't answer.

"What's wrong?"

"Rita, I'm scared," he told her. "You don't know what it's like. It's like I can't stop. I'm afraid you're going to ask me to make a promise, and I'm going to mess up. Then you're going to claim you gave me a chance and kick me out."

She took his hand and squeezed it. "No, I'm going to give you a chance. As long as you're working on the problem, I'm going to stand beside you."

He squeezed back. "I should have told you a long time ago."

"Let's leave it alone and move forward."

She kissed him and told him she still loved him. He told her he still loved her. She went in to see Greg, but he seemed to be asleep. She thought he might be pretending, but when she called his name, he didn't say anything.

She returned to bed, turned off the light, and lay down. Mike didn't bother her. He kept perfectly still. Feeling relieved of all the burdens that had been tormenting her, she went to sleep.

But she awakened to an empty bed. Right away she got up and looked for Mike. He was not in the house. She found a note from him on the kitchen table: "Gone out for a while. Be back soon. Love, Mike."

The torment came back. She was angry at herself for being so understanding and for being so easy on Mike. She should have made him tell her everything, made him prove it, made him explain all the entries in his little black book, and then made him agree to a set of rules that would ensure he would do no further gambling.

Loud music began to blare beyond the closed door of Greg's room. She went to his room and opened the door. "Turn it down!" she said over the music.

"What's wrong with it?"

"Turn it down or it goes off completely!"

Greg didn't argue. He turned down the music. Rita looked around at the room. It was trashed worse than ever. "Let me tell you something before you say anything."

"What?"

"You're not doing anything today until you clean this room."

"I see you're still in a bad mood."

"I'm not in a bad mood, but you're not going to live like a pig. I want this room picked up. Look at that"—her finger jumped from one pile of clothes to another—"there's one, two, three, four bath towels. What, do you just use one and throw it down?"

Greg smiled.

"I don't think it's one bit funny," Rita said. "I work hard, then I have to come home and clean up after you. You need to start using a towel and hanging it up. You can use the same towel at least a couple of days."

"Can I go to the mall today?" Greg asked, ignoring what Rita had said.

"You're not going anywhere until this room is clean."

"Okay, I'll clean it."

"I mean, clean it good."

"Mom, it'll be good."

"Under the bed and in the closet too. Get one of those big black plastic bags and put all your trash in it."

"Mom—"

"And you have to vacuum."

"Mom!"

Rita fell silent.

"I'll clean it."

Rita took a deep breath and let it out. "I thought you and I were going to do some Christmas shopping today."

"Mom, I've finished my Christmas shopping."

"We could go to the mall together."

"Mom, to be truthful, people my age don't go to the mall with their mothers."

Rita thought of Renneker. "I just don't want you running around, getting in trouble at the mall."

"Mom, I'm almost fifteen. You're going to have to start trusting me sometime. Soon I'll get my learner's permit. I'll be driving next year."

"With an adult."

"I'm back!" Mike called.

Greg used the opportunity to slip past Rita and head for the kitchen. Rita followed. Greg opened a cabinet and got out a large black plastic bag.

"Better be careful, Mike. Mom is being a real B this morning." Greg returned to his bedroom, where he closed the door and turned up the stereo again.

"Where did you go?" Rita asked, trying not to sound angry.

He held out a stack of pamphlets and small books. She looked at them. They were from Gamblers Anonymous.

"I have some friends. They told me. I went to a meeting. It was good. I met some nice people there." He shrugged. "Some strange ones, but some nice ones too."

Once again Rita began to feel better, like everything might turn out all right.

14

Charlie followed her to her office the moment she arrived on Monday morning, not even giving her a chance to take off her coat and gloves. More beard had sprouted on his face over the weekend. The long, wiry hairs were going this way and that. "Charlie, it still looks like hell," she told him. He was wearing a brown shirt, open at the neck, showing the hair on his chest, and a black leather coat that came down nearly to his knees.

He opened a folder and dropped a black-and-white enlargement on her desk. In the foreground of the photograph was Jim Swearingen. "See the dude in the background?" Charlie said. "See his eyes?"

She did. Without a doubt, the man had either taken a sudden interest in Jim or was watching him. Still, the photograph was so blurry that it was difficult to distinguish the features of the man. She squinted to try to get a better look at the face, but it didn't help. She tried moving the photograph away from her face. That didn't help either. She put on her bifocals. Nothing worked.

"I've had it enlarged as much as it can be enlarged," Charlie said.

She ran a hand through her hair. "Okay, here's what you do," she told him. "You get in touch with Ed McDonell down at the NASA Protective Services Office of the Kennedy Space Center. He's an old friend. His office can do this sort of thing. You tell him we need the most refined shot of this guy we can get." From her files she brought out a telephone number and gave it to Charlie.

He was on the way out the door when she said, "Charlie—"

He looked back at her.

She wanted to tell him about Mike, but the words wouldn't come. "You said you were going to do some discreet checking around about NationsCare. Have you heard anything?"

"Yeah, I made some inquiries," he replied, "but no one's saying a word."

"I wonder why."

He shrugged. His leather coat creaked. "Like NationsCare doesn't want to be dragged into any kind of a scandal."

She said, "What about J. D. Grove? Can you talk to him?"

Before Charlie could answer, there was a tap at her door, and Joyce stooped under Charlie's arm, which was stretched across the door frame. "Good morning, Charlie," she said. She was carrying a stack of books and papers.

Charlie said hello to Joyce, then to Rita added, "I can try. I doubt he'd agree, but I'll see what I can do."

"Thanks, Charlie." She was glad she hadn't said anything about Mike, because Joyce would have interrupted them before she got the entire story out.

She looked at Joyce, who dropped a stack of books and photocopied articles on the desk. Joyce commented, "I went over to St. Luke's Hospital library to do research. You can tell by the marks on the pages that I've copied and the marks in the books that someone has been researching this particular topic. I made copies of the articles and brought some of the books so you could see them."

Vince appeared, looking over Joyce's shoulder. He asked, "Where did you get those?"

She told him.

He reached past her and picked up one of the photocopied articles, tilting it toward him. "This is Jim Swearingen's work," he said. "Jim did this exact same thing. When he was researching, he always made little check marks on the copies he made."

Though Rita didn't say anything, she knew all about Jim's system. As he read and took notes, he liked to make little checks. One check meant the information was interesting. Two checks meant the information was important. Three meant the information was crucial.

Joyce didn't seem to think the observation was of much interest. "So Jim was doing research. We all do research."

Rita would have agreed except for one inconsistency, which she kept to herself. Jim would have never written in the original books or journals. He would have made the copies he wanted and would have then made his marks on the copies, not on the originals. "What's the research about?" she asked. She knew but wanted to hear.

"Drowning."

"Okay. Joyce, how about I hold on to these and take a look at them? I'll get them back to you."

Joyce nodded.

"Nice work, Joyce." To Vince: "What's up?" Joyce slipped past Vince, poking him in the stomach as she did so.

Vince sat down. "Isn't it odd that Jim was over at the hospital conducting research about drowning—the same way he was killed?"

She didn't say anything.

"Come on, you have to admit that it's more than a coincidence. And you know as well as I that Jim wouldn't have made marks in books that didn't belong to him."

She said, "I take it you've made some inquiries with the feds."

Vince said, yes, he had made inquiries. He

had talked with one of his friends. "Note, all of this is highly confidential," he added. "I promised my friend none of it would ever get back to him."

"What is it?"

Agents from the Drug Enforcement Administration, Internal Revenue Service, and FBI had been trying to break up a gambling ring in Milwaukee, a ring that included, it was alleged, even the chief of detectives in the Milwaukee Police Department.

Rita immediately thought of Mike. The thought scared her. She hoped he hadn't been spotted in the investigation.

"Apparently the task force had turned over some of its investigative notes to Jim because there was some overlap in an investigation they were both working on. From what I understand, not long after that the task force made a couple of raids that came up empty, and it became clear someone had blown the whistle. The task force began to search for its leak and discovered that part of the information they had turned over to Jim included references to Al Hoeveler. And in the process of checking, they discovered that Al was married to Diane, who was Jim's ex-wife. They decided Jim must have been the one who had leaked the information." From where he sat, Vince leaned back until his neck was on the back of his chair, creating a bow in his body. "The feds lost a big part of their investigation, and it had been a rather elaborate affair. A lot of time, energy, and money lost. They were pissed, to say the least."

She turned her chair to look out at the city. The thought of Mike involved in a gambling operation haunted her. How extensive was his involvement? she wondered. Outside her window, snow was falling. Now and then snowflakes whirled close to her window and rose, as if the heat pushed them up. Watching the snow, she asked, "What was Al involved in, do you know? Were you able to find that out?"

"My friend was tight-lipped about the particulars, except to say that Al was a big-time gambler."

Rita turned to him. Would Mike and Al have crossed paths? She was scared. How could Mike ever drag her and Greg into such a mess?

He shook his head. "I don't think Jim was the leak. Jim wouldn't do something like that, not even for a relative."

Her thoughts were elsewhere. "Thanks, Vince," she said. She turned back to the window.

Vince asked, "Do you mind if I do some follow-up on Al Hoeveler—see what I can dig up?"

"Go ahead," she replied, staring at the snow. She didn't want to tell him to go ahead, but if she didn't he might ask questions, and she didn't want to answer the type of questions he might ask. "But be discreet." What if people got to digging around and discovered that Mike was involved in one of the gambling rings? Something like that could destroy her career, especially on an investigation like the current one. Or, what if the reporter Susan Hall had dug up some dirt about Mike? Rita remembered the threat Susan had recently made.

A terrifying thought occurred to her. Jim knew the way her mind worked. First, there was the revelation that Debbie Sweet had made to her. Jim had told her the two of them had been having an affair. Then there was the envelope containing his mysterious note to her. And the mysterious swimming lessons. And the marks in the medical journals and books. Why had he marked up the books at the medical library? What if he really had been trying to protect someone? No, Rita didn't think Jim would try to protect Diane, but what if he had tried to protect someone else? Perhaps Jim had discovered that Mike ran the risk of becoming trapped in a gambling scandal. She was close to some new discovery. She could tell.

She thought of one other loose end that bothered her, the money in Jim's wallet. She couldn't be positive, but she did know that Jim was frugal. He was one of those who would go out of his way to save a dollar. On more than one occasion he had spoken his mind about ATMs that charged a dollar or so to customers from other banks.

She rocked in her office chair, remembering something he had said: "It doesn't cost a bank a dollar or more to process a transaction by computer," he had said. "So you stop by a bank machine that isn't owned by your bank, and you want ten dollars. You can end up paying twelve dollars to get the ten that belongs to you."

So why had he withdrawn money from a bank that had charged him a fee? It wasn't like him. He wouldn't have paid an extra dollar to get his own money. It didn't make sense unless he wanted her to notice the face that would be in the bank videotape.

She brought out Jim's note to read it again:

Dear Rita,
    You remember how you were reminded the hard way of something a lot of us forget?
    We look at crime and think it's out there somewhere—not really a part of us. The truth is, child abusers, wife abusers, thieves, and murderers are living right next door.
    Sometimes they're in our own homes.
    Best wishes and love always,
    Jim

Mike was involved. Jim had met with him to let him know that he knew everything. Don't jump to conclusions, she told herself, angry that she would even think such thoughts. No, it was Diane Hoeveler and her husband who were involved, which is how Al had finally managed to get a contract from NationsCare. Somehow Al's contracting company had found favor with the NCA system. Leave Mike out, she told herself.

She called Jerry Grier in Narcotics and asked if he was busy. He told her his unit was basically shut down until after Christmas. "That's what you should do too," he told her. "Shut down and take a few days off. We've been through a lot."

"Can I stop by and talk a few minutes?"

That brought a moment of silence. Then, "Something wrong?"

"Are you going to be in your office for a while?"

"Sure."

She found him in his office, smoking a cigar and reading a dirt bike magazine. He had two sons who owned dirt bikes. They did a lot of local racing, she knew. Personally, she never had figured out what people saw in the sport, but it seemed like Jerry was always out buying a new dirt bike for one of his sons.

Jerry dropped his magazine on the desk, leaned back, his hands locked behind his head, and put his scuffed boots on the desk. "You sounded worried about something." He looked rough. He hadn't shaved for a few days.

She sat down in front of his desk. "Bull, did you know about this recent federal task force that included DEA, IRS, and FBI agents?"

He took the cigar out of his mouth, rolled it in his fingers, and said, "Yeah, I heard about it. Some kind of gambling sting."

"Did you ever hear any rumors about Jim and that operation?"

Yes, he'd heard rumors.

"That he might be in trouble?"

His shoulders rose.

Why hadn't he said anything to her? she asked.

His boots dropped from the desk, and he leaned forward. "Because I didn't believe a damned thing I heard, and I don't spread rumors."

She stood and went over to his windows to look out. His view wasn't as good as the one in her office. His windows looked out at another office building.

"Listen, Rita, you and I both know Jim was a good cop. That's all there is to it."

She asked, "Did you talk to Jim in recent days?"

"Yeah, I talked to him."

"About what?"

"Of all places, I saw him on Wells Street, near Marquette University, going into a place called Zeskind's."

"Zeskind's?"

"It's a pawnshop owned by an old Jewish guy. In fact, it's rarely open. Every time I drive by there, it's all barred up and there's a Closed sign in the window. You know how rough Wells Street is anyway. But I saw him going in there one day, and I thought that was odd, so I stopped to see if he needed a backup."

"What did he say?"

"That he was all right."

She stared at him. "But you knew otherwise."

Jerry said, "Rita, let me tell you a fish story."

She sat on the ledge near the window. The heat was on, but it only warmed her jeans rather than burning.

"Jim and I were at a retreat down in the Ozarks one time, and we ended up at the cabin of this woman he had met. Jim was that way. He was always running into women who wanted to give him things and do him favors. Anyway, she had told him that there were some really big fish in the lake. All Jim wanted to do was relax, to get away from it all."

"I asked him if he wanted to fish the morning after we got there, and he said, sure, what time? I told him if we were going to go after the big ones, we should get up before daybreak. Jim said he would do it, but the next morning I couldn't get him out of bed."

"So I went down to the lake. I fished for a while and tied into something really big. I could tell the minute it hit my line it was big. I was more excited than I've ever been. I can even remember flying out of dust-offs in 'Nam and bullets popping through the belly of my chopper and not being as excited as I was that morning. Whatever I had on the line was huge." He stopped talking.

She watched him. What was he trying to tell her?

"I held on as hard as I could," he continued.

"Then the line went slack, and I reeled it in. Whatever had been on the line had broken it."

He smiled sadly. "I knew Jim was in trouble. But I also knew he was like that big fish. He had a mind of his own. In the end I figured whatever trouble had snagged him, he would just run out the line and break it."

Rita thanked him for his time.

From Jerry's office she drove to Zeskind's. Snow was falling even more heavily. The roads were slippery. The street crews couldn't keep up with the snow removal.

The shop was closed. Shielding her eyes, she pressed her face close to the glass, thinking there might be someone in the back, but she saw no one. There was a sign in the window with a telephone number.

She brought out her portable phone and dialed the number.

"Hello," came an old man's voice, someone with a light accent.

"Mr. Zeskind?"

"Yes." His voice was pleasant.

"Mr. Zeskind, my name is Captain Rita Trible. I'm a criminal investigator for the state of Wisconsin, and I would like to know if I could come by and talk to you about a friend of mine. Do you know a Jim Swearingen?"

"Of course we know a Jim Swearingen."

From the background came a woman's voice: "Who is it, Philip?"

He yelled out, "It's a friend of Jim's, Liddy.

She wants to know if she can come by and talk to us.''

The woman's voice said, "Why, of course she can come by and talk to us. Tell her any friend of Jim's is always welcome here.''

"My wife says you're welcome here." He gave her directions.

Rita glanced at the Zeskind shop again, all dark with bars on the windows and door. The shop stood out in a neighborhood that was being renovated all around it. Marquette University had bought up much of the property in the local area and expanded its campus. What was the connection? Was the pawnshop owner a loan shark? Was Jim going to settle up a debt for someone? The thought of another possible connection to Mike made her suddenly queasy. She really hoped it was unrelated but thought otherwise.

15

The Zeskinds lived in a secluded retirement community on the northeast side of Milwaukee, near Lake Michigan. The elegant condominiums had been built in a wooded area that, despite the snow, looked well landscaped and meticulously cared for. There were paved walking trails everywhere, all of which had been cleared of snow.

Philip Zeskind was waiting for her at the door. He was a skinny man whose thick glasses magnified the age of his mud brown eyes. His hair had thinned significantly, but it still had a smoky gray color to it. On his bony left arm, made prominent by the baggy short-sleeve shirt he wore, was a number tattooed in blue ink.

Liddy had a number too, though time seemed to have treated her better. Philip looked like he had just come out of a concentration camp. Liddy, on the other hand, was a short, robust woman.

"Come in, come in," Liddy said, stepping past her husband and holding out her hand.

Rita shook the hand, wiped her feet on the entrance rug, then followed Liddy across the thick beige carpet. Everything in the living room was neat and orderly, from the bookcases filled with books about the Holocaust, to the many knickknacks here and there. Rita sat down on a leopard-skin sofa and put her notebook on the glass coffee table in front of her.

"Can I get you something?" Liddy wanted to know. "Coffee, tea, sparkling water?"

"No, thank you." Rita mentioned that it was only the second time in her life she had personally met survivors of the Holocaust.

Philip said he had been at Buna of Auschwitz; Liddy had been at Birkenau of the Auschwitz camp. Philip said there weren't many survivors left, that he was beginning to worry that people would forget what had happened.

Rita smiled sadly. "You have a very nice home here," she said.

Liddy said it had been a good place to retire, and they were comfortable. "It keeps us near the grandchildren. You sure I can't get you something to drink?"

Rita said she would have coffee. Liddy seemed to insist on her taking something.

"Are you helping Jim with his case?" Philip asked, smiling.

As gently as she could, she informed him of Jim's death.

"Oh, no," Liddy said, appearing from the kitchen. Her face was pale, her eyes red. She reached for Philip's hand. "I told you something like this was going to happen," she told him. "These are evil people you got messed up with, like in the camps."

Rita asked what she meant by the comment. "What kind of a mess were you in?"

After spending several years in England, Philip explained, he and Liddy had come to the United States, where they had opened a pawnshop in Milwaukee in 1954. In recent years different parties had tried to persuade them to sell their shop and move on. First it had been Marquette University, which was trying to clean up its neighborhood. Marquette officials had tried to pressure him into selling the choice property across the street from Marquette's Alumni Center, which he described as "Marquette's gawdy castle in the heart of the slums."

Liddy looked nervous. She said everything had been fine until Philip had fallen into a trap. "Those three gentlemen who recently visited worried me," she told Philip.

What three men? Rita wanted to know.

From the beginning, NationsCare had tried to get them to sell the pawnshop and the land, Philip said.

Rita had suspected that's what they were talking about.

"We told them we were not interested, but I have this nasty habit, a habit that I thought had nothing to do with the NCA group. When people used to ask me how I survived the camps, I told them it was three things: luck, luck, and more luck. I thought I was lucky until three SS men show up at the store and say we either sell or they will ruin us because of my habit."

Rita said, "Let me guess, you ran up a gambling debt?"

Yes, he admitted, he had done some gambling and had gotten in over his head. "Not anything we couldn't pay off if we were forced to, but we would have had to take a big chunk of money out of our savings. I didn't want to do that. Next thing I know, these three SS goons started telling us how if I didn't pay up, our store might accidently burn down or something. Liddy and I talked about it, and we decided we have survived the Holocaust, we weren't going to let any evil men take away what was ours. I told them if the store burned down, we would rebuild a better store with the insurance we collected."

"How did you get Jim's name?" Rita asked.

Liddy laughed at him. "My Philip takes it into his head to write the governor," she said, "and so he did."

"You wrote to the governor?" Rita asked.

Philip smiled proudly and raised an index finger. "I always believe in going to the top," he said. "I didn't mind repaying the money I had lost—I've always felt that one should pay one's debts—but I wasn't going to let these goons push us around."

Liddy giggled at him. She said, "When my Philip makes up his mind about something, you better stay out of his way."

They made a delightful pair, Rita thought. "And what did the governor say when he got your letter?"

Philip told her the governor had never answered his letter.

"Do you still have a copy of the letter you wrote?" Rita asked.

"Oh, Philip's not that fancy," Liddy said, laughing.

He smiled at her. "Now, Liddy, I wouldn't say that. I would instead say I trust the people I write to."

Liddy said, "Philip trusts everyone. He doesn't even lock his car when he goes someplace."

"Liddy, I believe if someone is dishonest, a locked door doesn't make any difference."

Rita couldn't help but to laugh at the two. "You didn't keep a copy of the letter you wrote the governor?"

"No, I didn't keep a copy, but when he didn't answer, I wrote him again to remind him that he hadn't answered my previous letter."

Rita smiled. "And this time he answered?"

"No."

"But Jim came to see us after Philip wrote his second letter," Liddy said. "Philip wrote and told the governor we weren't going to be pushed around by some SS thugs, and Jim showed up at our shop."

"I take it, then, that the governor passed on your letter to the state police, and Jim was assigned the case."

While Liddy returned to the kitchen to get the coffee, Philip said, yes, he assumed that was why Jim had shown up at the shop one day.

"What did he say to you?" Rita asked. "Did he say the governor had sent him?" She didn't remember any such letter in Jim's files.

Liddy returned with a tray. On it were two cups, a coffeepot, sugar, and cream. "Jim was one of the nicest people we've ever met," she said, placing the tray on the glass table. "He didn't say anything about the governor, but he told us he had heard about the problems we had been having, and he thought he could help us."

Philip nodded. "But it was more than that. He wanted to be our friend too. He asked questions about the camps, a lot of questions. He said he hated what had happened to us."

After Vietnam, Jim hated all wars and what they did to people. "So, he started asking about the problems you were having at the pawn-shop, right?"

"Yes," Philip replied. "He asked us what had happened, and I was honest with him. I told him I had been gambling and had lost a lot of money, but that I thought the gambling was rigged. He told us that gambling operations were illegal anyway, and that no one could legally take our store away from us. He said that with a lot of the operations, the goon squad tried intimidation, and if it worked, fine, but if someone bucked, the goon squad would back off."

Rita asked them how NationsCare fit in. She opened her notebook and began to take notes.

Philip said all he knew was that when he ran up his gambling debts, the first thing the thugs suggested was that he could sell his business.

"To NationsCare?" Rita asked.

Liddy nodded. "That was the part that got us," she said. "When they mentioned this hospital system, we knew that wasn't right. A hospital shouldn't be involved in something like that. Philip can, as they say, smell a rat from a mile away, and he knew something was wrong from the beginning, didn't you, Philip?"

"So you told these thugs you weren't going to sell out to NationsCare, and they didn't like that?"

"No, they didn't like it."

"Has NationsCare ever made a written offer to buy your property?" Rita asked.

"No." He held up a finger. "And that's how you can always tell a crook. A crook doesn't want anything in writing. I know this Chad Whitaker. You knew he was born and raised here in Milwaukee? I knew him as a kid. He used to stop in the shop. A real wise ass."

Rita didn't know a lot about Whitaker. She let Philip talk.

"You heard how he tried to take over the big company his family helped set him up in, the Placard Health Company."

The Placard Company, Rita knew, was a pharmaceutical conglomerate.

"Chad Whitaker made it clear to the board of directors at Placard that he wanted to be the CEO, or he was going to jump ship. Right after that the CEO at the time, G. Holles Charlton, discovered he had cancer, and the board felt sorry for him, so they kept him in office, and Chad jumped ship. Moved to Colorado somewhere. Now he's back, and he wants to take over the entire city. He'd like nothing more than to build his hospital complex, then go somewhere besides Placard for his supplies, forcing Placard out of business."

Rita was getting a feeling for Chad Whitaker, but she wanted to get to the matter at hand.

Her impatience must have showed, because Philip said, "Anyway, we're not going to let NationsCare or anyone else take away what belongs to us." He waved a hand.

Rita said, "What you're saying is you knew something was wrong, and you weren't going to sell?"

Philip replied, "They were a bunch of crooks."

Liddy said, "Thank goodness, not everyone's that way."

He looked at her.

"The candle holders?"

He was silent.

She pointed at two silver candle holders that were in a glass case in the dining room. She said, "When my family and I were taken away to the camps, they took everything we had—our house, all of our personal possessions, everything, even the fillings in our teeth.

"When the war was over and we were liberated, I went back to the house where I had grown up as a child. I just wanted to see it again. As I was leaving, I met a woman who lived in the house next door. She looked familiar, and we got to talking. She was a German woman—"

"You're correct," Philip said. "One of the righteous gentiles."

Liddy nodded. "The more we talked, the more I remembered. One thing led to another, and I realized she had been our neighbor when we had been taken away to the camps. Funny how you shut out so much when you go through an experience like that. Of course, she had been only a young girl then—maybe eight or nine, or half my age—so I hadn't really known her at the time. She told me that when we were taken away, her mother had gone into our house and taken some silver candle holders that she had known were special to my mother—handed down from generation to generation. Her mother had carefully wrapped those holders and buried them in the backyard of their own house so the Germans wouldn't find them. The daughter returned them to me." She pointed toward the dining room. "There they are. So, see, Philip, get back to your position. Philip's an impossible optimist at heart."

Liddy seemed to have made a point because Philip nodded. "I didn't mean everyone was a crook," he replied, his tone as lighthearted as ever. "But when those SS thugs came around for their money, and said they would be willing to cancel my debt if I agreed to sell our property to NationsCare, what was I supposed to conclude about NationsCare of America?"

Rita asked them if they could describe who had visited. "Do you remember anything about this 'goon squad'?"

They were three football players, Philip told her. "What is there to describe?" he asked. "Each one filled the door as he came into the store."

Liddy laughed. "Two white men and a black man."

The descriptions didn't help, and it turned out neither Philip nor Liddy was good with details. What did help, though, was that Rita knew Jim had been working on a gambling investigation. And it might have been that he had been working on some kind of inquiry initiated by the governor, though she couldn't remember any mention of such an inquiry in Jim's files. A governor's inquiry would have stood out. Paul would have known. He would have mentioned something. Such an inquiry would have had to come through him—unless, of course, the inquiry had been a private matter. One of Jim's good friends, Ed Harding, was in charge of the governor's security detail. Had that been it? A private inquiry?

Rita's pager went off. She asked if she could use Philip and Liddy's telephone.

It was Charlie. He had arranged a meeting with J. D. Grove.

16

The snow was pelting by the time she got to Wells Street. It was no day to be out. She called the office to tell extra staff to go home. As for herself, all she wanted was to get finished with J. D. Grove as soon as possible so she could head home herself.

Rita began to have a bad feeling as she parallel-parked the car, not about the neighborhood, though it was no place to be alone, but about something else.

Mike's Christmas play, "The Ghost of Christmas Present," had juxtaposed the lives of the affluent with the lives of street people. How had Mike known about the street people? Rita bundled up, put on her gloves, and got out of the car. A little voice in her head kept saying, Mike knew something first hand.

She encountered a young black girl, six, perhaps seven years old. Standing in soaked tennis shoes in front of a corner store, the girl was crying. As she cried, she rubbed her nose, staring at Rita. Rita asked her what was wrong. The girl told her it was none of her business. Rita didn't push.

Not far down the street was a drunk, a black man without a left leg from the knee down, who lay in front of a pharmacy. He had passed out, and a blanket of snow had formed over him. Near him was another black man, this one with gray hair, whose penis was exposed. What looked like a urine stain spread from his crotch to the snow around him.

Along came a fat black woman with gray hair. She was trying to push a grocery cart through the snow.

"What did you expect?" asked an old black man with an intense expression on his face. Next to him stood Charlie. She recognized J.D., having seen his photograph in the newspaper enough times. His eyes were bloodshot and his Afro hair was unkempt. His lips, surrounded by wiry black hairs, were dry. "You expected that like your friend Jim Swearingen, you were going to come down here and it wasn't going to be that bad? That's what he thought, you know." That's when she noticed his nose was swollen. It had probably been broken at some point.

"Do we need to stand out here in the cold?" she asked.

An hour and a half later, they were in the back room of a tavern. J.D. and Charlie were playing game after game of pool. There were no chairs in the room with the pool table, a room that smelled like a mixture of urine and stale alcohol, so Rita stood leaning against the wall, which was grimy and riddled with holes in the plaster, holes where people had obviously kicked and hit it.

She realized before long that the bar was a center for bookmaking and that J.D. had some key role in it. He kept getting called up to the front, only to return with a wad of ones, fives, and tens. The money was worn. It had been circulating for a while.

J.D. admitted, among other things, that he was a bookmaker. Rita kept waiting for him to say that Mike was one of his customers. That was because J.D.'s eyes kept coming back to her, as if to say he knew all about her, but wasn't going to put her on the spot. Yes, he repeated, he was a bookmaker, though he said he was small-time compared to Chad Whitaker's operation. "That guy's big," J.D. told Charlie. "He knows what he's doing. He knows how to put people in his back pocket, and he knows how to run a crooked operation. He's been doing it since he was a young punk running the streets. As for me? I basically lose."

Was Mike one of his customers? she wondered.

J.D. shrugged. "I look at it as a way for me to take some of my income from the council and give it back to the people."

Despite how dimly lighted the room was, J.D.

had put on sunglasses now, and he chain-
smoked as he nursed cheap wine. He said he
liked wine because it gave him a more even high
over hours of drinking. Yet he didn't seem high.
As he played pool with Charlie, she could tell
that he took everything seriously, from his wine
to his bookmaking.

All the while he talked. He discussed the children in the neighborhood, children who without
the school lunch program would seldom get a
hot meal. He talked about the rats that openly
ran around buildings. He paused before he
made a shot, looked up, a cigarette dangling
from his mouth, and told Charlie, "You can
keep killing them but you can't ever seem to get
rid of them."

Then he shot, breaking a new rack, balls going
this way and that. He talked about the unemployment rates. He looked at her as he chalked
his cue. He told her, "You people measure it in
percents—as if six or seven percent isn't bad—
but most of you never come to this part of town,
where you can see the unemployment hanging
out in groups on street corners and in places
like this." He wiped his blued fingers on his
orange pants, then tried to slap the marks off.
"Your six or seven percent across the board happens mainly in those hidden sides of town like
the one you're in now—the side they tell you
never to drive through, especially at night."

Charlie asked about Jim. He had asked a couple of other times during the course of an hour and a half, and finally J.D. responded.

Yes, he admitted, he had talked to Jim.

"He came here?"

J.D. smiled. "He wasn't that crazy. Say, my man, you want to share some feet?"

From his front pocket Charlie brought out a money clip and pulled off a ten-dollar bill. He held it out. "And a beer," he said.

J.D. took the bill and left the room.

Rita didn't say anything.

Charlie smiled at her. From the pocket of his black leather coat, he removed a handkerchief and wiped his hands with it. Blue stains came off on the handkerchief.

J.D. returned from the tavern with a jar of pickled pigs' feet, a pepper shaker, a small bottle of wine, a Budweiser, and two glasses. He lined the items along the edge of the pool table, opened the jar of pigs' feet, reached into the pickle juice and removed a foot, which he covered with pepper. He began gnawing on the bony foot, pulling meat off with his teeth.

Charlie opened his beer, poured some in a glass, and got a pig's foot. He doused it with pepper and began eating.

J.D. said, eating, "No, Jim wasn't an idiot. He showed up at one of the council meetings. A sort of neutral ground, you dig." He was still talking to Charlie, but turned to ask her if she wanted one of the pigs' feet.

No, she told him. The thought of eating one

was repulsive to her, though she didn't tell him that.

She didn't have to. J.D. laughed. "Jim and I go back a long ways," he continued.

Yes, Charlie said, he knew that. "You two were in 'Nam together, weren't you?"

J.D. nodded. "Anyway, he shows up at a council meeting, pulls me aside, and tells me he's investigating some gambling operation, and that he thinks it has ties to NationsCare, which is what we're talking about at the council." He opened the small bottle of wine and poured it into a glass. The glass was just big enough to hold the bottle's contents. "I don't get the good stuff too often," he said, holding up the bottle.

"Was there anyone with Jim that day?" Rita asked.

The question made J.D. smile. "The man was all alone, one lone cop, and he comes runnin' this line on me about how he's investigating corruption, a gambling operation, and NationsCare." He laughed, lit a cigarette, and took a deep puff from it. To Charlie he said, "Isn't that just like how it is? If one of the brothers holds up a liquor store or something, they send in an army of police. If a big corporation like NationsCare is being investigated, they assign one man, and they tell him to clean up the town at the same time. Like the sheriff on the white horse in the movies." He laughed.

J.D. and Charlie ate more pigs' feet as J.D. continued to tell about Jim.

"But I didn't laugh right in his face," J.D. said. "Anyone else, and I would have told him to get lost, but I figured if Jim was on the case, he'd call in the reinforcements if he got on to something. Yeah, Jim and I were in 'Nam together. He was a stand-up guy."

Charlie said, "What was he trying to figure out?"

J.D. put the pig bones on the side of the pool table and shot the cue ball at a striped ball. "He wanted to know if NationsCare was putting any pressure on council members."

"And?" she asked.

"I told him, NationsCare was more sophisticated than that when it came to council members. With us, they were trying to wine and dine us, not to mention pad our pockets. If that didn't work, they tried catching us in embarrassing situations—such as to suddenly announce that it would be a shame if the public found out that Reverend So-and-So on the council had run up a fifty-thousand-dollar gambling debt, which was always followed by an offer to cancel the debt." He stared at her. "You look familiar to me. Have we met before?"

"Did anyone from NationsCare approach you?" she asked, trying to keep the focus off of herself.

J.D.'s attention went back to his game. "They knew better than to play me like that. They knew I'd tell them to get out of my face. But I did hear rumors about one member who was receiving some real pressure, Joe DeFalco.''

Rita wrote the name on a notepad.

''There were others, but I only give you his name because I like DeFalco. They're playing him for a fool, and it's too bad. If you ever meet him, you'll know why.'' He stopped speaking. ''No, I'll give you one other name.''

Rita expected to hear Mike's name.

J.D. shook his head. ''No,'' he said, ''never mind about that person.'' Then, ''How about a name of one of NCA's 'bone-breaker' squad, the one that was making rounds over in the area where the new hospital is supposed to be. There was at least one brother involved.'' To Charlie, he asked, ''Do you know a brother by the name of Leon Hampton?'' He spelled the name.

Charlie didn't acknowledge one way or the other.

''Leon is a small-time crack dealer who thinks he's big-time. He's been in and out of the joint. He's got a few girls. You know the kind of brother.''

Rita's pager went off, and she looked at it. It was Jerry Grier's number.

J.D. said, ''At least that will give you something to go on.''

Charlie nodded.

J.D. raised his hands to his surroundings. ''I mean, this may not look like much, but it's ours, and some of us are struggling to make it better. NationsCare doesn't want the brothers and sisters wandering around in the neighborhood. They want us completely off their streets. If they could build a wall around us and seal us off, they would."

Charlie slapped the open hand. "I hear you."

"Guns and walls and taking away what little we have isn't going to work."

She thanked J.D. for his information and told Charlie she would see him later.

On her way out of the tavern, she glanced at a couple of old black men, one of whom had a bottle turned to his lips. He took a drink, then handed the bottle to his partner, who seemed to be waiting to light a cigarette until he had taken a drink. In his hand was a cigarette and book of matches. She could hear one of the men mumble something about her.

She was glad to get out to the street, despite the snow and cold. She got in her sedan and started it. The windshield wipers took several sweeps to clean off the snow. She rolled down her window and looked out to get into the street. She saw the black man she had seen earlier—the one curled up on the sidewalk. On the radio she called it in so a rescue squad could give him medical attention.

Downtown, Jerry Grier was standing at his desk, clearing off papers and folders. Noticing her arrival, he said, "I liked Jim, and I know you did too. Come on, I have something I have to show you. I should have shown you before, and I'm sorry."

She followed him into the conference room, where there was a television and VCR set up. He pushed in the tape that was already in the mouth of the VCR. A surveillance tape began to show. "You didn't see this," he said. "It's an evidence tape I got from one of my friends over at the DEA. This is a gambling club they have infiltrated."

Rita sat down. She felt light-headed. She knew Bull was about to show her a tape of Mike caught in a gambling club.

He put the tape on FAST FORWARD. Human figures moved quickly about the club. Then, with a click, the tape resumed its normal speed.

There he was, Al Hoeveler, entering the club and taking a seat at one of the card tables, where he wrote out a note, and someone counted out a stack of chips.

Rita let out a deep breath. She could feel the perspiration at the back of her neck.

"Each of the dark chips is worth a hundred dollars," he said. "The light chips are worth ten dollars. Al just wrote a note for two thousand dollars."

In FAST FORWARD, they watched him as he played cards. He lost again and again. He wrote out another note.

He said, "This goes on for several hours, and this is only one tape."

Even with the tape in FAST FORWARD, Rita could see the frustration in Al's demeanor. He was bending the edges of the cards, so the decks had to be replaced frequently. Bull commented, "The only thing I can think of is he's trying to cheat—mark the cards." Al began throwing around cards and chips. He was no longer smiling.

Bull stopped the video. He said, "I think you get the picture."

"Do you know how much of a debt he ran up?" she asked.

"My buddy at the DEA said he ran up sixteen thousand on this day alone, and this is nothing."

"Why didn't you show me this before?"

Bull lit a cigar. "It wasn't that easy."

She didn't know quite what to say.

"Damn it, Rita." He fast-forwarded the tape again, and there he was—Mike. As abruptly as Mike appeared, Bull stopped the tape.

She breathed out deeply. "How long have you known about this?"

"Not long."

"Come on, Bull, don't play that game with me."

"I swear, Rita. I didn't know he was on there. It was by accident I saw him. It's not like he was a big player someone was watching. The important person is Al Hoeveler. Those notes he was writing out were IOUs. And I understand he ran up fifty to sixty thousand dollars' worth of IOUs, which he's now paid, or at least the IOUs have been canceled."

She looked at Bull sharply. "Do you have any idea why they were canceled?"

"From what I understand, the FBI was investigating him for some kind of an organized-crime hit down in Chicago, a real sloppy job." He sat on the edge of the conference table. "They had a tap on his line, and at one time he was talking, then someone—the feds think it was Jim—tipped him off that he was being investigated or set up, and he became as quiet as a church mouse. Aside to the references to the hit he had been linked to in Chicago, the feds couldn't get enough evidence to link him to anything. The trail suddenly turned cold."

"What do you know about the Chicago hit?" she asked.

"It's a twenty-six-year-old Asian woman who they found floating facedown in a canal of the Chicago River."

"What else do you know?"

"That she had been tortured and then thrown into the river while she was still alive." He stood. "Her name was Miss Yuan Zhang, and the cause of death was drowning, which is kind of interesting because they first thought it was homicide by stangulation, but it turned out to be drowning."

She asked him if she could have the tape. As soon as she asked, she felt dirty and cheap. Would he think she was trying to destroy the evidence about Mike?

Without comment, he gave her the tape.

She returned to her office and locked away the tape. She was about to leave when she noticed a note on her desk. A telephone message from her bank. She called. The bank was closed, but some of the employees were still there. One of them checked the computer to find out what the call was about. Rita discovered that her checking account was overdrawn.

"What? That's impossible. My account?" She had kept her own account even after she and Mike had been married.

"That's what we thought too," the employee told her. "We know from your history that you've never overdrawn your account. Right now we're willing not to charge you any fees if you'll make sure your account is covered right away."

Rita asked how much the account was overdrawn. The official told her it was only $180. Rita said she would cover the amount. She said she had a couple of CDs with the bank, and she would transfer one the next morning.

The official said, "One other thing—"

Rita could feel the tears of anger and embarrassment welling up inside her.

"Is it possible someone might have stolen some of your checks?"

"I'm not sure, why?"

"We've been looking at a couple of the checks, and your signature and handwriting look forged."

17

Rita was even more shocked when the bank faxed her copies of the three checks in question. Sure enough, she had not written the checks, though someone had crudely signed her name to them. No wonder Mike had immediately gone to Gamblers Anonymous as soon as she had confronted him. He had had more to hide than he had acknowledged.

On her way home, the snow was thick, so she was extra cautious. She listened to a talk show on the radio—she thought that might take her mind off of things. The DJs were inviting members of the listening audience to call in. The question: If your spouse cheated on you, would you forgive him or her?

A woman called in and said it would depend upon the circumstances.

One of the DJs, a male, asked, "What do you mean, it would depend upon the circumstances?"

"I mean, if he got drunk and happened to go

to bed with another woman and he was sorry for it, then yes, I guess I would forgive him. But he'd have to be really sorry."

A female DJ asked, "How would you know if he were really sorry?"

"You know what I mean. It depends. If he came and said he was sorry, he felt terrible about it, and it'd never happen again, then I'd probably forgive him. But if I confronted him about it, and he said he was sorry, then I tried to talk to him and he said, 'Look, I said I was sorry, now get over it,' I probably wouldn't forgive him."

Both DJs laughed. The male DJ said he would forgive his wife. "I'd have to," he said. "She means so much to me that even cheating I'd have to keep her."

The female DJ said, "You'd forgive and forget?"

"That's what forgiveness is."

"I don't know. I might forgive, but I'm not sure I could forget."

The male DJ laughed. "Oh, so you're one of those. One of those people who keeps bringing things up year after year. I can hear it now: 'Honey, you left the lid off the toothpaste.' 'So, at least I didn't try to ruin our marriage by cheating on you.' "

Rita turned off the radio. Why hadn't she remained single? she wondered. Life would have been so much simpler. It was the first time she had had such a thought, and the thought scared her. Hadn't she forgiven Mike? If she had wanted to ask questions, why hadn't she done so at the time she had confronted him?

Why hadn't he told her everything, though?

She hadn't asked.

She went back and forth like that.

Didn't she have a responsibility, especially to Greg? She could tell Mike she still forgave him, but she needed him to understand how serious things were. Then if he continued to be remorseful, she would continue to forgive him. If he became belligerent, then that was another story.

But he was not at home. Greg was there. He was talking on the telephone.

"Get off the phone," she said.

"I just got on."

"That's what you always say. Get off."

"Mom, I swear, I just got on."

"Get off now or take the punishment."

"Can I call you back?" Greg asked, speaking into the telephone receiver. "Thanks." He hung up. "What's wrong with you?"

"Greg, you can't tie up the phone all day."

"Then can we talk about me getting my own line?"

"No."

"Can't we just talk about it?"

Rita looked around at the kitchen. It was a mess. "You know your job is to do the dishes. Why don't you start by keeping up your end, then we can go from there."

"Then can we talk?"

Rita sorted through the mail. There wasn't much. A couple of bills—there were always bills—and a catalog. Greg always ordered catalogs. Whenever he was reading a magazine, he sent off for everything that had an address or offered a catalog.

Greg started to do the dishes.

"What did you do today?" she asked, tearing open a credit card bill.

"I watched TV."

"And talked on the phone all day. It was a good thing there wasn't an emergency."

"I didn't talk on the phone all day."

"Did anyone call?"

"Mike called. He said he was going to be home late."

She looked at him. "Why?"

Greg was filling the dishwasher. "He said he was running behind."

"Rinse those before you put them in there. A dishwasher isn't a garbage disposal."

Greg rinsed a plate. "Merry Christmas," he commented.

"Don't talk to me like that."

"My gosh, what's wrong with you today?"

He was right. Why blame him? He hadn't done anything. "I'm sorry," she said. "You're right. If I had a rough day, I shouldn't take it out on you."

"That's okay."

"Tell me about your day."

"That's okay," he repeated sarcastically.

"No, I want to hear about it."

Greg got a plastic bottle of Coke from the refrigerator. The two-liter bottle looked like he had been working on it for a while. He unscrewed the lid, took a swig from the bottle, and screwed back on the lid.

She wanted to say something about him drinking out of the bottle but didn't. That would be finding fault with everything.

"Okay, I've got something we can talk about." He continued to fill the dishwasher. "If I were to earn my own money and could buy a television, would you pay the extra amount to hook up cable in my room?"

"I thought we weren't going to get in an argument."

"Would you think about it?"

Rita thought about saying nothing so there wouldn't be an argument, but then she decided it wouldn't be good to leave it like that. Next thing she would know, Greg would go to Mike and tell him she had promised to pay for an extra television hookup. "You watch too much television as it is."

"Would you just call the cable television company and find out how much an extra hookup would cost?" He put in dishwashing soap, closed the dishwasher door, and set the timer. The machine started to make noise. "That would be a good Christmas present for me."

If she let him badger her, she'd blow up at him. Instead she walked into the bedroom, dropped her things, then went to the living room, where she plugged in the Christmas tree. Even the tree didn't look as good as it had in previous years. Once upon a time it had been exciting to decorate the tree, her and Greg together. The past couple of years, however, tree decorating had become a chore. The tree looked it too. There weren't as many lights because it was a chore to untangle them. Not as many ornaments either because some of them had lost their hooks, and no one had gotten around to buying new ones. Rita sat down and stared at the tree, its lights flashing. Two days before Christmas, and Christmas was the furthest thing from her mind. She could hear Greg on the telephone.

Greg came into the living room, carrying the portable phone. "Mom, do you remember meeting someone named Steve Brown?"

Rita looked at him. He was such a handsome boy. Slightly overweight but handsome. Soon, he would be driving. "Who?"

"He was at the play. He wasn't in it, but he was there. Tall. Plays football."

No, Rita said, she didn't know him.

Into the phone, Greg said, "Mom says she doesn't remember you." He laughed. "I know. Makes you feel real good, doesn't it?" He left the room. He returned, still talking on the phone. "Mom, Steve wants to know if I can come over for a while. He just lives two blocks from the church. His mother can pick me up and drop me off."

"That's fine," she said absentmindedly. "For a little bit."

"You mean it?"

"Write down the address and telephone number in case I have to get in touch with you."

Greg smiled. "I need to write down your telephone number and address." He laughed. "I know. That's how moms are." He went into the kitchen. "I'll be waiting on the front porch. Bye."

"Be good. I love you."

"I love you too."

Then the door closed and Rita was all alone in the house. For the first time she realized how depressed she was. The world was closing in on her. What was life all about? She unplugged the tree. It didn't even look pretty to her.

The front door opened. She thought it was Greg returning, but it was Mike.

She didn't know how long she had been sitting there. The room was almost dark. She looked numbly at him.

He said he had been to a "meeting." She took that to mean Gamblers Anonymous. One of his hands was behind his back. She hoped he hadn't bought her a gift. She didn't feel like one. He said, "They tell you whenever you feel depressed or you feel the urge to gamble, you need to get to a meeting, and if you can't get to a meeting, you're supposed to contact someone on the support group list.''

All the while she hoped he wouldn't bring out a gift. A gift would be like he wasn't sorry, like he was being extravagant again, or like he was trying to pay her off.

"That's why I'm late. I went to a meeting. It was a rough day." He produced a rose, so deep red it almost looked like blood. He said, "I wouldn't have been as understanding if the tables had been turned, I don't think. You knew how much trouble I was in, and when I admitted it, you didn't rake me over the coals or make a lot of stipulations." He held out the rose. "I'm sorry for all the trouble I've gotten us in, and I just wanted to let you know I was thinking about you today."

She took the rose. She didn't want to, but she took it anyway. It was easier to take the rose at that point than it would have been to bring up the matter of the forged checks. Besides, the telephone rang, and she didn't think she'd be able to answer it until she had either taken the rose or refused it.

Mike gave her the telephone. He told her it was Paul Clowers.

Paul told her to turn on the television to channel six.

She turned it on and used the remote to turn to channel six. There she was, Susan Hall, microphone in hand, speaking to the camera:

"This is Susan Hall for WITI-TV's Contact Six, and this is a special investigative report."

Paul, still on the line, said, "I just got a call from the television station saying they were going to air a report and asking me if I wanted to make a comment."

Susan Hall was standing on the shore of Lake Mendota in Madison, and in the background was the fishing shack where Jim's body had been found.

"It all began early last week in that shack right behind me"—she turned to point—"when the body of a top criminal investigator for the state of Wisconsin, Major Jim Swearingen, was pulled from Lake Mendota here at our state's capital. Contact Six was on hand shortly after the investigator's body was retrieved from the icy water."

The camera came back to Susan. "Since then this case has become one of the most bizarre cases in the history of Wisconsin law enforcement.

"First, there was the rumor that the investigator had committed suicide. But everyone said privately that such a story would be a scandal. State officials wanted to do anything to keep word of suicide from getting out. Next thing we knew, the death was linked to a serial killer." A photograph of Scott Renneker flashed on the screen.

"Then there was another shocking revelation. Everyone knows the sad story of the little girl by the name of Brittny Neuland, who was sexually abused and murdered, her body recently found north of Madison." A photograph of Brittny came on the screen.

The television camera zoomed in on Susan Hall's flawless face. "How convenient," she said. "State investigators had a potential scandal on their hands, so they tried to link it to the murder of Brittny Neuland." Susan shook her head. "The truth of the matter? We've been doing some digging, and privately officials are saying that Major Jim Swearingen might have committed suicide in order to escape the scandal that was about to catch up with him."

On the screen appeared the image of an Asian woman. "This woman, Yuan Zhang, was strangled in Chicago, allegedly by a relative of the state investigator who committed suicide. The investigator apparently let the guilty people go, destroyed official documents and crucial evidence, and then killed himself."

The cameras zoomed in on her. "Officials are still refusing to comment, but this is only the first of several special reports we'll devote to this matter. Stay tuned to channel six for all the latest updates. This is Susan Hall, Contact Six, reporting."

Paul said, "Rita, this isn't good."

Rita knew someone had told Susan about Yuan Zhang, and there weren't many possibilities. Jerry's was the only name that came to mind.

Paul asked her if she knew who Yuan was.

Rita admitted she had only recently uncovered the lead.

"Why didn't you tell me?" he asked.

"Paul, I haven't even had a chance to look into the matter yet. A lot's going on. Tomorrow's Christmas Eve."

"It seems our Susan Hall is hard at work two days before Christmas," he said. "Maybe I should put her on our staff."

"Paul, that's entirely up to you," she said. She didn't feel like playing games at that hour, not with everything already on her mind. "News reporters don't have to be as careful as we do. We have to worry about chains of evidence, laws, procedures, et cetera. There's always going to be a Susan Hall out there somewhere, trying to stir up a juicy story, but if you want her to work for us, you go ahead and hire her. She'll stab you in the back as soon as you get her employment paperwork processed, but go ahead."

Paul took a deep breath. "I'm sorry. I just don't like to watch television in order to find out what's going on in my own department. I want a report as soon as you can put some details together. More than likely the attorney general will now launch his own investigation, and the feds are going to follow up on what they were doing in the first place. There's no stopping it now."

"I know."

"And one other thing. You need to make sure whoever you have working on this is a little more discreet about what he or she's saying and doing. Someone's talking too much."

The moment Rita got off the phone, she buried her face in her hands. Then she ran her hands up through her hair and held her hair back for a moment. She dropped her hands and blew out a long sigh.

Rita looked around. Mike, who she thought had been standing with her, was gone. She went down the hall. He was in the bedroom. In his hands were the photocopies of the forged checks. He put them back on the bed with the other papers she had dropped there. He looked embarrassed.

She didn't say anything, but went into the bathroom. When she came out, Mike was not there. He was in the living room, watching television.

In the kitchen, she saw the vase containing the lone rose. He must have put it in water for her. She heard Mike turn off the television. She could feel him behind her.

He asked her if she had left the photocopies out in the open on purpose.

No, she told him, but wondered if subconsciously she had wanted him to find them. She could feel the tension between him and her. Do you forgive him or not? she asked herself.

18

Mike returned most of the items he had purchased with the five thousand dollars. As a result, Christmas was a simple affair. She got Mike some tools he had been wanting for his workshop in the basement. He gave her an electric blanket for the bed, which Greg said illustrated where Mike had his mind; and a miniature tape recorder, which she said she could put to good use in her work. Together they had gotten Greg clothes, CK cologne he had been wanting, and CDs for his stereo.

Once Christmas was over, Rita, accompanied by Charlie, headed for Chicago. On their way, she told him about Mike. Charlie said he knew to some extent that Mike had been gambling. She asked him why he hadn't said something. He told her it had been J.D. who had mentioned it to him. He said, "He told me he had been able to tell by looking at you that you knew. I figured if you wanted me dipping into your private business, you'd say something to me."

She said she respected that.

"I have some news," he said. "Claudia's pregnant."

"What!" She slapped his shoulder as she drove. "Charlie, that's great! Congratulations."

He had a tense grin on his face.

"What's wrong?"

He said, "We didn't really want another child right now."

She didn't know what to say.

"We've been thinking about this whole business of leukemia, and we hate the thought of something like that ever happening again."

"Charlie, you can't stop living because you're afraid."

He was silent for a few moments. "The other thing I've been thinking about is how Keisha's been in and out of remission," he said. "That Claudia's suddenly pregnant again makes me wonder if this is some way of getting us ready for something bad that's about to happen to Keisha."

She said, "Don't even think something like that." The way he was talking scared her. Such thoughts, she knew, had a way of getting carried away with themselves.

After that, they were relatively quiet until they got to Chicago.

Detective Tony Donato of the Chicago Police Department Homicide Division brought out the case file of the Yuan Zhang investigation, beginning with the photographs. He said, "This was a troubling case from the beginning, especially as the lab reports began to come back. You can see from the photographs that her head was burned badly. The lab reports indicated a catalyst."

"Gasoline?" Charlie asked.

Donato shook his head. "Whoever did this is sick. Do you know how flammable aerosol hair spray is?"

Neither she nor Charlie responded.

"There were heavy concentrations of hair spray on Yuan's head, which means that someone apparently set her on fire using it."

Rita glanced at the crime photo. It depicted a woman whose hair had been burned off and whose head and face had been badly burned.

"Then whoever it was tried to make it look like she had tried to commit suicide. They apparently hung her from a bridge that passed over the canal, but the clothesline or whatever that had been used broke, at which point Yuan dropped into the river and drowned." He looked up from the photographs he was studying, a young Italian in his thirties. "You know how it is when you find a body and the marks of injury don't appear right away?"

Both Rita and Charlie sat without comment.

"That's how it was in this case," he continued, and one at a time he held out black-and-white photographs of Zhang. "These are early photos. Note how there aren't clear marks on her neck."

Rita studied each of the photographs. It was true. There weren't distinct marks. She passed the photographs along to Charlie.

Donato held out a photograph. This one he didn't release, but instead held it so he could see it at the same time they could from across the desk. With the eraser end of a pencil, he outlined a distinct mark on Zhang's neck. "Notice how the constriction mark on the right side of her neck extends up behind the right ear?" Without waiting for a response, he said, "See how it travels diagonally across the windpipe and to the base of the neck on the left side?" He traced the line with the pencil eraser. "Jim Swearingen pointed it out to me. He pointed out that we were looking for someone who was truly sick, someone who tortured his victims to the very limit of human tolerance."

Rita thought of Renneker.

"If she had tried to hang herself, the cord or rope would have pulled up equally on both sides of her neck," he said, "which gives us some clues about the killer." He produced another photograph, this one an anterior nude shot. With the eraser end of his pencil, he pointed out several abrasions and scratches on Zhang's chest and legs. "What we think," he explained, "is that whoever murdered her, beat her first, stripped her naked, making it appear to be a sex crime, burned her—this asshole likes fire—tied a cord around her neck, and dragged her, facedown, to the river and hung her. From the constriction mark on the neck, and the abrasions and scratches, it looks like her assailant was left-handed."

Charlie said, "Then she was definitely alive when she dropped into the water?"

"That's correct," Donato said. "There was water and plankton in her lung bronchi. She seemed to be trying to get her breath when she dropped into the water. The actual cause of death is listed as homicidal drowning." He shook his head. "That's how bizarre all of this is. The killer knows death inside out. There are clearly burns of a serious nature, but they are first- and second-degree. Given all that happened, that tells us something. Third-degree burns are so serious that they don't even hurt. The killer in this case wanted the victim to suffer. Then the petechial hemorrhages on the victim's face and the constriction mark on her neck show strangulation. More torture, not quite enough to finish the job."

"So someone wanted everyone to think that it wasn't really a professional killer who had done the job," Rita commented, running a hand through her hair.

"That's right," Donato replied. "This was someone who wanted it to seem like a moron had attempted to kill someone and couldn't seem to get the job done."

"The killer would have had to be a big man," Charlie added, "someone strong."

"Very strong," Donato agreed. "Once we went back over the crime scene, we saw that Yuan had been dragged quite a distance."

"And how did Al Hoeveler become a prime suspect in the investigation?" Rita wanted to know.

According to Donato, Hoeveler had traveled to Chicago, where he had attempted to buy a gun in a pawnshop. "Apparently he thought if he came here, no one would know about his prior criminal record, and no one would do any checking. He hit several pawnshops, but every time someone submitted his name to Alcohol, Tobacco, and Firearms, it came back with a flag on it. After several days he left town, but we do know he was staying in the same general neighborhood where Zhang lived, he was seen hanging around near her apartment, and in one pawnshop, owned by a local Chinese family, he had claimed to know Zhang, apparently in an effort to get them to sell him a gun. It was the same time frame as her murder."

"But all circumstantial?" Charlie mentioned.

Donato admitted it was. "But Hoeveler was clearly a prime suspect. He seemed to be stalking her for some reason. Either that or he was hanging around for some reason." He shrugged. "Perhaps he was angry about some previous encounter he had had with her. Perhaps it was a hate crime. We see a lot of that."

Rita asked, "What do you know about her, about her past?"

"Not much," Donato replied, and explained about the difficulties of investigating such a case that involved language and cultural differences. "From what we can figure out, up until about six or so months before she moved to Chicago, she had lived in Milwaukee. Then she lost her job there and moved to Chicago, where she had family and friends."

Where had Zhang worked in Milwaukee? Rita wanted to know.

Donato consulted the investigative notes. "NationsCare of America."

Rita glanced at Charlie.

Donato said, "Maybe she got fired. Otherwise she could have probably moved back here and worked for them. They have a hospital here, you know. In fact, they have hospitals all over."

Charlie asked, "Did you get a chance to interview Hoeveler?"

Yes, detectives had interviewed him, Donato explained, but there never was enough evidence to link him directly to the murder of Yuan. "There were problems with identification, and so on. You name it."

Rita then asked about Jim.

"Nice guy," Donato replied, "though we didn't agree on certain things."

"Like what?" Charlie wanted to know.

"He didn't think Hoeveler was the one who murdered Miss Zhang," Donato said. "He came here, looked over the investigative notes, like you did, looked at the photographs, examined the body, watched our videotaped interview, then said he didn't think it was Hoeveler. That rubbed people the wrong way." He laughed.

Rita asked if they could watch the taped interview. "You say you videotaped it?"

Yes, they had, Donato said, and she and Charlie were welcome to review the tape.

Donato set up the tape in a small room that was so hot that Rita even had to close the heat vent while she and Charlie watched the tape on television.

The tape started unremarkably with Al sitting at a table, his hands folded in front of him.

Detectives advised him of his rights and not only orally got him to waive those rights, but they also had him sign waiver forms in front of the camera. Sure enough, Hoeveler was left-handed, as the killer was. At least he signed the forms with his left hand.

Then the camera, indicating the time and date on the black-and-white image of Hoeveler, remained on him as detectives took him through a grilling interview:

What was he doing in Chicago?

He wasn't.

Why had people seen him there?

They must be wrong.

Why was his name on the Alcohol, Tobacco, and Firearms forms for a gun?

"I guess someone tried to buy one in my name."

Why would anyone want to do that?

He didn't know.

The interview went on like that for approximately an hour. At least in superficial details, Hoeveler was at ease while answering questions. In fact, he remained unruffled until Donato asked him, "Why did you murder Yuan Zhang?"

That question flustered him. He said he had not murdered Yuan Zhang, that he didn't even know her. Then he asked if he could smoke a cigarette.

Yes, that was fine. From a drawer in the table Donato removed an ashtray and slid it across the table.

Hoeveler lit a cigarette, took a deep puff from it, and blew out the smoke.

"You did use her name," Donato told him. "We have three witnesses who can attest to that."

"It wasn't me. The witnesses must be wrong."

"Then where did they get your name and description?"

Hoeveler shrugged. "I guess someone gave it to them." He took a nervous puff on his cigarette, then tapped it on the side of the ashtray, knocking off ashes.

Donato told him it would be better if he didn't try to hide anything from them because they were going to find out the truth sooner or later anyway.

Hoeveler calmed a little after that. He insisted he had nothing to hide, and the questioning resumed.

Producing a photograph, Donato asked Hoeveler if he had ever met Yuan.

Hoeveler, smoking as he talked, explained that he was a contractor and had a company in Milwaukee. He said when NationsCare had announced that it was hoping to build a hospital complex in Milwaukee, he had contacted NCA and expressed interest in having his company participate in the construction of the new complex. "I believe I might have met her during one of my contacts."

"How did you contact NationsCare?"

"By telephone. A couple visits."

Rita leaned forward and put the VCR on pause. She told Charlie, "Whatever Jim saw on this tape, it led him to believe that Al hadn't murdered Yuan. Have you seen anything that strikes you as being odd?"

Charlie was leaning back in his chair, his feet stretched out in front of him. "Not really, though Hoeveler seems to be acting like there was no written record of his contacts with Chad Whitaker, or NationsCare."

"That's true." That's what she had noticed too. "It might establish a motive. Let's say that Yuan was supposed to have destroyed all copies of the correspondence, but she kept copies for herself, only they didn't know that. So someone at NationsCare figured that all that needed to be done was to eliminate the only person who could possibly testify to the fact that there ever was any correspondence in the first place." She touched the REWIND button on the VCR, then pressed PLAY.

"—did you contact NationsCare?"

"By telephone. A couple visits."

"What, you picked up the telephone and said, hi, I want to work for you?"

Hoeveler laughed. He seemed to appreciate Donato's sense of humor. No, he replied, the process was more complicated than that. His call had been switched from office to office until he had been connected to Yuan Zhang, who had explained that no bidding had started for the construction phase of the project, but that she would add Hoeveler's name to a list of interested parties—

This time Charlie leaned foward and stopped the VCR. He touched REWIND, then PLAY:

"—list, and that all the companies on the list would be contacted—"

He pushed STOP, touched REWIND, then PLAY:

"—she would put my name on a list, and that all the companies—"

He played that same section again and again. Rita wondered what he had heard that struck him as being odd.

Then he played the section in slow motion and touched STILL when the moment came.

There was Al, his eyes glancing at a turned left wrist. No wristwatch, Charlie pointed out.

This time when Charlie replayed the section, she noticed the subtle movement immediately. Al was looking to see what time it was, only to discover that he wasn't wearing his watch.

Rita stood. "You know, we need to see if we can get a copy of this tape because there are probably dozens of little things like this that we're missing." She went out to find Donato, who said he would be happy to make them a copy of the Hoeveler interview.

As she and Charlie left the homicide division, she was still puzzled by the watch. She could remember times in her own day-to-day routine when she had looked to see what time it was only to discover she had forgotten to wear her watch. What had Jim seen? she asked herself.

Charlie commented, "I guess I'm still surprised that Hoeveler finally got a contract from NationsCare."

She admitted she was puzzled by the same thing. "Are we both in agreement that someone at NationsCare apparently wanted to get rid of Zhang?"

Charlie said he could concede that.

"Which means she would have had to have been some threat to the organization. Let's go home."

Charlie tried to get her to talk about what was on her mind, but she didn't say anything specific until they were back in Milwaukee. There she brought out the envelope that had been in Jim's locker at the University of Wisconsin. There they were: Zhang's initials on the typed correspondence that had gone out from Chad Whitaker. The initials "YZ" beside the initials "CW" were too much of a coincidence to refer to anyone other than Yuan Zhang. She had been Whitaker's personal secretary. Rita was certain of it. She pointed out the initials to Charlie.

"Yes," Charlie said, "but I find it too much to believe that Chad Whitaker would arrange to have his own private secretary murdered. That would be taking a serious risk." He pointed at the letters spread out on Rita's desk. "The letters indicate that Whitaker had his act enough together that he didn't want Hoeveler anywhere near his organization. I don't blame him. One look at our man Al was all I needed to tell me he wasn't exactly the caliber of person Whitaker would have anything to do with." He shook his head. "I simply can't see a connection between Whitaker and any murder. I mean, if he wanted to avoid scum by keeping distance between himself and Hoeveler, why end up crawling into the same bed with him by becoming involved in a murder?"

They finished watching the videotaped interview of Hoeveler. Rita said, "Let's consider what we have so far. Al tried to lie about Yuan, then he cleaned that up; it's obvious he's lying about how he got on with NCA, though we don't know how that ties in; and he doesn't have a watch on, which he seemed to realize during the interview."

Suddenly, once the interview was done and before the tape ended, Hoeveler returned to the interview room, where he picked up a package of cigarettes from the table. With the disposable lighter, he tried to light a cigarette. The lighter wouldn't light. Hoeveler adjusted the flame with a switch on the lighter. Still it wouldn't light. The detective who was accompanying him said, "Here," and tossed Hoeveler a lighter, which Hoeveler caught with his right hand. Hoeveler lit his cigarette and tossed the lighter back—using his right hand. The camera went off, and the screen was replaced by fuzz.

Rita and Charlie looked at each other.

She commented, "It looks like Al writes with his left hand, but does other things with his right." Was that what Jim had seen? Rita turned in her chair to look out the window. "Let's expand our surveillance to cover Diane Hoeveler. Somehow they've got Whitaker over a barrel."

There came a tap at her door. It was Bev Smith, her administrative aide. She held out a Federal Express package. "This just came for you," she said.

It was from the NASA Protective Services Office of the Kennedy Space Center. As Bev stood there, Rita tore open the package.

Bev had two slips of pink paper. "You had two calls," she said. "One was from a Debbie

Sweet. She said it wasn't important. She wondered how things were going. I told her I'd pass along the message to you. She sounded like a nice girl."

Rita was thankful when she opened the FedEx package. The face in the photograph was clear now. It wasn't Mike. At the same time, she realized it wasn't anyone else she knew. She had hoped that the face would be of someone Jim wanted her to see, had hoped she'd recognize. Instead, it was the face of a stranger. She handed the enhanced photograph to Charlie, who had the same reaction. He shrugged. The face meant nothing to him either. "A slight resemblance to Hoeveler, but it clearly isn't him."

Bev was still there.

"Who's the other call from, Bev?" Rita asked, taking the photograph back from Charlie.

"Isabel."

Isabel Sardas, the child abuse task force's psychiatrist. It couldn't be good news. "Okay. Everybody out," Rita said. "I need to make a couple calls."

At the door, Charlie said he was going to watch Leon Hampton for a while. Hampton was the person whom J.D. had identified as a "bonebreaker" for Whitaker's gambling operation. Charlie left before she could say anything, pulling the door shut behind him.

She called Isabel. The parents of Bianca Willis had signed her out of the hospital, AMA, against medical approval.

The news took a few moments before it sunk
in. "Wasn't there anything you could do?" Rita
wanted to know.

"Rita, you know the law as well as I do. We
had nothing to stop them."

Rita looked out the window at the bright winter sunlight. She hoped Bianca would be all
right.

19

City Councilman Joe DeFalco was there to see her, Bev Smith told Rita. At first Rita was surprised, but when she thought about it, his showing up was logical. Her office had been making inquiries about NationsCare of America, so they'd sent someone to do some reconnaissance work.

Bev mentioned, "He's a sweet old man who said he thought you might like to talk to him."

Rita looked at the yellow slips indicating calls she hadn't returned, at the reports that needed review and signature, and at the notes she had been taking on the Swearingen investigation. She didn't want DeFalco looking at any of it. She told Bev, "Give me a few minutes to put some things away."

Bev left, and Rita began to organize the loose papers and notes in front of her. She turned over some reports so that DeFalco wouldn't be able to see their contents.

At the tap at her door, she looked up. In the doorway stood a short, balding Italian man with a salt-and-pepper mustache. It reminded her of Jim's mustache. She guessed DeFalco was in his sixties. The hair on his head was still dark, at least around the sides, where he still had hair. He had obviously had a stroke at some time in the past. His right hand was giving his left hand support, and there was some drooping in the left side of his face.

She smiled and stood. "Mr. DeFalco," she said.

"Please, call me Joe." He let his left arm dangle while he reached out with his right hand.

She took his hand and shook it. "Please, sit down," she said, and motioned to a chair.

He sat down, and with his right hand he placed his left hand in his lap.

"It was kind of you to stop by to see me today," she said.

"Did your secretary tell you why I was here?"

"She only said you wanted to talk for a few minutes."

"I heard you were asking questions about me."

"About you? Who did you hear that from, Mr. DeFalco?"

"Please, Joe."

"Joe."

"I was born and raised in this town," he said. "My heritage goes back a long ways here. Even the mention of my name gets back to me."

Rita leaned back in her chair. She smiled. "You sound like a very popular person."

He smiled, though it wasn't much of a smile—more of a sad expression. "I've been a good Catholic all my life, and when I hear someone's asking questions about me, I guess I get a guilty conscience, and I want to confront it. Catholics hate to carry guilt around."

"I don't know why you should have a guilty conscience," she told him. "Can I get you a cup of coffee or anything?"

He said, no, he was fine.

Rita asked, "Why do you have a guilty conscience?"

"Let's say we all have skeletons in a closet somewhere. That's why I'm here."

What was he getting at? Rita wondered, but was afraid to ask. Was it Mike? Was DeFalco here to say that Chad Whitaker knew about Mike's nasty habits and was going to expose them unless she backed off?

There was a tap at the door. It was Bev. She had a strange expression on her face, like she might be sick.

Rita asked not to be disturbed.

Bev seemed not to hear. "Charlie has been shot!" she said, too disoriented to say more.

"What!"

Rita didn't remember leaving DeFalco. She was with him at one moment, and the next moment she was in the winter air. After that, everything was confusing. She remembered running,

and driving fast—she almost had an accident—
and praying.

Only Charlie was not there by the time she
reached the tavern on Wells Street. According
to traffic on the police scanner, that was where
the original distress call had come from, and
there were a lot of emergency vehicles on scene
to prove that she was at the right place, but
Charlie was not there. Only blood in the snow.
Someone mentioned that an ambulance had
taken him to St. Luke's.

Someone else said he was dead.

The area around the tavern was chaotic, police
cars everywhere, more arriving even as she
moved among an army of police and detectives,
trying to figure out what had happened.

She came upon the body of J. D. Grove. He
was clearly dead, his life spread out in a large
pool of blood beneath him. She could see he had
been shot in the neck. A charred, ugly hole. It
was thick blood, a lot of clotting in it.

Where was Charlie? she asked.

A rookie pointed at another body. "He's over
there," he said. "He's dead."

Before she had realized what she had done,
she had actually knelt in the blood of the other
body and had touched him.

Someone pulled her away. "This is a crime
scene, lady," a uniformed officer said.

She didn't know the officer. She looked at herself. She had blood on her hands and clothes.
The man she was standing over was Leon

Hampton. She knew from his mug shot. He was big too, like Charlie.

A detective told the uniformed officer who she was, and he released her, apologizing.

Where was Charlie Dalton? she asked the detective. It was Joe Kestner, a city detective. She and he had been on a guard detail together once when the president of the United States had visited Milwaukee.

There had been a shootout, Joe said. Charlie had been hit. "He went down hard," Joe told her. There hadn't even been time to wait for an ambulance, Kestner said. Officers had thrown him in a cruiser and rushed him to St. Luke's. Kestner pointed at another pool of blood. It was big, enough that he must be hanging in the balance between life and death.

Jerry Grier took her by the arm. "Come on, Rita," he said. "I'll take you there." She was thankful to see Bull. He smelled like a cigar.

All she could think of as she sat in the backseat of a souped-up narcotics car was that she was responsible for what had happened to Charlie. Bull was holding her, telling her to relax. A longhaired narcotics agent was driving. Rita kept asking herself why she had insisted on digging for information. Didn't she ever know when to stop? If she had hadn't asked Charlie to see what he could find out, it never would have happened.

Suddenly she hated Chad Whitaker, and she didn't even know him. He was going to get

what he wanted, and he wasn't going to let anyone or anything get in his way. He was going
to have his new hospital. He was going to have
his high-rise apartments on Wells, and he was
going to raze Zeskind's pawnshop. She hated
him for sending Joe DeFalco to make inquiries.
She hated him for how he was going to squeeze
her about Mike.

Charlie had been taken directly to surgery.
Rita found Claudia in the surgery waiting room.
She looked too stunned to cry. She was
trembling, like someone who couldn't get the
chill out of her. There was a uniformed policewoman with her.

Rita went to Claudia and hugged her tightly.

"He was shot," Claudia said weakly.

"I know, I know." Rita was out of breath.

"They say he is close to death." She began
to weep.

All Rita could do was hold her. She was afraid
to say anything, afraid what she said might turn
out to be wrong. What if she were to say, "Don't
worry, he'll be fine. He's a fighter," and he
died?

"They wouldn't let me see him. They said it
wouldn't be good to see him. They had to cut
open his chest to get his heart to start again."
Claudia's watery eyes focused on Rita. "What is
that, massaging the heart?"

Rita knew but didn't want to say.

Claudia described what the doctors had done,
then asked, "How could this happen?"

With her arm around Claudia's shoulder—the two women were the same size—Rita walked her to some chairs, where they sat down. The policewoman stood out of earshot. Rita whispered, "I'm so very, very sorry this has happened."

"Why should you be sorry? It's not your fault."

Yes, it is, Rita wanted to scream.

"What I just can't believe is that first it was Jim, and now it's my own husband. How can this be? It doesn't seem real." She was trembling. "Why is all this happening?"

"I don't know."

"I thought he was working with you."

No, she hadn't been with Charlie, Rita explained. He had been on a surveillance detail. She had been at the office when she had received the news.

Again Claudia looked at her with teary eyes. "He wasn't working with you?"

"No, I wasn't with him."

"He told me he was working with you. What was he doing?"

"Claudia, I haven't talked to him yet. I don't know what happened. I'm only at this moment figuring out things for myself."

Claudia stood up. Her complexion was pasty.

"Claudia, you need to sit down," Rita told her, and pulled her back into the chair.

Charlie's parents were flying in from Detroit, Claudia said weakly. "The doctor said to call

the family. That's not good, is it? When they tell
you to call the family and get them here?''

"The family should be here together. That's
what a family's all about." She thought of Mike.
Why was it she suddenly thought of him? He
couldn't be blamed for any of this.

Claudia said her family was driving in from
Fort Wayne, Indiana. "They can't afford to fly.
Besides, by the time they could get a flight, they
could already be here by driving."

Soon the waiting room for surgery began to
fill with friends and Charlie's family.

Mike arrived with Greg. To her surprise, all
she wanted was to hug Mike.

Sean and Julie arrived. They took Greg home
with them. Rita and Mike walked down the hall.
They went out the exit door and stood in the
stairwell. To her surprise, she didn't cry. She
didn't know why that was. Perhaps she was too
numb. Perhaps she had gone beyond that point.

Mike asked if Charlie was all right.

She told him Charlie was still in surgery.

What had happened? he wanted to know.

She could only tell him what she had told
everyone else: Charlie had been working on a
surveillance detail. She had been at the office
when she had heard the news. The rest was a
blur.

Did she know where he had been shot?

A bullet had nicked his aorta, she told him.
According to what she had heard, the only reason Charlie had lived was because two rookies

had heaved him into the backseat of their car and had rushed him to the hospital, where doctors immediately went to work on him. "Claudia said he was so close to death that the doctors didn't even have time to scrub or administer anesthesia. They cut him open and began to work even while they were in the elevator on the way to surgery." Finally she broke down crying. She couldn't help it.

Mike held her. He told her he was sorry.

She kept her face buried in his chest. She remained that way for a long time, until she knew she should return to the waiting room. She said, "Let's go back to the others." There was nothing else to do. She had wanted to ask Mike questions, but had felt the thought was too vicious and ugly to pursue.

They went back to the waiting room, where everyone was gathered, and she and Mike sat with other friends and police officials. Bull knelt before her and took her hands in his.

"How you doing?" he asked.

She nodded. "I'm making it, Bull. Thanks."

He told her she should wash her hands. At the same time, he nodded toward the others in the room. "It's hard when they see something like that," he said.

For the first time since coming to the hospital, she noticed the dried blood on her.

In the rest room, she stood for a long time at the sink, rubbing her hands together under the warm water. Without looking in the mirror above the sink, she was aware of her reflection, though she seemed a million miles away from it. She even dried her hands in front of the mirror, but never looked up. She was afraid if she looked up she would cry, and she didn't want to cry anymore. She wanted to be angry.

In the waiting room, she didn't feel like talking, but conversations went on here and there. She didn't even feel like listening and tried to make that known by the way she stared at her hands instead of looking at anyone in particular, but it seemed that no matter how hard she tried to ignore everyone, someone would inevitably ask her a question, so that she found herself compelled to listen to what was being discussed—in case someone asked her something.

"Did you see that new printout on our caseloads?" someone asked.

"Oh, I know. For the life of me I can't read it," someone else said.

"Why do they use all those decimals? You get like a three point two in one area, and it doesn't make a damn bit of sense. Where do they get those numbers anyway? Rita, do you know where they get them"

She knew. She had attended a two-hour seminar on reading the new performance evaluations, but she didn't feel like explaining anything at that particular moment. Instead she said, "Oh, it's nothing. It's something that managers use to determine caseloads and assignments."

Everyone fell silent as a surgeon wearing surgical greens entered the room. He went to Claudia, who stood up hurriedly.

"Can we talk outside?" the surgeon asked, and the two went out into the hall.

Rita could see the surgeon explaining and Claudia asking questions. It seemed like they talked for a long time. Claudia remained in the hall as the surgeon reentered the waiting room.

He said, "I'm Dr. Coscia, and Mrs. Dalton has asked that I pass along a message to all of you. Mr. Dalton is out of surgery and in intensive care. He's in critical condition, and we won't know for twenty-four hours or so whether the repairs we have made are going to be successful. She has asked that all of you go home. She's said there's no reason for everyone to be sitting here waiting for the next couple of days. She promises to let you know the minute she has any news whatsoever. She has authorized me to answer any questions you might have. Are there any?"

No one said anything.

Dr. Coscia nodded and left the room, at which time the people who were waiting began to file out of the room, heading for the elevators.

Claudia was very cordial. She nodded to some, hugged others. Amid the leave-takings Paul Clowers rushed in. He went right up to Claudia, cutting in front of others who were waiting in line to express their concern and support. With him was his wife, Donna. Everyone stood back as Paul hugged Claudia and spoke privately with her. He seemed genuinely shaken.

Paul approached Rita. In a kind voice, he asked, "Are you all right?"

Rita nodded.

He patted her shoulder. "Don't worry, everything's going to turn out okay." Then, "What happened, anyway?"

She told him what she had told everyone else—she still didn't know what had happened. Everything had happened so quickly, she hadn't even had a chance to make any inquiries.

Paul sighed. "Okay, okay," he said gently. "Let's get this thing together. Let's find out what happened to him. Let's find out who's responsible." He told her he was going to take his wife to a motel; then he and other investigators could meet at the CID office in an hour.

Paul patted Mike's shoulder. "Mike, how are you?"

"I'm fine."

Paul nodded. To Rita, he said, "I'll see you at the office."

After saying good-bye to Mike, she returned to the Commodore Inn, the tavern on Wells Street where she and Charlie had first met J. D. Grove. The bodies were gone, though where they had been had been marked, and the bloodstains were still there, as were many police officers and detectives.

The lead homicide detective in the case was

Sergeant Will Moore, a dark-skinned black man from the Milwaukee Police Department. She knew him. They had worked a number of homicides together. She went up to him and shook his hand. He asked how Charlie was doing. She told him what she knew.

He said he had once worked a case in which a black teenager had shot a white teenager the same way. Will touched his chest near his heart. "The bullet grazed the white boy's aorta, and there wasn't a thing anyone could do."

She asked him what he had been able to find out about the shooting.

According to the three witnesses who had been nearby—two of whom weren't reliable because they were drunk—Charlie and J.D. had been coming out of Commodore's when Leon Hampton had suddenly appeared. "From what I can put together, Leon was yelling at J.D., calling him an Uncle Tom, and shoving his chest." Will hit his own chest forcefully with his fingertips several times to illustrate what Leon had been doing. "Next thing people knew, Leon yelled he was going to kill J.D. He pulled out a .25-caliber automatic and began shooting, which caused Charlie to draw his own piece and fire." Will shook his head. "Here's the bizarre thing. The one good witness we have said it didn't seem like Leon was even going to shoot at Charlie, but Charlie's first shot hit Leon on his left side, which spun the automatic toward Charlie. You see what I mean?"

She nodded.

"Leon was still shooting," Will continued, "and the spin caused the automatic to go off in Charlie's direction. It hit him once, and he went down. All three witnesses said Charlie dropped like a tree limb in an ice storm." He shook his head again. "You know, people always say that a .25 automatic isn't anything—you can put it in the palm of your hand and no one can see it—but I always say it can kill someone, and that's all that matters."

She asked Will, "Between that time when Leon was pushing at J.D., and the time he yelled he was going to kill him, and pulled out a gun, what was Charlie doing?" All she could think of was how quickly Charlie had gone after Scott Renneker the week before when he said he had seen Renneker reaching for her service weapon. Wouldn't he have as quickly stopped Leon?

Will flipped open the small notebook he was holding. "Let me read you verbatim what the one good witness told me. He said that when Leon was pushing J.D., calling him an Uncle Tom, Charlie reached out to stop Leon, but J.D. distracted him, saying, and I quote, 'Charlie, don't waste your time with this simple-ass nigger,' end of quote. Leon answered, and I quote, 'I'll show you who's a simple-ass nigger. This simple-ass nigger's going to blow your fucking head off.' And that's when it happened."

"Anything else?"

"I'm afraid we're not going to know much else until we can talk to Charlie."

She walked away from the scene confused. Charlie was supposed to have been watching Leon, so what had he been doing with J.D.?

Rita went in search of Joe DeFalco. His family business was the Milwaukee Fruit and Produce Company, off South Broadway Street across the Milwaukee River. He was gone for the day, she was told, wouldn't be back until the next morning.

At the office, everyone was waiting with their own questions, questions she didn't feel like dealing with. Then there was Paul.

She and he went into her office. Even as good-natured as he was, she could tell he was concerned. He asked her, "Have you seen the latest?"

She didn't know what he was talking about.

"Susan Hall is on the warpath again."

Another special report? she asked.

Yes, another special report. "She's basically asking why you're on the case. She's wanting to know why this entire office is on the case. She's asking whether child abuse and neglect is a legitimate problem in our communities, and if it is, why is the entire special task force working on another investigation?"

Rita looked out at the snowbound city. She wished she could go home.

Paul was pensive also. He said, "There was a time when if a cop died in the line of duty, everyone grieved. Everyone dropped everything and went to the rescue of the downed officer. You wouldn't ever see a bloodsucking Susan Hall walking around stabbing people in the back." He shook his head. "These days if a cop dies in the line of duty, people ask what he had been doing to deserve it. They're going to ask the same thing about Charlie."

She sat down, the air rushing out of the plastic cushion in her chair. "I know."

"There's really not much choice. I need to take you off the investigation."

"What—"

"This whole thing has gotten out of hand, and I've got to get things under control. When I first asked you to help, I had no idea it would blow up in our faces like this. We'll handle the investigation over in Madison, which is where the jurisdiction should have been to start with."

She protested. "Paul, there are too many loose ends. At least let me tie some of them up."

He was not going to be budged. "The longer this drags on, the worse it gets. That's apparent now."

"Just a few days."

His voice continued to be pleasant: "You know as well as I do, I can't justify any of this. Before, I could, but now it's turning into a disaster, and it's all in the front of the news. People are asking why I brought Milwaukee in to investigate something that happened in Madison."

"Paul, come on."

"Rita, if it were up to me, you know I would say, do what you have to do. But it's not as simple as that. Look at it from my point of view. The media, especially this Susan Hall, keeps bringing you into the picture. People are saying, 'I thought she ran the Milwaukee unit. What's that have to do with what was going on in Madison?'" He stood and walked past her desk to look out the window.

She turned in her chair to follow him. "I'll take the heat."

He was staring out. "Like I said, it's not that simple. The taxpayers pay our salary. People come to me if we're not doing what we're paid to do."

"Please."

He looked at her. "I'll give you a couple of days," he told her. "That's all I can do."

A couple of days was better than nothing.

"And you work alone. I can't justify your entire office working on this. As it is, I'm in hot water for calling you away from your duties here."

"I understand."

He patted her shoulder and was about to leave her office when she said, "Paul—"

He looked at her, a pleasant smile on his face.

"You say you've been getting some pressure on this?"

"Yes, I have been."

"I was just wondering, do you know anything

about a case Jim might have been working on through the governor's office?"

For an instant Paul had a blank look. "What do you mean?"

Yes, he knew something. She could tell. "I mean, have you had any contact with, say, Ed Harding, the chief of the governor's security detail?"

He sat back down. "This doesn't go outside this room," he said. "If it does, I'll deny I ever said anything, so help me God."

"What?"

"Yes, the governor received a complaint about someone he's received a lot of campaign money from. He wanted Ed to look into the complaint in a discreet manner, and Ed passed the complaint on to Jim, who told me about it."

"Who was that person who gave all the money to the governor?" She knew. Chad Whitaker.

Paul slowly enunciated each word, "Rita, please, leave this alone. This has nothing to do with anything."

She ran a hand through her hair and sighed. "Okay, Paul, I'm not going to put you on the spot."

"A couple of days," Paul announced, rising. "Then we need to get on with life."

"A couple of days is all I need."

After he left, she began to gather the materials pertaining to the investigation. She needed to consolidate them so there wasn't the appearance that the investigation was commanding all of her attention. Then she remembered some papers she had locked away. Key ring in hand, she tried to unlock the middle drawer of her desk. The key was stiff in the lock, though, and wouldn't turn all the way. She leaned down to look at what was blocking the way and noticed that the drawer was ajar. Plus there were scratches in the metal at the top of the drawer. Someone had tried to pry open the drawer. She took a pair of scissors and busted open the drawer. There was the envelope she and Charlie had retrieved from Jim's locker at the University of Wisconsin campus. She sighed. Thankfully, no one had gotten to the envelope.

Had it been Paul? He didn't know about the envelope, and he would have never opened her desk without her permission. No one else in the office would have either. She stared at a name she had scribbled on her desk calendar: Joe De-Falco. She remembered what she had been doing when she received the news about Charlie. She was filled with a strange sensation, the kind she got when she woke up from a nightmare and tried to piece together the fleeting details. It all seemed vague to her, but she remembered that Joe DeFalco had been sitting in her office when Bev had burst in, and she remembered having left him behind. If he had tried to open her drawer, she intended to find out why.

20

Rita and Mike lay in bed and talked well into the night, but when he finally fell asleep, she was still wide awake. He had answered her questions, but she had been careful not to grill him, so there were many gray areas in his answers. Then, no sooner had she drifted to sleep than she awakened again. The room was still dark. Mike couldn't sleep with a clock facing the bed, and she guessed it was around five-thirty. She got out of bed, only to discover in the bathroom that it was barely two-thirty. She didn't know how she had made that mistake, so she went back to bed, only to toss and turn all over again.

No matter how hard she tried not to think about Jim and Charlie, she ended up thinking about them anyway, and that kept her awake too. One moment she was thinking about the envelope of letters she and Charlie had retrieved from Jim's locker at the University of Wisconsin;

the next she was thinking about the ATM photograph. One thought spun off the other like that. She finally got out of bed at five till six.

Outside, the morning was overcast. There were a few patches of blue, and the slightest hint of sunlight in the east, but mainly the sky was a striped gray. She stopped at Shoney's, off the interstate, where she got a booth and spread out her notes on the table. Countless thoughts were still passing through her head. She didn't know quite how they all fit together, but knew somehow there was a pattern. She also knew that sooner or later she was going to be confronted with Mike's past and the confrontation was going to come in the form of blackmail.

Sallie Cramer, who worked the midnight to eight shift, brought Rita coffee. "Good morning," she said, a big smile on her face. She was a short, heavy woman in her fifties, who could be a talker when she wanted to.

Rita told her she didn't need anything at that moment, only some time to do a little work. "That and keep the coffee coming."

Sallie tittered. "Okay, then, I'll keep out of your way, but don't forget to try some of the hot apples on bread this morning. The bread's fresh out of the bakery, and it's delicious."

Rita took a sip of coffee to get the taste of night out of her mouth—something that not even brushing her teeth would do—and began to jot notes on a yellow pad. Jim was dead, and he had been murdered in such a fashion as to

make it look like suicide. He had been watching
Scott Renneker, who had turned out to be a serial killer. The common link: Placidyl, the rape
drug. Renneker used it so he could gain control
over his victims, and Jim had a large dose of it
in his bloodstream when he had died. But Renneker didn't kill men. At least that wasn't his
modus operandi.

Sallie brought more coffee. "You ready for
those bread and apples yet?" she asked.

"Not quite," Rita told her.

Sallie said, "Holler when you're ready," and
left before Rita could reply, "I will."

Rita hated making small talk, but in this case
it had certain advantages. It gave her clout in
the restaurant. Wherever she wanted to sit, she
got to sit, and Sallie kept other customers away,
which meant Rita could keep things spread out
on the table without having to worry about anyone gawking at what she was doing.

Everything kept coming back to Chad Whitaker, a man who seemed to live with a foot in
two worlds. One was in the world of legitimate
business; the other was in the underworld. Rita
remembered the videotape of a gambling operation Jerry Grier had played for her. The estab-
lishment had a bar, which could explain how
Whitaker could hook up with the likes of Renneker. If Renneker had worked in one of Whitaker's clubs sometime, then it wouldn't be
impossible, or even unlikely, that someone in
Whitaker's hierarchy would get wind of Renne-

ker's particular appetites. A Renneker would probably fit well into Whitaker's underworld. As for Al, he didn't fit as well. He was more of a liability than an asset.

Rita finally ordered the hot apples on bread. Sallie went for them.

From the letters Jim had in his possession, clearly Hoeveler knew about Whitaker's shady past, and he somehow had Whitaker over a barrel. Rita guessed that at some point Whitaker had tried to get Hoeveler out of the way by implicating him in the murder of Yuan. Since that clearly hadn't worked, Hoeveler must be in possession of some kind of insurance plan. What did Hoeveler have that was making Whitaker now keep his distance? Al Hoeveler didn't seem shrewd enough to handle the likes of Whitaker. Rita guessed Diane Hoeveler was somehow involved.

The apples arrived. They were steaming and smelled like cinnamon.

How would Diane manipulate Whitaker? Had Jim given her something that would keep Whitaker in his place?

Sallie wanted to know how the apples were. Rita took a bite. "Mmmmmmm," she said, "they're delicious."

Sallie giggled. "Didn't I tell you?"

They weren't really that great, but Rita didn't want to hurt her feelings.

When Sallie was walking away, Rita keyed the pager in her pocket. When the beeper went off, she brought out the pager, glanced at it, and began to collect her papers.

Sallie returned to the table. "You have to go?" she asked, looking disappointed.

It was the only way, Rita thought. "Yes, I've got to head for work."

Writing on a pad, Sallie said, "You haven't even eaten your apples."

Rita drove to the hospital to see how Charlie was doing. He was still unconscious and in critical condition, on a ventilator, though Claudia told Rita that every passing moment gave her new hope. Claudia stepped out of the police-guarded intensive care unit to have a cup of coffee with Rita. They had hugged, then had stood in the hallway near the intensive care doors and talked as coffee steamed off their styrofoam cups.

There was wire-mesh windows in the doors of the unit, and Rita could see Charlie through them. He looked dead, surrounded by medical equipment and monitors.

Claudia looked drained. She told Rita the nurses had explained that part of the reason Charlie looked so bad was because he had been paralyzed with drugs and sedated so he wouldn't fight the ventilator or any of the other equipment. The doctors didn't want him to move and possibly tear open the aorta. Claudia said, "I look at it this way. He's made it through the night."

Rita drove into the city after that. The traffic

was heavy, especially as she got downtown, but the streets were cleared of snow. She drove to the Milwaukee Fruit and Produce Company, a business that had been in the DeFalco family since the early 1900s, when the family had immigrated to the United States from Italy.

Joe was there, wearing a dirty white apron and walking through the warehouse with a clipboard in his right hand. His left hand hung loosely at his side. In the air was the smell of fresh fruit, especially fresh citrus.

At first he didn't see her. When he did, he came over and asked her if her friend was all right. Apparently someone had explained what had happened, or he had followed the news reports and put two and two together. Charlie was still in critical condition, she told him.

Suddenly she had to move aside to let a man pass. He was pushing a two-wheel dolly, upon which were stacked eight boxes of lettuce. It looked like a feat to be able to balance and control so many boxes at the same time.

Joe said he was sorry to hear about Charlie. "I never met him," he admitted, "but the way you ran out yesterday, I knew you were good friends with him."

"Yes, we're good friends." She wanted to ask what he had done once she had left the office. She knew he was the one who had tried to break into her desk.

They stood together awkwardly for a couple

of moments. He seemed more nervous than he had been the day before.

She asked him if they could go to talk someplace. "I promise I won't keep you long," she added when he didn't seem thrilled by the idea.

He said he had a few minutes to spare, but then he had to get back to work as soon as possible because it was a busy day at the warehouse.

He led her to an office that overlooked the ground floor of the warehouse. "What can I do for you?" he asked after he had closed the door. There were mountains of invoices on the desk.

"I hope someone saw you out of the office yesterday and didn't keep you sitting there." She noticed his cheeks took on a shade of red.

"I found my way out," he said.

"How did you get trapped?" she asked. "Gambling debts?"

The red grew darker. He sat down at his desk. He held his left arm in his lap. From the expression on his face, she thought his arm might be aching. At least he was holding it that way. "I don't know what you're talking about."

She sat down too. "I'm afraid our conversation was cut short yesterday," she said. "Why did you say you had come to see me? Or were you looking for something?"

Awkwardly, he said, "I heard you had been asking questions about me."

"That's what you told me. I thought about that afterward, and to tell you the truth, I don't remember anyone from my office asking any questions about you."

"That's not what I heard." The tone of his voice had changed from the day before. He was no longer friendly. There was even a tone of animosity in his voice. Maybe he had been chewed out because he hadn't gotten what he had been sent for.

"So, you say you came down to my office because you heard I was asking questions about you?"

"Yes, that's what I did. If someone has something to ask or say about me, I want that person to do it to my face."

"Joe, let me set the record straight. I wasn't asking questions, which means that whoever told you that was putting you on the spot. It makes me wonder why someone would put you on the spot. But for the record, you need to understand that we're talking about human lives here. This isn't a game of spreading rumors and talking about people. This is a situation in which real people have been getting killed and seriously injured. It concerns me that somehow you appeared in my office right in the middle of things, but you claim you know nothing about what's going on. Doesn't that sound a bit strange to you?"

He nervously said, "No. In any city there are going to be murders. Just because I happen to be driving by your office when something like that happens doesn't mean I knew a single thing about it."

She thought she would try a different approach. "You mentioned something else that struck me as being odd. You said something to the effect that everyone has skeletons in his or her closet. Can you explain that?" She wasn't sure she wanted to hear the answer, but if someone had told him about Mike and suggested that she might be vulnerable, she wanted to know.

"I just meant that no one's house is perfectly clean. I'm sure that goes for you as well as me."

"Explain."

"I simply made a general observation, nothing more."

"Joe, that almost sounds like a threat."

"Let me put it this way, you don't close down a city because of a few skeletons."

That was an odd thing to say, she thought. "Who said anything about closing down a city?"

"That's what happens when you start pushing someone like Chad Whitaker too far," he told her.

So, the name was finally out in the open. "What?"

"Come on, everyone knows you've been making inquiries about him."

She didn't deny the statement.

"He already left once. If he leaves again, I don't think he'll be back, and we'll miss an opportunity of a lifetime for Milwaukee."

"Let me get this straight. If someone rich and

powerful decides to have his way no matter what"—she noticed the slight paleness that came over his face—"we shouldn't get in his way because next thing you know that person might decide to leave town and take all his money with him." She tried to be very careful with her word choices because she didn't want the likes of Chad Whitaker accusing her of making inflammatory comments about him.

"I'm not saying that at all. Business is competition. Someone big might have to push a few people around. Sometimes you have to get the broom out and sweep the floors. What I'm saying is that the more that happens like what happened yesterday, the more bad publicity we get. The more bad publicity we get, the more problems we have with people who are willing to invest big money to help this city grow. No one wants to invest in a city that's having street shootings and violence like that. For people like me, that means our businesses dry up, and all that our families have worked for for generations goes to waste. As far as I'm concerned, and I hate to say this, but if your people weren't so anxious to play cops and robbers and were more professional, things like yesterday wouldn't have happened. Most of us around here don't go in for the Dirty Harry type of police work."

"I get it. We're finally getting to the topic of our conversation. All of this is about investors, isn't it?"

"Investors and a lot of other people, people that might be considering moving to Milwaukee, people who want Milwaukee to move ahead."

"You're thinking if Chad Whitaker builds his complex here, your business is suddenly going to expand."

"I didn't say that, but I think it's going to be good for the city."

She sat forward. "What's the bottom line, Joe? I want you to tell me because I want you to be on the record as having established where you stand."

"I can't help you, that's the bottom line. I think you've gotten yourself into a mess that you created yourself, and besides, you're not even in your own jurisdiction. You're out asking a lot of questions about things that you don't even have the authority to investigate."

"Who said that?"

"It doesn't matter. What does matter is that if you were doing your job, you'd be taking care of some of the crimes you have authority to enforce. Instead you're running all over the state, worrying about all kinds of other things. Remember the saying, Get the log out of your own eye before you try to get the speck out of someone else's eye?"

She stood. "Joe, yesterday you seemed like a nice man, someone who really did have a conscience. Today, I don't know. I think you know more than what you're saying, and you're letting people get hurt left and right because all you're worried about is the almighty dollar you stand to gain. You're worse than he is. As for my jurisdiction, I'm a state investigator. I have jurisdiction anywhere in Wisconsin." She turned and left.

He came out of his office yelling at her. Everyone else in the warehouse stopped to look. "You have no business coming here. If you come in here again harassing me, you'll be hearing from my lawyers!"

Before she could say anything, he went back inside. She walked out into the cold December air. Rita realized Paul had been right. It was only a matter of time before people began to question her role in the investigation. She had to close this up, and the quickest way to do that, she decided on the way to her car, was to confront Chad Whitaker herself.

As it turned out, though, he was not what she had expected. She had seen him on television, but TV could be deceptive. He was short and skinny with a big head and a loud, boisterous voice. "Hi, how are you? Good to meet you," he said as if meeting an entire crowd of people. He shook her hand with a firm shake. His short brown hair, combed to one side, was thinning, and his skin looked weathered. Tanned, but weathered.

They met in a second-floor conference room in a stone building near the Marquette University campus. It was an old hospital that NCA was renovating for its Milwaukee headquarters. The conference room had piped-in classical music and a highly polished table that looked too big for the room, so big that Rita wondered how anyone had managed to get the table into the room in the first place.

She and Whitaker sat down on opposite sides of the table. He kept the music playing. She thought it might be because he didn't want her recording their conversation.

He said, "Now, how can I help you?"

She didn't know if he was upper class by birth, but she had heard that his family had made its wealth in industry. Whitaker, in turn, had apparently been astute enough to invest in a field that would always have a future—health care. She said, "Wasn't your grandfather one of the founders of Milwaukee?"

He smiled. "My great-grandfather. My family helped build this city."

"And you left a few years ago. Where did you go, Texas?"

"Colorado. I'm a surgeon, so I can basically establish a good practice anywhere, but Milwaukee has always been home to me. Now, what did you come to see me about?"

The inference was clear: time was valuable to him. "During a criminal investigation I came across some old correspondence of yours."

"Oh?" Whitaker hesitated, started to say something, then changed his mind.

She nodded. "Some correspondence between

you and an Al Hoeveler, typed by a young woman who was found murdered."

"You will forgive me if I play dumb, but I would have to see the correspondence in order to refresh my memory."

Yes, she had caught the hitch in his steady, composed voice.

"I'm sorry," she said. "I thought you might know the correspondence I was talking about, and that we'd be able to get right to the point."

Whitaker's face turned red. "If I'm a target of a criminal investigation, I have a right to know," he said.

She acted concerned. "Did I say you were a target of a criminal investigation? I don't recall saying that."

"All I have to do is pick up the phone, and I can have an army of lawyers after you."

"I'm sorry. What are you talking about?" She put on her best confused face.

"The letters you mentioned. Letters about me."

"Wow, we must have had a breakdown in communication," she said quietly. "I had no idea you'd hire a team of lawyers about some letters I intended to return to you. I thought the letters meant nothing and were of no value. Maybe I should rethink all of this and hold on to the letters for a bit longer."

The pupils of his eyes widened steadily. His clenched fists loosed and color returned to them. Still, she knew she'd struck a nerve. She had bluffed him and won. Not a very good poker player.

"Let me tell you something," he said. "You're fooling with the wrong person. I suggest you cover your own ass. You see, I know quite a bit about the nasty gambling habits of your husband. Mike, isn't it?"

She felt very little reaction since she had been anticipating this moment.

"If what I know gets in the wrong hands, you'll be destroyed." He seemed comfortable delivering threats. Obviously he was accustomed to giving them.

She stared into his eyes, eyes that were fiery with boldness. "Let me tell you something, Mr. Whitaker. Give it your best shot, because I don't scare."

She walked out of the conference room without saying anything further. Now it was up to Mike. If he had told her everything, she was safe. If he had lied . . .

21

Why she drove from seeing Whitaker to Madison, Rita wasn't positive. She didn't even tell anyone she was going. By the time she got to Debbie Sweet's duplex, snow flurries were falling. She left footprints in the light dusting on the sidewalk and knocked on the door.

Debbie was home. She was wearing navy sweats, which were stained with water and what looked like cleanser. She smelled like Windex. "Rita, this is a surprise," she said, smiling. "Come in."

Rita stepped inside.

Debbie apologized for the way she looked. She said it was her cleaning day, and she never showered until she had finished.

They went into the kitchen, where they sat at a round table. That was because the vacuum cleaner and cleaning supplies were in the middle of the living room.

"Coffee?" Debbie asked.

Rita glanced at the coffeemaker. There was coffee made. "Sure," she replied.

Debbie poured cups of coffee for both of them. The coffee smelled strong, like it had been sitting for a while.

"When does school start back up?" Rita asked, making small talk.

"Around the middle of January."

"Must be rough having this much time off." Rita smiled sarcastically.

Debbie smiled back.

From where she sat, Rita could watch the snow falling. She hoped it didn't pick up, making for a hard drive home.

Debbie looked over her shoulder. "I heard on the radio we're supposed to have a heavy snow," she said. "It seems like we're getting more this year than we normally get."

"Debbie, have you heard the news about yesterday?"

Smiling, Debbie said, no, she hadn't heard any news. She rarely watched television, she said, and she almost never bought a paper. Why? What had happened?

Rita told her about Charlie, and a visible change came over Debbie.

"What's wrong? Are you all right?"

"Yes, I'm fine."

She didn't look fine. Her voice sounded nervous too.

"Debbie, I can't help but think that I've overlooked something, which is part of the reason why I'm here. Too many things aren't adding up. I know Jim wouldn't have shared details about a criminal investigation with you, but he might have said something that might not have seemed important to you, but would be very important to me. Do you mind if we go back to the beginning and run through the whole story again?"

No, Debbie said, she had no problem with that. She started at the beginning, telling how she and Jim had been forced to share a table at a university coffee shop, and how while she was sitting there, she noticed that Jim was looking at gross photos of dead bodies. "I noticed he was reading about drowning, which especially caught my attention because I'm a lifeguard, and you always think about that. You always wonder when you're going to have to pull someone out of the pool, and you always worry that it's going to be too late."

Had she ever worked as a lifeguard at a lake? Rita wanted to know. The question didn't seem relevant, but sometimes irrelevant questions had a way of tripping someone up, especially if the irrelevant questions came in the middle of a rehearsed story.

Yes, she had been a guard at a lake one summer. She told a story of how as a child she had almost drowned while swimming in a lake. A lifeguard had pulled her out, and after that she had always wanted to be a lifeguard. "The sad thing is he got killed a few years later. A motorcycle accident. I've often thought about how he saved my life and ended up losing his. Odd how life works out that way, isn't it?"

"Is that why you became a lifeguard at a lake?"

"I guess I really never thought of that. I suppose."

"So, you were saying about how you and Jim met?"

Debbie was precise about all of her details, including dates, which didn't bother Rita except for one illogical date. Rita explained why she was troubled. First she told what she knew about Yuan Zhang without saying the name or gender.

According to records at the medical library where Jim had done his research, she explained, he had been researching drowning around the time that Yuan's body had been discovered. Based upon the letters Jim had, Rita went on, it seemed logical that he knew Yuan would be in danger, and when he learned of her death, he went to Chicago to figure out what had happened.

"What's not logical is that according to you, Jim was doing research about drowning before the death."

Debbie's fingers were tangled together.

"It could be that Jim had been researching about drowning on two separate occasions but that doesn't seem very likely. Homicide drownings aren't that common. Debbie?"

Debbie looked at Rita.

"It seemed you left me for a moment. Were you thinking about something in particular?"

Debbie sighed. It was a forced sigh. "I guess I'm just tired," she said. "I've been cleaning since this morning."

"Did you ever hear Jim mention the name Yuan Zhang?"

"Who's she?"

Rita smiled. "That's odd that you should ask that," she said. "I'm just curious, why did you assume I was talking about a woman? Why couldn't it be a man?"

Debbie's cheeks reddened slightly. She looked over her shoulder again. "It looks like it might not be as bad as they said it was going to be."

Rita didn't respond. She was willing to wait, see what came out.

Debbie bit on a thumbnail. "You think you're going to catch these people who are responsible for Jim's death?"

Rita stared at Debbie. That was an odd response. "These people?"

"What?"

"You said you hoped we caught 'these people.'"

"You know what I meant."

"Yes, I know what you meant; and, yes, I think we'll catch whoever's responsible, especially with your help."

Debbie quit gnawing her thumbnail. "I'll help in any way I can, though I don't know how much good I'll be. I guess I'm not too good with dates. I might have been wrong about a couple of them."

Suddenly Rita knew why the dates were wrong. "Debbie, did you ever work for Chad Whitaker?"

Debbie's face turned dark red.

"For NationsCare?"

Debbie's eyes seemed to bulge, and her complexion became sickly pale. "I don't feel very good," she said. "These past couple of days, I've felt a little run-down. I think I might be coming down with the flu or something. Can we talk about this later?" She stood up, but looked like she was about to collapse. "I think I need to lie down."

Rita helped her to the sofa in the living room, where Debbie sat down and leaned back. Rita moved the cleaning supplies and vacuum cleaner.

Lying on her back, Debbie said, "I guess all the smells of the cleaning supplies made me light-headed. I haven't had anything to eat all day."

Rita sat at Debbie's feet and leaned forward, her elbows on her knees and her hands cupped together beneath her chin. "Debbie, let me try a theory on you, and you stop me whenever I go wrong."

Debbie didn't say anything. She was looking at the ceiling. Her eyes had become watery, and a tear slid out of her right eye.

"You didn't meet Jim Swearingen last year. You met him only several months ago when he came investigating NationsCare. You started working for the NCA chain, and Chad Whitaker took notice of you and asked if you wanted to work in his office. Perhaps you became his personal secretary. You can type, can't you?"

Debbie didn't answer.

"In fact, I bet you took Yuan's job after she was fired. You discovered some correspondence that Yuan had typed for Chad Whitaker. Or maybe Mr. Whitaker had told you to shred some documents, and you kept copies of them because when you looked at them, you thought they might be important. I'd almost venture to say you discovered the documents about the same time you discovered what had happened to Yuan—that is, after her body had been found. You either contacted Jim, or he contacted you. In any case, he was the one who set you up over here at the university, and he was the one who set you up in this place." Rita raised her hands to it. "Am I right?"

"No."

"No?"

Debbie was still staring at the ceiling, but each time she blinked, tears slipped from her eyes. "Yes, Chad gave me a promotion, but it was to become the secretary for the chief nursing officer of the new hospital there. Yuan and I sometimes had lunch together. One day we were supposed to have lunch, but she didn't show up. Later I heard she had been fired for stealing eleven hundred dollars in petty cash from an account she kept for Chad. Naturally I was shocked"— she sat up and dried her eyes—"but I didn't know what to think because what I was hearing sounded like it was true.

"Chad Whitaker kept a petty cash fund at the office, and everyone knew it. Every time Yuan put money into that fund, according to Chad, she would always deposit less than what she had been given. She hadn't realized, apparently, that Chad kept his own set of books. This supposedly went on for several months, at which time Chad did an audit and discovered eleven hundred dollars missing and fired her."

Rita said, "Let me fill this part in, then. Chad Whitaker had had his eye on you, and when Yuan was fired, he asked if you would step in and fill her position?"

Debbie didn't say.

"And you ended up having an affair with Chad?"

"I felt sorry for him. Sometimes he would invite me into his office, and we would talk for hours. He would tell me all these things about his marriage, and about how his wife never gave him what he needed in the marriage, which was why he was such a workaholic."

"So you were working as Chad's personal secretary, and you were having an affair with him. What happened then? What went wrong?"

"Yuan called me at home one night. She told

me she hadn't stolen any money, and she was going to fight. She asked me if I would help her."

"What did you say?"

Debbie shrugged. "At first I was scared. I didn't even want to be talking to her. I wanted to hang up on her, but then she made a confession. She told me what had really happened."

"But how would you know what she told you was true if you already didn't trust her?"

"She told me she thought she had gotten pregnant with Chad's baby. When she told me that, then I believed her, especially when she told me how her affair with Chad had started. It seems he ran the same line on all of us—about how he and his wife had grown apart, and how he had thrown himself into his work. At least when she told me all that, I was willing to listen. She asked if we could get together for a cup of coffee, which is what we did."

Debbie fixed one of the cushions so she could lie back on it. "Over coffee she told me that she was partially at fault. She said she had over-reacted, that when she thought she was pregnant, she had gone to Chad to see what kind of arrangements he would be willing to make for the baby. He had insisted that she have an abortion, and she had refused. From what she told me, she had made threats to him, and he had made threats to her, all of which were premature because it ended up being a false alarm. She discovered she wasn't really pregnant." Debbie forced a smile. "According to Yuan, it wasn't long after that that the whole business of the eleven hundred dollars came up."

"Then you believed her story?"

Debbie seemed less than certain. "I didn't really know what to believe."

"Yuan was the one who gave you the envelope of letters involving Chad's correspondence with Al Hoeveler, wasn't she?"

"Yes."

"Why? What did she say about them?"

Debbie held open her hands. "Nothing. She said if anything ever happened to her, she wanted me to have the letters."

"And you had no idea what the letters meant?"

"None. All I know is that when I was Chad's personal secretary, and I did some snooping around about this Hoeveler person, I discovered that his company was an approved contractor for NationsCare. It didn't make sense given what I had read in the letters Yuan had given me. In fact, I couldn't find any record of the letters at all. Had she not given me copies of them, I would have sworn they didn't exist. I did mention Hoeveler's name one time, and I remember getting the distinct impression that Whitaker didn't like him."

Rita took a deep breath through her nose, and let out the breath. "Then you weren't having an affair with Jim, were you?"

"No. I wouldn't have minded. He was a nice man, but no."

Rita messaged her temples. She could feel a headache coming on again. "Debbie, I need to tell you something, and you need to listen very carefully to what I have to say. Okay?"

Debbie's head nodded almost imperceptibly.

"These people we're dealing with probably murdered Jim and Yuan. They've killed a city councilman, and they've critically wounded another friend of mine, a state investigator. What you need to understand is that it's just a matter of time before they find you. In fact, there's a good chance that since I know where you're at, they know too."

Tears leaked from Debbie's eyes, but she didn't cry openly.

"It's going to be better if you tell me everything and stick with me on this. I'm going to get you someplace where you'll be safe, and once all of this is over, we'll get you set up with a new life somewhere."

"Chad will find me no matter where I go," she said.

"Don't worry about him," Rita said. "I'm going to take care of him."

Debbie shook her head.

"Why did you leave NCA anyway? And how did you find Jim?"

She forced a smile. "Jim came to see Chad at the office."

That sounded like Jim, Rita thought. He liked the direct approach too.

"Chad was real upset afterward. Next thing I know, Jim showed up at my apartment. He told me what had happened to Yuan, and told me he didn't want the same thing to happen to me—"

There came a scraping noise. Debbie started to get up. Bringing a finger to her lips for Debbie to be silent, Rita went to the front window and looked out. Two boys were shoveling the sidewalks and entranceways of the duplexes. She told Debbie that, who replied that the owner of the duplexes was very good about keeping the snow cleared. "What I think I should do is talk to Chad. Maybe he'll understand."

"Debbie, why don't you talk to me, and let me do the talking to Chad Whitaker? It'll be better that way."

Debbie fell back on the cushion. "Jim said he was going to help also, and look what happened to him. Everyone who gets in the way ends up getting hurt or killed. I just think I should go to Chad personally and let him know I'm going to keep my mouth shut about everything."

"Debbie, we can't live in a world like that, where someone like Chad Whitaker can walk all over other people, hurt them, and even kill them, can we?"

Debbie didn't have an answer for that.

"How do you think Al Hoeveler fit into Whitaker's plans?" Rita wanted to know.

Debbie said she didn't know.

What about Joe DeFalco? Did that name mean anything?

Debbie said she thought DeFalco was helping Chad swing votes on the city council. "Mr. De-Falco visited the office one day," she said. "I remember when he was leaving, while he was still standing in Chad's open doorway, I heard Chad tell him that the new complex was going to need a lot of fruit and vegetables, and that NationsCare hoped he—meaning Mr. DeFalco—would be able to supply all the needs. Mr. De-Falco had laughed and said it was no problem." She shrugged. "I assumed DeFalco was cooperating in some way, or Chad had him over a barrel."

A strange thought occurred to Rita. "Debbie, did a Scott Renneker ever visit Chad Whitaker?"

"Who?"

"A young man named Scott Renneker. Did he ever come asking for some kind of contracting work? His uncle, Rich Spiker, is a carpenter—"

"Rich?"

"You know him?"

"Yes, Chad and he are good friends. In fact, I've often thought they might be lovers of some sort. They used to go once a week to this sauna place. I guess they've been friends since child-hood." Debbie smiled. "They look like the odd couple. Rich is this big ox with a lot of muscles, and Chad is this skinny, short little man. Oh, wait a minute, wait a minute! I know the young man you're talking about. Yes, he did come to visit Chad one day. In fact, he called several times before and kept asking to see Chad. Yes, I remember. Chad finally saw him, but that was all there was to it. Chad knew him, you could tell, but didn't like him, or didn't want to be seen associating with him. I guess—what's his name?"

"Renneker. Scott Renneker."

"Okay, I guess this Scott Renneker came and wanted some money, and put Chad off. He hates people like that. He's got a lot of money, but he hates beggars and people who aren't willing to work for a living."

Rita stood. "I've got a photograph in the car I want you to see. I want to see if you recognize someone."

She didn't make it to the car. When Rita opened the door, the man from the ATM surveillance tape was standing there. She was sure it was him, though he wore wire-rimmed glasses. His eyes had a peculiar wildness to them. He was in his fifties, and his grimy, long hair was so sparse that she could see the distinct features of his scalp.

"May I-uh-come in?" He had a catch in his speech that called attention to itself, as did the pistol, whose barrel was barely visible from his side, where he held the gun close to him. A .357 Magnum, she guessed. "In-uh-uh-uh case you have any funny ideas, you see my-uh-uh-uh"— he held his left finger up and made the sign of a cross, as if that had some power over the speech problem—"friend is behind you."

Rita glanced back. Sure enough, there was a burly giant who looked like he could shatter the patio window at a moment's notice. The friend, who was in between a shave and a beard, tapped on the glass with the barrel of his own gun. He made no attempt to conceal the weapon.

The stutterer said, "Why-uh-uh-don't you be a good girl and let my-uh friend Howie in."

Rita did as she was told. She went to the patio door and unlocked it.

Howie slid open the door so abruptly that he almost threw it off its track. His face vaguely resembled Al Hoeveler's face.

"Wipe your shoes off, Howie," the stutterer said. He had gone into the living room to sit down with Debbie, who stood backed to the fireplace.

Howie stepped inside the kitchen-dining room, closed the door, and stomped his feet on a throw rug.

Rita could see whitish gray in Howie's beard, a color that was close to the gray of his eyes. From the glazed look in them, she imagined that he was on some kind of drug, perhaps something for depression. Oddly enough, he had sunglasses fixed on top of his head, probably so people couldn't see his eyes if he didn't want them to.

As Howie was escorting Rita into the living

room, he stopped at a watercolor painting of a house in the tropics. "Hey, Lou, did you see this?"

"No, Howie, I didn't." He came over to look at the painting. "It's-uh-uh"—he raised his left index finger and made the sign of a cross—"nice." Then he looked in the direction of Debbie. "Uh-uh-be a good girl and sit down, Debra-uh-uh." With his .357 he motioned toward the sofa.

Debbie sat down.

To Howie, Lou said, "Make-uh-uh-sure our friend isn't armed."

Howie smiled at Rita, saying, "It'd be better if you just tell me where it is rather than make me find it for myself, though I'd be happy to find it if you wanted me to."

She nodded down at her sweater, which he lifted. He removed her 9mm from its holster.

They all sat down in the living room.

Lou ran his hands through his greasy hair, pushing back some loose strands. "Well, dear," he said, looking at Debbie, "you've-uh-uh-uh"—he made a cross—"given us quite a run for our money."

"You obviously all know each other," Rita said.

Howie was sitting back all comfortable in his chair. He smiled. "Of course, you know us, don't you, Debbie?" he said, smiling. His head was tilted slightly—in an arrogant posture. "We go back a ways."

Rita was still waiting for some kind of explanation, and Debbie gave it. Howie and Lou worked for Chad Whitaker.

Howie said, "Debbie, I knew from the moment I set eyes on you, I didn't trust you." He somehow looked angry or offended, as if he wanted to get up and slap her.

"Now-uh-now, Howie, we got her and that's all that counts. Tell me, uh-uh-dear, what do you have to drink?"

Debbie told him she had a bottle of vodka and a bottle of tequila in the kitchen cabinet above the stove.

Lou suddenly looked refreshed. "Well, uh-uh-uh"—he signed a cross—"Howie, go get us some drinks and let's have a toast or two to our success. Chad's going to be extremely pleased. Besides, we have a few hours to kill before it gets dark."

Howie got up. The chair creaked as he did so. He went into the kitchen. Doors slammed. Glasses rattled.

He returned with four wineglasses, a bottle of vodka, a bottle of tequila, and a carton of orange juice.

Lou laughed. "The-uh-perfect host. Screwdrivers and sunrises."

Howie made them each a drink, heavy on the tequila and light on the orange juice. "Come on, drink up," he said.

Rita and Debbie didn't drink until Howie pointed his .357 at them. Then they each took a sip. He shook a finger at them. "More than that," he said, a smirk on his face. "Drink your orange juice. You'll need your vitamins." Rita took a big gulp. The tequila burned as it went down her throat, but she was somehow glad to have a drink.

Lou laughed, which caused Howie to smile at him. "There's uh-uh"—he made the cross—"woman who knows how to drink." Lou and Howie then had a race to see who could finish his drink the quickest.

Howie immediately made another round of drinks for everybody. As he did so, he said, "Say, Debbie, you remember that swimming hole we all went out to?"

Debbie didn't reply.

Howie pointed his .357 again. "Drink up," he said. They all drank again. "That was the first time I saw those big tits of yours, and I realized what Chad saw in you."

Lou laughed loudly.

Rita could feel the alcohol begin to nudge her with a sense of euphoria, as if no matter what kind of a problem she was in, she could get out of it. The problem was, Howie kept mixing drinks. She didn't want to drink that much, but he was insistent. She felt like the child whose parent tries to force her to finish the food on her plate.

"What are you going to do with us?" Debbie asked.

Howie said, "Let me put it this way, Mr. Whitaker doesn't like people to put pressure on him."

Lou said, "Now, Howie-uh-uh, don't tell them too much."

Rita told them, "Don't you know that sooner or later, someone's going to come looking for me?"

Lou got a big grin on his face. "Don't worry, they won't find you." The alcohol seemed to be curbing his speech problem. He laughed loudly again. "It'll be like that famous teamster leader who disappeared. Who was it?"

"Jimmy Hoffa," Howie said.

Lou nodded. "Vanished without a-uh-uh-uh"—he raised the index finger of his left hand, but managed to say "trace" before he needed the cross.

Rita made her move, but Howie hit her in the head with the side of his gun. That stopped her, and blackness swirled all around, but she was still conscious. She distinctly remembered bleeding into the carpet of Debbie's condo and Howie standing over her. She also distinctly remembered him raising the side of his gun to hit her again, as if his gun were a hammer and he was using it to pound in a nail.

22

Rita and Debbie sat on the floor with their backs to each other as Howie tied them with rope. Rita had a vague idea where they were. She had revived enough to know they had been brought to Milwaukee, to the general area where Chad Whitaker wanted to build his medical complex. She also suspected she was in a part of an old hospital wing, because the windowless room where they were kept looked like a hospital room. She asked, "Howie, why are you doing this? Why are you getting yourself into this huge mess?"

He stopped tying. "What do you mean, why am I doing this? You come around asking a lot of questions and bugging people, and you ask what we're doing? You're endangering one of the biggest, best projects that's ever been set up. A lot of money. A lot of important people have come together to make this thing work."

"I noticed," Rita commented. The side of her

head was sore, running down into her jaw. "By threats, coercion, blackmail. Yes, you've managed to herd a lot of people together."

He smiled at her. "Let me tell you something. I could put you loose on the street, and there are a lot of hotheaded people who, if they knew what you were up to—all the questions, the digging around, and the stirring up of trouble—would kill you in a minute and probably do it for free." He continued to bind their hands and feet, creating an elaborate web of ropes.

Rita told him, "Then why don't you let us loose and let us take our chances?"

"No, there's not going to be any more of that attention-grabbing stuff. Mr. Whitaker says these sidewalk shootouts and things have to stop. He's tired of it."

Rita tried to keep herself tense so that when she relaxed, there would be some play in the rope.

Howie said, "When the time comes, we're going to torture you, and you'll tell us where the letters are, and then you'll beg us to kill you and get it over with."

She watched him efficiently cut the rope at her feet with a knife. "Like you tortured Yuan?"

"Yes, like I did to Yuan. Brought her right to the point of death and then loosened the rope to let life back in her. When she thought I might tighten the rope again, she told me where she had hidden the letters. Only I found out she was lying, and she really shouldn't have done that."

"Was that when you burned her?"

"I was angry by then. It was really by coincidence that I saw the can of hair spray on the floor of her car. I was so angry that I lit my lighter near the side of her head and shot the hair spray into it." He smiled calmly. "I think it surprised me as much as it surprised her. The entire side of her head caught on fire, and she tried to put it out with her hands. By that time she was willing to tell me anything. She told me about the letters and Jim Swearingen."

"After which you threw her into the canal."

"I knew there wasn't enough life left for her to fight by then. She didn't know that, but I knew. You get a feeling for it after a while, a feel for how much someone can tolerate."

Howie gagged Debbie. Before he gagged Rita, she asked, "One more question—why the letters?"

Howie gave her a big smile, gagged her, and said, "Because that idiot Hoeveler was so dumb that he happened to bring out in the open the names of a couple of our contractors. Those contractors, as a matter of fact, had paid a lot of money to keep their records clean, and Mr. Whitaker didn't want anything like that in writing. He's real conscious about such things."

Howie left, locking the door behind him.

Rita waited until his footsteps faded, then looked around at her surroundings. She wasn't waiting for them to come back. At last her eye stopped on the old baseboard heaters. That was it.

"Debbie, come on, we gotta move."

Rita began to scoot in the direction of one of the heaters. Debbie remained still, and Rita said, "Come on with me."

Debbie got in the rhythm with her, and together they were able to get close enough to one of the heaters that Rita could shove the top off with her foot. Inside were shiny, almost paper-thin coils. Rita nodded. That's what she wanted. Again she and Debbie began to rock and scoot, lurching closer to the heater. Rita kicked the heater once again, breaking off the front. It fell forward with a metallic clatter. Debbie looked sharply toward the door, but Rita shook her head. "These are thick plaster walls. They can't hear us."

She leaned down to the heater, straining against her bindings, and began rubbing the hand ropes against the coils. They were razor-sharp, and the ropes began to fray. Within five minutes of straining effort her hands were loose, and she freed herself from the rest of the ropes. Once she was completely free and had her gag off, she released Debbie. Dazed, the young woman remained on the floor, massaging the rope impressions left on her wrists and ankles.

Rita tried the door, but it was locked from the outside. She pushed it open enough that she could see a padlock holding the door shut.

"Who are these people?" she whispered to

Debbie. Rita massaged her jaw, especially near her right ear. She could feel a huge lump in the side of her head.

They were a part of Chad Whitaker's private security team, Debbie told her. "Lou Albert, the one with the speech impairment, is the chief of security."

Rita massaged her own rope burns. "We don't have much time. We've got to get out of here. As soon as Whitaker gives the word, Howie and Lou are going to be back to work on us."

Debbie shook her head. "I think they're only trying to scare us. What difference do a few letters really make, anyway?"

"Let me put it this way: Lou and Howie went through a lot of trouble to get rid of my car and bring us here. I guarantee you, as soon as Whitaker gives the word, they're going to make sure both of us disappear for good."

She felt amazingly clearheaded and focused. She knew what had to be done. Her attention turned to the top of the space heater, laying on the floor. Twisting back and forth, she worked the corner brace free. She had already spotted an air return vent on a wall near the ceiling. Standing on her chair, she used the brace as a screwdriver. The head of one of the screws she stripped trying to get it loose, but the other three screws she was able to pop free. Then she jerked the vent out of the wall, breaking the fourth screw.

The opening looked about eighteen by eighteen inches, which would barely be big enough for the two of them to crawl through, one at a time. Rita looked into the opening. There was a thick black growth inside it. "Do you want to go first, or do you want me to go first?" she asked Debbie.

"You go," Debbie said.

Rita took off her coat, then her sweater. She put back on her coat. She said, "When I get in there, there's not going to be room to turn around. I'm going to hold one sleeve of my sweater, and you're going to have to pull yourself up with the other sleeve. You think you can do that? Otherwise you better go first so I can give you a boost up."

"You go first. I can do it."

"Bend your knee and lock your fingers together." Rita showed her how to make a foot-hold with her hands.

The moment Debbie had made one, Rita used it to boost herself into the square opening. She squeezed into the dark shaft, trying not to think of the dirt and grime she was crawling into. Strands of a cobweb brushed her face, and she shook her head violently. Using her feet, she pushed the sleeve of her sweater toward the opening. Finally one end dangled free. She kept pushing it downward until next thing she knew, Debbie grabbed it. With it stretched taut, Debbie pulled herself up into the shaft. Debbie's arms were strong, and she got in easily.

Rita whispered to her, "Just keep holding the

sleeve of my sweater so we don't lose one another."

They crawled forward. The shaft was hot, sweaty hot, and it closed in on her. Rita had no idea where she was heading because she had no light.

Feeling her way forward, she came to a crossroads in the duct system. She took the left passage. She crawled along it for fifty or so feet before she came to a dead end. Then, with Debbie withdrawing first, they had to back out of the dead-end shaft.

Once they got back to the intersection, Debbie had to back into the original shaft far enough that Rita could back in also. Then, moving forward again, Rita took the shaft to the right. This led to a larger shaft, where warm air was blowing. The larger shaft also had light to some degree because there were openings to adjoining rooms and hallways.

Soon Rita heard voices. She tried to crawl as silently as possible, though the aluminum shafts tended to buckle under their weight. She was about to pass the vent from which the voices rose when she heard a familiar voice, Lou's. She signaled for Debbie to stop so that she could hear better.

The vent fed out of the top of what looked like an old surgical arena, a two- to three-story room that had since been converted into a library. In the ceiling near the vent was the old dome light of the arena, a concave dish that reflected the light of an intense bulb. Far below was a huge oak table, around which sat a number of people. A couple of them Rita couldn't see because of her angle, but she thought there were seven, maybe eight people at the table.

"We're so close," Chad Whitaker said, "that we can't jeopardize everything we've worked so hard for up to this point."

From her pocket Rita brought out the microrecorder Mike had bought her for Christmas. After checking to make sure the recorder had a tape in it, she pushed the RECORD button and put the recorder near the vent.

"Everyone needs to be calm, as calm as possible," Whitaker went on. "We can't afford any more mistakes."

The room, Rita could see, had a glassed-in front, three stories tall, which overlooked a courtyard. Apparently the walls had been knocked out and a glass front reinstalled to give the administrative wing the flavor of a medical facility. Beyond the windows, snow was falling heavily. It was the middle of the night. Mike must have called someone by now. Surely he had called Paul.

Lou was irritable, perhaps disgusted with his speech impediment. He said, "Can't—uh-uh-uh"—Rita saw his left index finger rise and make a cross—"you put her to good use like the others?"

"No, that wouldn't work at all," Whitaker replied. "We can only use children. There is no substitute for a child's immune system."

"Chad, I'm beginning to feel a lot of pressure on this," said a man Rita recognized immediately. She was surprised she hadn't recognized him before. It was Dick Groucher, Milwaukee's long-time member of the United States House of Representatives. A chill shot through Rita. Groucher had been around for eight or nine terms, and when he wanted something, he got it.

"I know, Dick," Whitaker replied politely. "And I promise, this is the last loose end. We didn't anticipate this latest wild card, but now that we have it in our hand, there won't be another problem, I promise you. Meanwhile, the project is going well."

"How well?"

"Let me put it this way, it looks like we have a drug that will eliminate rejection in over ninety-nine percent of organ transplants. If that happens, all of us who hold stock in NCA will have more money than we could imagine."

"Chad, I can appreciate all of that, but like I said, there's a lot going on. How much longer do you need on this?" Before Whitaker could answer, Groucher continued, "I really wish you would have come straight to me in the first place. I could have taken care of this Trible person."

"I didn't want to get you involved."

"Believe me, it would have been much better

for me to be involved then than it is now for me to be pulling strings."

"I appreciate all you've done, Dick."

Was that why Paul had tried to remove her from the investigation? Rita wondered. She wished she knew who all was around the table, but she knew if she did much more moving about in the vent shaft someone would hear her, and that would be the end. Besides, she knew she had to get out of the building as quickly as possible. The moment Whitaker sent someone to the room where she and Debbie had been tied up, and discovered they weren't there, it would all be over within a matter of minutes. She shut off the recorder and put it back in her pocket.

As quietly as possible, she backed up until she bumped into Debbie. She whispered, "We have to get out of here."

"I'm ready," Debbie whispered back.

After crawling a ways, Rita found a vertical shaft. She started down, wedging her feet and hands against the walls. Debbie was right above her when she suddenly slipped. One of Debbie's feet glanced hard off Rita's head, and the other crashed onto her shoulder. She was thrown wildly off balance. The next thing Rita knew, they were plummeting down the shaft together. Rita felt her right arm rip across metal. She didn't scream, but she felt the metal tear off flesh. She had barely time to feel the screaming pain when the shin of her left leg hit something solid. In another second a vent beneath her burst open and she plunged toward a laundry cart below. She landed halfway on a ribbed side, which caused the cart to flip up on end. This broke Debbie's fall, who landed right behind her.

Disoriented, Rita got to her feet, her right arm and left leg bleeding. She was filthy black from the air shafts. Debbie was also black, and though she didn't seem to be hurt, she was stunned from the fall. Rita helped her up.

"You're hurt," Debbie said as she saw that Rita was bleeding.

"We have to get out of here," Rita said. "There's no time. They'll be coming for us soon."

Together they ran down a basement corridor. Rita lagged behind, having trouble running on her left leg, which looked to be bleeding freely. Behind her she was leaving a trail of blood.

They got to a door, but its red handle indicated that an alarm would go off if they tried to open it. "We can't go this way," Rita said. "Come on. We have to find another exit."

They were halfway back down the hall when Rita found an opened door. She yanked on Debbie and said, "This way." She pulled her into a room and locked the door behind them.

One wall of the dimly lighted room was stainless steel, lined with rows of doors. There was a freezer also, and what looked like an ice machine. Rita knew exactly where she was. "The morgue," she said. She found some gauze in a cabinet, made a pad of the gauze, and wrapped it around her leg, creating pressure to stop the bleeding.

"This place is giving me the creeps," Debbie said. She started to open the door, but Rita caught her hand. She heard the crackling of a two-way radio in the corridor. A finger to her lips, Rita signaled for silence. The radio passed.

"I don't think they're looking for us yet," Rita whispered, "but we don't have much time."

"Where do we hide if someone comes in here?"

Rita glanced at the refrigerator doors.

"That's sick," Debbie said. "I saw that in a movie once. Someone had to hide in one of those things, and it had a body in it."

Rita told her, "This isn't the movies, and this morgue hasn't been used for years." To prove her point, she went and opened one of the refrigerator doors. She barely got her hand to Debbie's mouth in time.

The refrigerator wasn't empty. Inside the freezing container was a body bag.

"Turn around," Rita told Debbie. Debbie did so without argument. Rita pulled out the drawer and unzipped the bag. She knew right away who it was. It was Mary Jane Dunn, otherwise known as "M.J.," a thirteen-year-old who had been listed as a runaway. Her photograph was on the wall of Rita's office.

Naked, the child had recently had surgery. On

her stomach was a scar, outlined by a surgeon's orange Betadine wash.

Rita opened a second door. Michael Alderson was in there. He, like M.J., was frozen.

In a third container was Beth Tuma. They all bore the scars of surgery. Some of the scars were more extensive than others. What in the world was going on? Rita was about to open a fourth door when keys rattled in the door.

The door opened, and there stood a security guard. "Hey!" he shouted. Before Rita could react, he bolted from the doorway, probably to get backup.

Without a moment's hesitation, Rita jumped up onto a freezer case. "Come on!" she called to Debbie, whom she helped pull up.

The window above the freezer case wouldn't open no matter how hard Rita jerked its handle. Starting to panic, she jumped off the freezer. "We need something . . ." She ran to the ice machine, where she got the metal scoop from the machine, and returned to the freezer. This time Debbie helped her up.

"Watch your eyes," she said, and hit the glass with the metal scoop. The glass cracked but didn't break. Suddenly Rita could hear voices in the hallway. Using the metal scoop, she jabbed the glass as hard as she could. This time it shattered, and she smashed out the pieces around the frame. "Let's go!"

They came out behind the bushes fronting a brick wall. From there, she and Debbie raced into an alley. They ran blindly, as fast as they could, and finally collapsed behind a Dumpster.

"We can't stay here. We have to get some-place safe. Catch your breath, and then follow me."

Debbie didn't argue.

Though exposed by occasional car lights, they made it across the bridge and the interstate and down to the rail yards. "I'm pretty sure they'll be looking for us out in the open," Rita said. "They'll be expecting me to try to flag down a police officer. Come on, this way." With Debbie at her side, they followed the railroad tracks toward downtown Milwaukee.

They needed a place to rest, to plan what to do next—so they both could stay alive.

23

Rita and Debbie found an abandoned warehouse near the rail yards below the interstate. The warehouse was a shelter from the wind, but most of the windows were broken out, so the cold still got in. She and Debbie had made themselves a temporary shelter out of some cardboard and trash they had found, but not even that kept them warm, not with the cold that seemed to penetrate everything.

Their resting place gave Rita a chance to examine herself. Drainage from her wounds had stopped—the wounds were caking over with dried blood—but she could feel an occasional cold trickle from her arm whenever she moved too abruptly.

Debbie said, "You need a doctor."

A doctor wasn't important to Rita at all. She told Debbie what was important, namely what she had overheard. Ordinarily she wouldn't have passed along such information, but she figured that if anything happened to her, she wanted to make sure Debbie knew what to tell others.

Debbie didn't seem to care, though. She acted like the less she knew, the better.

With that Rita got to thinking again. Why had Yuan, at the point of death, given Howie and Lou Jim's name? That's what Howie had told her. Yet according to Debbie, Yuan had turned over the Hoeveler correspondence to her. Why wouldn't Yuan have given up Debbie's name instead of Jim's, if that had been the case? After all, Howie had tortured Yuan. Wouldn't she have finally told the truth at the point of death? Rita didn't want to confront Debbie just yet. Instead she brought out the microrecorder. She pressed the REWIND button—but the recorder didn't make that familiar whir a recorder makes when its tape is rewinding. With an open hand, she tapped at the recorder. Nothing happened. She popped open a compartment on the back of the recorder. Mike had given her a gift without batteries.

She arched her back, smiling. "Damn," she mumbled. She ached. She decided that even had the recorder worked, it probably wouldn't have picked up the conversation anyway. She glanced at Debbie, who had her arms huddled around her to keep warm.

"Where are we going next?" Debbie asked.

"Well, we have a couple of choices. One depends on whether you want to stay here and wait until I send help, or—"

"I'm not staying here by myself." Her tone was emphatic.

"Then we're going to have to do some walking."

"How far?"

"Far enough that we can get you someplace safe and warm, then I'm going to get to my office." Even as she said that, she knew her office was being watched. A chill shot through her. Mike and Greg would be watched also. Greg would try to be strong, but he would be shaken to learn she was missing.

"How far is your office?"

"Where I'm taking you is twenty minutes or so."

"Let's go."

"Debbie—"

"Yes."

"There are a couple of things that I need the truth about."

"What?"

"How did you end up leaving the employment of NationsCare? You admitted you were Whitaker's personal secretary, and that you ended up having an affair with him, but you didn't get to the part that happened after that."

Debbie was silent.

"There's more, isn't there? You've been lying to me, haven't you?"

"No, I haven't been lying."

"Then let me ask you this. When Howie was tying us up, he mentioned that Yuan had given him Jim's name as the person who had the letters. Why didn't she give Howie your name?"

"I suppose because Jim had already contacted her, and she knew I had turned over the letters to Jim."

Rita said, "Let me tell you something they teach us in criminal investigation. It's about dying confessions again."

Debbie was silent again.

"If someone makes a dying confession," Rita continued, "that is treated by most courts as carrying a great deal of weight. Do you know why that is?"

Debbie didn't answer.

"It's because courts tend to think that someone who is dying has little to gain or lose by confessing the truth." Rita moved closer to Debbie. Only then did she realize how sore she was. "I've been trying to figure out why Yuan, at the point of death, would lie about whom she had given the letters to. Why wouldn't she have given Howie and Lou your name if she really gave the letters to you in the first place?"

Silence.

"And why would she give the letters to you anyway? What would they mean to you, and what could you do that she couldn't do?"

"I told you, she wanted me to get the letters into the hands of the authorities if anything ever happened to her."

"And so Jim showed up one day at NationsCare, and you decided to give the letters to him because he had the courage to stand up to Chad Whitaker?"

Debbie didn't answer.

Rita said, "You see what I mean? The more I think about all this, the more confused I become. The way I figure it, Howie and Lou would want to know more than who had the letters. They would also want to know who knew about them and their contents. Wouldn't that include you in Yuan's dying confession? You know something about those dead children in the morgue too, don't you? You can jump in here anytime you want now."

Debbie began slowly, telling about a party Whitaker had thrown one night. The entire floor of the hotel had been reserved for Whitaker and his guests, and all the doors had been open, so that guests roamed from suite to suite. She said, "Chad and I had an enjoyable evening in his suite. We took a long bath together—you know, one of those baths you see in the movies, where there's all these suds and the two lovers have champagne and make love together in the tub.

"Then after the bath, we ate and drank more. We made love again."

Rita could hear Debbie take a deep breath and let out the air.

"Next thing I know, we were enjoying ourselves, and there came a pounding at the door. Chad opened the door and there was an entire group of men, including Congressman Dick Groucher."

Rita tried to see Debbie's eyes. So, she did know.

"You know who he is, don't you?"

"Yes, I know."

"They all told Chad they wanted me. Chad went out to talk to them, pulling the door partially closed behind him, and I could hear him telling the men—they were obviously all drunk—that they could have any man or woman on the entire floor, but they couldn't have me."

Debbie's voice was trembling.

"I was glad and thought that would take care of them because I knew Chad had ordered a lot of men and women from an escort service. That's what all those escort people were there for—to make sure all the guests were satisfied in any way they wanted."

Debbie was crying now. Rita moved closer to her and held her.

"They argued with him," Debbie said in a strained voice, "and Chad told me to do him a favor and go out to them. I wouldn't, so he shoved me out to them."

Rita was holding her and rubbing her back. "It's all right," she said.

"In the morning, they carried me out to his door and dropped me there. I couldn't even move." She began to wipe away her tears. "Next thing I know, Chad opened the door. He was all showered, shaved, and dressed, and he told me, 'Come on, we need to get to work.' "

Rita felt her trembling, and she held her tighter.

"I couldn't even move. Chad had to have Howie and Lou pick me up and carry me into the suite. That's when I took the letters. It was me. I knew about them, stole them, packed my things, and ran away." She added, "Yuan said Jim had the letters because that's who had them. I know because I gave them to him, and he went to see Yuan. He was the one who helped her get moved to Chicago. He was trying to take care of us both. When Yuan got fired, she hadn't had a chance to get the letters, but she told me about them, and I was the one who found them. I stole them and went to see Jim."

"It's all right," Rita told her. "Everything's going to be all right."

"Jim was the only one in the entire time I worked as Chad's personal secretary who had enough courage to walk right into his office and tell him face-to-face he was going to bring him to his knees." Debbie fell silent for a moment, then she asked, "Have you met Chad?"

"Yes," Rita replied. "I met him briefly."

"He's an evil man."

"I know."

"He's arrogant about it too. I used to watch how sly he would be when he slipped tips to waiters, and bellhops, and so on. He would always shake their hands, leaving money in their hands, and even without looking back, would say loudly, 'You have a nice day, you hear?' " Debbie's tears became a laugh. "Jim must have been watching Chad for a while because the day he came to the office, when he left, Jim reached across my desk, shook my hand, and said, 'You have a nice day, you hear?' I looked in my hand after Chad returned to his office, fuming, and there was Jim's home number on the back of a card."

Rita asked, "Did you know what he was doing with those children we found?"

"I knew he was developing some kind of medication that would stop the rejection of transplanted organs, and I knew he was paying good money for bodies, but I thought it was all legitimate."

"Did you know that those children were run-aways—children Whitaker had found on the street?"

"After what he let happen to me, I'm not surprised. I guess that's how Rich Spiker's nephew fit in. He got the children. He seemed to know just where to find them."

Rita got to her feet. She was stiff and sore. Now that she had had some rest, she realized how hard her earlier fall had been. "Once we get out there, we have to keep hidden. If I tell you to get down, don't argue with me or anything. Just drop right to the ground when I tell you. If I tell you to run, you run like you've never run before."

"Won't they know you're going to try to get to your office? I don't think you should go back there."

Helping Debbie up, Rita said, "Don't worry."

"I'm sorry I haven't been more truthful. I just didn't know who to trust anymore." Debbie was sniffling. Her nose was running from so much crying. Rita wished she had a handkerchief to give her. She seemed like a nice girl, someone who had gotten tied up with the wrong people. Rita had seen it happen too many times to too many people.

Outside, dawn was appearing in the eastern sky. There was not much light, but a half-moon made foot travel possible. Under the interstate, however, the going was not so easy. It was pitch-black there. Cars and trucks rattled and roared overhead. Each vehicle that passed seemed to shake the entire network of tons of concrete and steel.

Once out from under the overhead ramps, Rita and Debbie passed through a poorly lighted parking lot belonging to Marquette University. There were a few cars here and there, but for the most part the parking lot was empty. Christmas vacation, Rita thought. The students were gone.

Immediately in front of them, two black men appeared from behind a car. She and Debbie must have startled them because at first they backed away as if about to run. Then it became apparent what they were doing—stealing wire rims from cars—because one of the men held up a tire iron while the other tried to conceal a hubcap.

"We don't want any trouble," Rita said. "We're just passing through."

The black man with the tire iron made a circling motion with his finger, and the two men spread out.

The second man produced a knife. Strike, she told herself, don't get trapped.

Rita's right foot lashed out, kicking the hand with the knife, sending the knife flying. In the same swift motion, Rita's fist slammed upward into the knife-wielder's windpipe.

Debbie let out a scream.

Rita jumped back and threw a kick from the rear into the other man's chest. The tire iron dropped from his hand. Rather than run, allowing the man to grab his iron and chase, she attacked him, kicking him first in the groin, then throwing an elbow up into his throat. She thought she had dislodged his windpipe because she could feel the cartilage give way.

Then she grabbed Debbie, who was still stunned, and ran. At a purple light, she almost stopped long enough to set off the emergency alarm for help. Within minutes, she knew, Marquette security would be on the scene. Something told her not to do that, however, that the alarm would give away their location. Police would start searching the area, as would Whitaker's people.

They continued running and didn't stop until

they were behind the Episcopal church off of Wisconsin Avenue. In the bushes she and Debbie stopped to catch their breath.

There was a light on at the soup kitchen. Rita tapped on the door. A gray-haired man with a white collar opened the door. She recognized him. Louie Benoit. She had monitored a protest in which he among others had been arrested.

She told him who she was and showed him her credentials. Shaking his head, he told her the soup kitchen was closed—to come back during regular hours. He tried to close the bright red door. She stuck a foot in the door and told him she was on official business.

Sighing, he stepped aside and let them in. He locked the door behind them.

She repeated that she was Captain Rita Trible of Wisconsin's Criminal Investigation Division, and she was in trouble. She needed help, she said. She needed to use a telephone.

He didn't seem to have heard. "I can give you a sandwich and something to drink. I believe there's some milk. That's all I can do. You'll have to find your way to the shelter. It's several blocks from here. I can call, if you want, and find out if they have any beds."

"I need to use the phone," Rita repeated.

"We don't have a public phone here," he said.

"This is an emergency," she told him.

He studied her. "Have they raped you?" he asked. "Come on, people show me badges all the time. Half the people who come here carry a badge. If that's what you carry to protect yourself, and it works, that's fine, but a badge doesn't get you any special privileges around here."

Rita said, "Please," and added again, "this is an emergency."

Finally he led her and Debbie to a private phone in the kitchen. He even stood there, waiting for her to make the call.

She dialed her office number. "It's a local call," she told the priest as he watched every button she pushed.

Paul answered.

"Paul," she said, relieved to hear his voice. "Thank God, you're there. I need some help."

Before she could say anything more, he asked, "Rita, where are you? Is everything okay?"

She told him where she was.

He said they would be there in less than five minutes.

Once off the phone, she turned to Louie Benoit and told him he had to offer sanctuary to Debbie. "You have to let her stay here until I can get her to safety. She's in grave danger."

He seemed finally to believe what she was saying. At least he didn't argue with her.

Debbie did, though. "I want to go with you," she said.

"Debbie, please just stay here until I can get everything set up. I don't want anyone to know where you are right now. It's like you said, they'll be watching my office. As far as I know, you know who will be there personally."

Debbie gave in.

At the door, Rita thanked the priest. He let her out and locked the door behind her.

Before long she recognized the state sedan that pulled to the side of the chapel. Another sedan stopped up on Wisconsin Avenue, blocking off the one-way street. She saw another sedan approximately a block away.

Good, she thought, they're doing it by the book.

She ran out and jumped into the waiting car.

"What's going on?" Paul asked her, concerned.

She told him she needed a weapon. "Let's get to the office."

He didn't argue. He handed her a 9mm and put the car in gear. On Wisconsin Avenue, he asked her, "Where have you been?"

She checked the weapon. It was loaded. She threw a round into the chamber. "Right now I'm fine."

"Where's the girl?"

"Who?"

"Debbie Sweet."

"How did you know about her?"

He looked uncomfortable.

Slowly she pointed the gun at him.

"How did you know about Debbie Sweet?"

"You haven't heard?"

"Heard what?"

"Charlie's okay. That's how I heard. What in the hell are you doing!"

She sighed.

"We talked to him. He told us everything. Why didn't you tell me?" He reached out a hand, but she moved the gun back. It was still pointed at him. "Everyone's been worried sick about you. I'm hoping you have this girl in protective custody. We can't afford any more mistakes."

"She's in a safe place." She still had the gun trained on him. "Paul, there are too many coincidences here, too many things that only you would have known about."

"What are you talking about?"

"You killed Jim, didn't you?"

"What!"

"What, had he discovered some dark secret about you and confronted you about it? Did Dick Groucher call you and pull a few strings?"

He turned into an empty parking lot next to the parking garage off of Wisconsin Avenue.

"What are you doing!" she demanded.

He turned the car around and headed back up Wisconsin Avenue. They passed Howie, who had been following. "Whitaker's men are following us," Paul said, gunning the car.

She told him, "Paul, you can stop pretending. In the Renneker investigation, Charlie and I both noticed right away that the report wasn't written by Jim. Charlie didn't think anything more of it. It was on Jim's computer, and Jim had hard copies of things in his files, so Charlie probably thought it was just one of those things Jim had written in some distraught state. He hadn't read enough of your reports to know your writing style."

Paul chuckled. "Well, I'll be damned. You are good."

Another car did a U-turn and joined the chase. Rita recognized Lou, Whitaker's security chief, at the wheel of the car. She shook her head. "And we know about Renneker too. Don't you find it ironic that everywhere Renneker has been, Chad has had an NCA hospital; or is it the other way around?"

Paul was concentrating on his driving. At Marquette, he turned onto Tory Hill. He gunned the engine, and the car fishtailed. She saw the parking lot where they had been earlier that evening. At the stoplight, he turned left on Ember Lane, which he took under the interstate. At the next stoplight, he turned right on St. Paul Avenue. "Call for backup," he told her. "Don't be foolish!"

It was strange to be heading in the same direction she had come from, the abandoned warehouse district. Keeping him in her sights, she glanced at her side mirror out of the corner of her eye. She saw the headlights of two cars following. "I want the truth, Paul!" she said.

"Okay, I'll tell you the truth! I didn't kill Jim. Renneker did."

"Paul, come on!"

"I promise! Renneker did it. Jim and I had been working together. Renneker killed him, I knew he did. I knew the only way to point the finger in the right direction was to put Jim's body in the right place—"

Just then the back window exploded. The car jumped the curb, shot up the incline below the interstate, and flipped. After that, it seemed like things went into slow motion, taking forever to happen. The car rolled. The air bags inflated. She didn't know how many times the car flipped over. It seemed to be several times, but maybe it was only once. The air bags deflated suddenly, followed by the crackling of gunshots.

Paul fell back against his door, and she flew on top of him. They both hit the ceiling of the car, then flew to the passenger side, before sitting upright in their seats again.

Paul was in shock. The left side of his face was bleeding from where he had flown into his door and the window had smashed. She tried to get her door open, but it was jammed. "I had to," Paul mumbled. Aiming her gun at the glass, then turning her eyes away, she pulled the trigger. She used her foot to kick out the rest of the glass, and lunged out onto the embankment.

She could hear gunshots. Bullets were flying everywhere. A tracer shot by her like a fiery red dart. She tried to get back to the car to help Paul. The next thing she knew, a tracer hit the car, which exploded, throwing her. She landed hard on the pavement. As she passed out, she noticed the flames leaping into the night sky.

24

When Rita came to, she noticed that Lou and Howie were gone. She had assumed they had done the shooting. Undoubtedly a tracer had ignited the gas tank. The two men must have thought both she and Paul had been killed in the explosion. She stared at the yellow-orange flames and the thick black smoke that rose into the night. She must have blacked out for a few minutes.

Someone was calling from the highway.

Rita felt as if she were in a different world, and the person on the highway wasn't yelling at her. "What?" she yelled back, but her words sounded like nothing. She thought her eardrums had burst when the car had exploded.

"Are you all right!" Someone was standing over her.

"Call for help!" she yelled because she couldn't hear herself very well. She tried to get to the car. She looked for Paul, but she didn't see him. Good, he had gotten out. She collapsed on the snow.

Other cars were stopping on the highway above. She could see emergency flashers jumping in the darkness. In the night she could hear sirens.

Someone from the highway jumped the fence and slid down the snowy embankment. "Are you all right?" he asked. He had a cell phone in his hand. He told her he had called 911. He said he was an emergency medical technician.

She tried to sit up. The EMT told her not to move, but she insisted, so he helped her. She told him there had been someone else in the car. "Please help him," she said. The EMT skirted the car, trying to get close to it, but the flames were too hot.

The first police vehicle on scene was a Milwaukee County sheriff's car. She knew both deputies and told them what she knew about Lou and Howie so that they could be detained as soon as possible. One of the deputies called in the information. The other deputy sprayed the burning sedan with his car's fire extinguisher. It was a futile effort.

The EMT returned. He hadn't found anyone else, he said. Somewhere Paul was burning, though she couldn't see his body. She thought she could smell burning flesh—like the smell of burning hair, only stronger—but she hoped it was only her imagination.

A friend of hers, Tim Smith with the state police, arrived. She asked him if she could use his car phone. Smith and the EMT helped her to the police cruiser. She called Mike and Greg. Rita assured Mike she was fine, then talked to Greg. He tried to act like he wasn't concerned, but she could tell by his voice that he was scared. He asked when he could see her. She told him Mike would bring him to St. Luke's, where she would be heading in a few minutes. "I'm all right," she said. "I just have a small cut that has to be sewn up."

She called Vince. She told him to arrange for the state police to put a police watch on Mike and Greg.

After that she felt better.

A fire truck arrived. Almost as soon as they arrived, firefighters had the fire out. They had, Rita thought, probably put out hundreds of similar fires.

She realized she was light-headed. Things around her seemed to be moving, trembling ever so slightly. The warmth of the state police cruiser was such a dramatic change from the cold she had experienced all night that she actually felt dizzy.

She telephoned Jerry Grier and asked him if he would go by the Episcopal church and pick up Debbie Sweet. "Take her somewhere and put her in a safe motel, Bull," she said. "Then order protection for her—a lot of protection."

Jerry said not to worry, he would handle everything.

When Rita called the hospital, the intensive care nurse called Claudia to the phone. Claudia said Charlie's condition had been upgraded to fair condition. She was bubbly with enthusiasm, talking about how it would be a matter of days and Charlie would be moved out of the intensive care. She kept saying that she was cautiously optimistic, but Rita could tell there was nothing cautious about it. She was ecstatic.

Then came the bad news. They'd discovered a body in the sedan. Oh, God, she thought. Tim was trying to get her to go with the ambulance attendants, but she refused. She was going to wait until the coroner arrived. She got out of his car and stood, aware of little more than the reeling scene, the smell of smoke, and the salt taste of blood on her lips. She looked at the charred car, which was still smoking. It was her fault, she thought. Paul had died because of her. She should have helped him out.

Once the coroner arrived, the remains of Paul's body were removed from the car. Rita didn't go look. She had seen burn victims, and she didn't want to see this one, not Paul. The coroner said he doubted that fire had killed the man in the car. He said there was a gunshot to the head. Had he shot himself? she wondered.

Tim told her she needed to go with the ambulance attendants. This time she didn't argue. There was no need to. What was done was done.

In the back of the ambulance, she rode to the

emergency room of St. Luke's, where she walked in on her own. A nurse escorted Rita to a gurney, handed her a hospital gown, and told her to change into the gown, the doctor would be with her shortly. The nurse pulled the curtain, creating a cubicle around the gurney.

Rita undressed and put on the gown. There was a lot of dried blood on her arm and leg. She suspected the wounds looked worse than they really were.

The nurse came in and set a large blue package on a stainless-steel table. The doctor arrived. He introduced himself. He made a couple of sounds as if the wounds were somehow communicating to him and he was responding: "Ummhmmmm. Umm. Umm."

The nurse opened the blue package, and the doctor pulled out sterile gloves. He began to scrub her leg wound with an orange soap. He said, "This is pretty close to the artery. You're lucky."

Rita looked at the doctor. He was at least ten years younger than she was.

The doctor displayed a syringe. "I'm going to inject a little something to deaden the area," he told Rita.

She felt a couple of pricks, and then her thigh filled with a cold numbness. Next thing she knew, the doctor was sewing her leg with black thread and what looked like a fishing hook. She thought of her father's fishing jacket, the one with all the pockets. There had been hooks and line in it when she had finally cleaned the pockets out. All of that was in her past.

Instead of using his fingers to do the sewing, the doctor was using what looked like a thin pair of pliers. They would lock on to the needle, and with a twist of his wrist he would push the needle in one side of the open skin and out the other. He quickly tied off each suture, which in the process pulled the wound closed.

Rita tried to make some sense of what had happened, of all she had experienced in the past couple of weeks. She wished putting it all together was as neat and straightforward as sewing torn skin.

The doctor cleaned, numbed, and sewed the wound on her arm. The nurse bandaged the leg and arm once the doctor was done.

Tim Smith brought her a portable phone. "You have a call," he said.

She asked Tim what he was doing at the hospital, and he held up a stack of papers. "Paperwork," he said. "A mountain of it, all because of you."

She shrugged.

On the telephone was Paul's boss in the attorney general's office, Ivan Liss. She had met Liss at a number of social events, and occasionally she had accompanied Paul to meetings with Liss. He was a vintage bureaucrat. She told him everything she knew, including about the dead children in the basement of Whitaker's hospital complex. She told him about Debbie and how

Jerry Grier had her in protective custody. The only thing she held back was what had happened between her and Paul. She didn't know why she held that back, but she did. The moment she told Liss everything, he said he had to brief the attorney general and the governor. He said he would be back in touch as soon as possible.

Rita was exhausted. She wanted to go home. What else could she do? she wondered. She could talk to Diane Hoeveler, but what was she going to tell her? What was Al going to tell her? Or Joe DeFalco or Dick Groucher? No one was going to say anything, she knew, not until the damning evidence was recovered from Whitaker's hospital, then everyone would disavow everything.

On her way out of the emergency room, Rita encountered Susan Hall. The two women looked at each other. Susan didn't rush forward, asking a lot of questions. All she said was, "If you make a press release, would you think of me?" It was a strange reaction. Rita nodded. It was as if Susan was a different person.

Then her face broke into a huge smile. In front of her were Mike and Greg. No two people had ever looked so good to her. She embraced them, one in each arm. When she kissed Greg's forehead, she asked him if he was okay. He smiled and said, "I would probably be happier if you had a job that was more exciting." She laughed and hugged him, despite her soreness.

Together, the three of them went to the hospital cafeteria, where they sat and talked. It was good to be together as a family. Once they had talked and drank Cokes, they went up to the intensive care unit, where Rita was allowed a few minutes to go in and see Charlie. He was still on the vent but awake.

She asked, "Are you all right?"

He couldn't move. He was still paralyzed from drugs, according to Claudia, but his eyes did bob up and down.

She took his left hand in both of her hands. It was a big hand. Even both of her hands had trouble wrapping around it. In the background, she could hear the ventilator feeding Charlie with air. It was an eerie sound. One artificial breath after another filled his chest. But he was alive. That was all that counted.

Outside, Smith handed her a telephone again. Liss was on the line. He had briefed the attorney general, he said, who had briefed the governor.

She asked him, "Can we get a search warrant to retrieve the bodies from Whitaker's hospital offices?"

Liss said it wasn't necessary. Chad had already given sheriff's detectives permission to go through the entire old hospital complex. "They didn't find anything. There were no bodies."

"But I saw them."

"Did anyone else see them?"

"Debbie Sweet did."

Calmly, Liss said, "I checked with Jerry Grier.

He's talked to Debbie, and she said she didn't actually see the bodies. She said you told her not to look."

"I saw them," Rita said.

"There wasn't anything there—no evidence of any bodies. Mr. Whitaker was very cooperative." Liss went on to say that Whitaker had turned over her service weapon, and the weapons registered to Lou and Howie, who had already surrendered themselves to authorities at the Milwaukee Police Department.

Slick, she thought.

Liss said, "Mr. Whitaker was very apologetic, and assured us that his security team hadn't been in any shootout. He said that his security team had wanted to talk to one of his previous employees, the young woman by the name of Debbie Sweet, but that there had been a case of confusion. It appears that Miss Sweet stole some money from a petty cash file, and Mr. Whitaker's security personnel got carried away."

Rita thought of Yuan. The same allegation had been made with her.

"I told him you would have a right to prosecute if you wanted, especially if his security personnel overstepped their bounds, but I hope that's not going to be necessary. He was very apologetic and, well, Mr. Whitaker is quite influential. He's even talked to the governor about this, assuring the governor he'll cooperate fully in any investigation."

Rather than lose her temper, Rita tried to

think as lucidly as she could. If Lou and Howie had turned in the weapons that were registered in their names, she was sure those weapons would not have been used in shooting at her and Paul. In fact, she was sure that the weapons used in the shooting would never be found.

She ran a hand through her hair. Be patient, she told herself. "That's fine," she told Liss. "If his security team has admitted that it overreacted, and Mr. Whitaker has apologized, I'm not going to push at this time."

She would go to see Renneker. He would know something.

She could feel the ease of tension on the other end of the line. "Good, good," Liss said. "I was hoping you'd say that. You know, I always knew you were levelheaded, fair, and understanding, but it's good to see all that under these conditions."

She commented, "Sometimes you have to back up and regroup."

Liss laughed. "That's the spirit," he said.

She turned and looked back at the intensive care unit. "I've got to go," she said softly.

"I'll keep you informed as I hear things," he told her. "In the meantime, keep me informed."

"I will." By the time she got the words out, she realized Liss had already hung up.

"Let's go home," she told Mike and Greg.

On their way, the car was silent. Rita knew she wanted to talk to Mike, ask him more questions, but she didn't want to talk in front of

Greg, didn't want to upset him any more than he probably already was. Her entire body was sore. The first thing she would do when she got home was pour herself a stiff drink.

"Mom," Greg said.

"Yeah, hon," she said.

"I'm glad to see you."

She looked at him, surprised. She wanted to hug him, or reach out and hold hands with him, but she knew that would embarrass him. "I'm happy to see you too," she replied. "In fact," she said, thinking of the frozen bodies that had been in Whitaker's private morgue, "you don't know how happy I am to see you."

25

Clyde Jenkins, the medical examiner who had performed Jim's autopsy, pulled a dead leaf from a potted plant on the windowsill in his Madison office. Rita had gone to Madison to wrap up loose ends in the investigation. He looked up and smiled at Rita, a flash of yellowish teeth in a goatee he was trying to grow. "Do you think it's because it gets too much or too little sunlight?" he asked, holding up the plant, whose other leaves had a blight on them.

She said she didn't know.

He looked at it for a moment, then pointed at a folder on his desk. "Do you remember when you asked me whether I had taken samples of the water from which Jim's body had been retrieved?"

Yes.

"If you'll recall, I said I had personally taken the samples."

Yes, she remembered that too.

"That was perceptive of you," he told her. "Most investigators wouldn't have thought to ask about samples of the water the body was pulled from."

"I thought it was routine."

He shook his head. "Let me put it this way, the others automatically wrote this off as a suicide. They didn't care about water samples. In a suicide, what difference does it make?"

She held out her hand for the folder. He gave it to her.

He said, "I've been doing this sort of work for twenty years. Sometimes something as simple as a water sample pays off big."

She put on her bifocals and looked at the report. There was a lot of technical language. "And your conclusion?" she asked.

"You've either got homicide on your hands or some other type of foul play," he told her. "At least there's enough evidence to warrant further investigation."

She stared at him over the top of her bifocals. "What makes you say that?"

He shrugged. "For one, the Placidyl."

"I don't get it. Before you said that was too circumstantial."

"By itself it was. But then I studied the stomach contents. Swearingen had ingested quite a bit of water, you know. Odd thing about the stomach contents too. There was a lot of mud and algae in the water, along with other sediment. I compared it to the water samples I took from Lake Mendota, and I was able to make a couple of interesting observations."

She folded her glasses and put them in her coat pocket.

"One, the contents of Swearingen's stomach indicated that he had drowned in shallow water—that he was down near the mud and bottom of the water when he drowned—"

"Yes."

"The second has to do with where Swearingen's body was pulled up at Lake Mendota. It's more than twenty feet deep in that particular location. He wouldn't have been at the bottom when he drowned."

"Okay." She knew what he was going to say—had already heard it from Paul—but she wanted him to put it in his own words.

"His body had been moved. He didn't drown in Lake Mendota. The water samples aren't even the same. The water Swearingen had inside him wasn't the water from Lake Mendota. Someone moved the body to Lake Mendota to make it look like that was where he had drowned."

Just as Paul had confessed. Holding the folder in one hand, she ran the fingers of her other hand through her hair.

He paused, frowned, and then went on. "I know you're busy, and I won't keep you long. Briefly, let me tell you what else I discovered. I also did the Neuland girl's autopsy, you know." He shook his head. "That was awful, wasn't it? Do you mind if I smoke?"

No, she didn't mind.

He turned on an electric air filter, which hummed, opened the middle drawer of his desk, and removed a cigarette, which he lit. He stood near the air filter so the cigarette smoke wouldn't circulate in the room. "Anyway, when I got those reports on Swearingen"—he nodded at the folder she held—"I got to thinking about where I had picked up the Neuland body."

Rita remembered the place well, thought she would never forget it.

"I started to put everything together as I thought about some of the things you had said about Swearingen and Renneker. Do you remember seeing a pond down from the electric lines where the Neuland girl was found?"

Yes, she told him.

"I went back to the Neuland scene and went down to that pond to take some water samples." His head was bobbing. "That's the exact place Swearingen drowned."

There was little doubt about drawing the same conclusion when Rita got down to the pond. After meeting with Clyde Jenkins, she drove to the site. She began to collect evidence and take photographs. She found the place where it looked like Renneker had gone into the water. Apparently he had been carrying Jim.

When she went to photograph the shore where the drowning had apparently taken place, she noticed a mound in the snow at her feet. She kicked some snow away to reveal a pair of rusty wire cutters that had red plastic grips. With them was a bundle of wire that had been overtaken by rust too. She carefully packaged the items as evidence, then radioed for a forensic team.

Members of the team arrived within the hour and began to comb the area for evidence. They found more. While they processed it, Rita returned to Madison to reinterview Renneker.

He was as arrogant and self-confident as he had been the first time she had met him. He smiled. "Where's your sidekick?"

He knew about Charlie. Word like that spread like wildfire in a jail. Ignoring the comment, she advised him of his rights and gave him a waiver form to sign. She told him she was back to investigating the murder of Jim Swearingen.

He smiled, reminded her he had already told her he hadn't murdered Swearingen, and signed the waiver form. "Ask me what you want." He walked nonchalantly to a chair, pulled it out, and sat down.

"Why don't we start with the topic of Chad Whitaker? You do know Chad Whitaker, don't you?"

"I've met him a couple of times. He's basically a childhood friend of Uncle Rich's. That's how I know him."

"I think there's more than that."

Renneker smiled serenely. "I don't know what you're talking about."

"Are you living comfortably while you're in jail?" She smiled back.

"Sure, I'm comfortable."

"I see Chad Whitaker has been keeping spending money in your jail account—so you can buy things at the jail commissary."

"Uncle Rich deposited that money."

"I think if I talked to your aunt Pat, she would tell me where the money was from."

"She's a whore anyway. I don't care what she says. So what if the money's from Chad? What do I care?"

"Do you think he's going to let you live?"

That pulled Renneker up short.

"Let me ask you this, how could he let you live? He can't continue to support you. If he does, sooner or later word's going to get out, and someone's going to trace Whitaker back to you. He can't have that. He can't have anything to do with you."

Renneker looked uncomfortable. "Like I said, the money in my account has come from my uncle."

"Right. I know a television reporter who's chomping at the bit for a story like this."

"Why do I give a shit what reporters you know?"

She shrugged. "The way I figure it, something went wrong." She stood up and walked to the two-way window. She knew the booth was empty, but she stood there as if the observation booth was occupied.

"Go ahead," Renneker said. "Tell me what you think since you seem to have all the answers."

She stared at him, keeping eye contact until he looked away. She knew she had him. "I guess you were pretty surprised when Jim Swearingen's body turned up in your uncle's fishing hole."

Renneker chuckled. "We all were."

"But I guess you in particular wondered how that happened, didn't you?"

He laughed again. "To tell you the truth, I bet a lot of people wondered how it happened."

"You more than others, though, since it must have been like his ghost got up and walked after you had killed him." Renneker's face lost some of its color, she noticed. "Did you have nightmares after that?"

"I'm sure I don't know what you're talking about."

"Sure you do, Scott. We already know where you did it. We've found the wire cutters and the wire. The wire cutters have your prints on them." She didn't know that yet, but there was no sense letting him off the hook. "The wire matches the wire on Jim's hands and ankles."

"You'll never prove it," Renneker said, "not when someone tampered with the evidence by moving the body." He fell silent for several moments, realizing that he had already said too much.

"Who said anything about anyone moving the body?"

He didn't say.

"How about if Chad Whitaker moved it, or had it moved?"

He started to scowl. "Why would he do something like that?"

"Because Chad doesn't like the likes of you hanging around him. Sure, he'll take what you have to offer. He'll get what he can from you, but then he'll wad you up and throw you away like a piece of trash. First he has to get you where he wants you. In here he has you by the balls. You're not going anywhere, and he knows it. Someday when you least expect it, someone'll stick a knife in you, or bash in your head with the handle of a mop or broom."

"I don't want to answer any more of your questions. First I want to talk to my attorney."

"Scott, Scott, you've lost some of your cool," she said. At the door she told him, "Funny thing about Jim Swearingen is that you couldn't get away from him even when he was dead, could you?" She shook her head. "He sure enough had you on the run, the way I figure it. Now you're in the same predicament. You're not going to be able to get away. All I have to do is call the television reporter who's been hounding me for an interview, and you're a dead man."

Renneker looked sick, like he really had been having nightmares that he couldn't shake.

Outside the interrogation room, Jim Beck, the detective who had first escorted Renneker out to the Neuland body, greeted her, holding out a portable telephone. He said, "Someone wants to talk to you about something happening down in Chicago."

It was Vince. He was with Chicago homicide detectives, who had arrested Howie for the murder of Yuan Zhang. The detectives had found the watch Rita had told them about, the watch that belonged to Al Hoeveler. Vince said that Detective Tony Donato had already said that the band on the watch was consistent with scratches on Yuan's body. Rita knew that much. She had studied the scratches as shown in the photographs, had seen Al look for his missing watch, and had seen him give it away during one of the surveillance tapes that Bull had turned over to her. The way she figured it, Whitaker's people had intended to leave the watch as evidence at Yuan's crime scene—physical evidence to frame Hoeveler—but Howie had gotten greedy and had kept the watch for himself.

She wondered what would now happen with Whitaker and his NCA project. The thought was depressing. The project would probably still go ahead, she thought. Whitaker would probably walk away unscathed. People like that usually got what they wanted. She remembered that from a news article about Whitaker—nothing would get in his way.

26

Absentmindedly, Rita ran a hand through her hair. Telephone receiver at her ear, she looked out the window of her spacious new office in Madison. The sky was blue and slightly misty, but otherwise clear for February. In the reflection of the plate glass, she could see the disbelief in her face. Her complexion was ashen, her lips looked bloodless. Howie had escaped. The first thing she thought about was Mike and Greg. Were they safe? Howie was ruthless. She knew that. He was the kind of killer who derived pleasure from torturing his victims, someone who would readily seek revenge with little or no real provocation. All the while such thoughts were going through her head, Detective Tony Donato of the Chicago Police Department was explaining what had happened. He said that Howie and other inmates had been taken outdoors into a fenced-in exercise yard at the county jail, where he was being held for trial.

Once the exercise period was over, and the inmates were being escorted from the yard back to the jail, several inmates had made a break for freedom. Since the fleeing inmates scattered, Donato said, all the guards could do was get the remaining prisoners back inside the building before pursuing the escapees. Howie had gone over a back wall, where there was a trailer parked. Donato said, "He climbed up on the trailer in order to get to the top of the wall. It's about a fifteen-foot drop from the wall to the parking lot on the other side of the wall. The parking lot is part of the bus station. Two witnesses said they saw someone meeting Howie's description drop from the wall. According to the witnesses, Howie seemed to have been injured in the fall. He was limping as he crossed the street and got into a waiting car. The car drove off."

None of it was what Rita wanted to hear, but at the same time, it was exactly along the lines of what she had been dreading would happen. "When?" she asked, a sick feeling inside.

"Two days ago," Donato admitted.

"Two days ago!" Rita felt anger rising.

"I know how you feel," he said. "That's why we didn't call you right away. We thought we had him and could get him locked back up before you knew anything, but he slipped through our fingers. Now we've got a lead on him again. He's been seen over in Rockford. In fact, we've sealed off the area where he was last spotted.

It's a remote area, and he's not going to get away from us. I'm calling to see if you want to be in on the apprehension."

Rita's response was an emphatic "Yes." Only afterward did she realize that it was Friday afternoon, and she had promised to spend the evening and weekend with Mike and Greg, who were coming into town from Milwaukee. They had been spending their weekends in their new home. She looked at her watch. Now that she was working out of Madison, she knew that within an hour or so, she could be in Rockford. Two o'clock. An hour at most to apprehend Howie. She would be back by five. Six at most.

She called Mike. He was home from school and waiting for Greg to get packed. She told him she was running late and wouldn't be home until around six. She said six to be on the safe side. He seemed to understand. She appreciated that.

He asked if she still wanted to attend a Gamblers Anonymous meeting with him.

She said, "Sure."

He even said, "You are all really wonderful, you know?" It was something new she had discovered in their relationship, a sort of freshness she hadn't experienced since they had first met. She liked it.

Greg got on the phone. He asked her if she would be home in time to take him to the paint store so he could pick out the color of his bedroom. She said if she wasn't able to take him that evening, she would for sure take him the next day.

"You swear?" Greg said.

She laughed at him. These days he tried to get her to swear to everything. It had been like that since Charlie had been shot and she had fallen into the hands of Howie and Lou. She told Greg, "I don't need to swear. I said I'd take you, and I will." That seemed to suffice.

Feeling better, she hung up and dialed Charlie's extension. He had been reassigned to desk duty while he recuperated from his gunshot wound. She had brought him to Madison as her assistant. He had been happy to leave the big city. She told him she was leaving for the day, and would see him, Claudia, and Keisha on Sunday, when they were invited to the new house for dinner.

With that she was out the door and on her way to Rockford, Illinois, which was a quick trip, despite the rain that had begun to fall. The rain cut into the snow of the fields along the highway as she got to Illinois. Odd how two adjoining states could have such different weather. The weather reminded her of the day Scott Renneker had led her and other investigators to the body of Brittny Neuland. By the time she got to Rock Cut State Park on the northeast side of Rockford, the rain was pouring.

At the entrance to the park, Detective Donato met her. He escorted her inside a command center truck the Illinois State Police had stationed just inside the park. There he introduced her to Captain Earl Crumpton, a detective with the Illinois State Police. Crumpton looked like a young Jim Swearingen—clean-cut, professional. He looked like the Jim she had known in the early years. At a map spread across a table, Crumpton outlined the layout of the park. He placed the tip of his fountain pen on the map. "Right here on the north side of Pierce Lake is a shelter," he said. "That's where our man Howie Michaels was last seen. We figure he'll try to get up to I-90 and catch a ride. We're waiting for him up there. We'll go in from this direction and flush him out. Major"—Crumpton looked at Rita—"if you want to pull your car up into the park, you and Detective Donato could wait for us here"—he put the tip of his fountain pen on the southern side of Pierce Lake—"that way you'll be able to see what's going on. No offense, but I'd just as soon not have any problems later on with questions about jurisdiction."

Rita nodded. At the same time, she glanced at Donato, who shrugged.

She and Donato did as they were told. She drove her sedan to a spot where they could see the other side of the lake. The other vehicles crossed the dam on the south end of the lake and went up into the woods. Donato adjusted the radio to the frequency of the Illinois State Police, and they listened to the radio traffic that mixed in with the sound of the rain hitting the car.

Not long after the last car had driven up into the woods, Howie appeared. He bolted up over an embankment and shot down the other side of the dam. While Donato called for a backup, Rita jumped out of the car and chased Howie. She ran down the road, jumped the guardrail at the dam, and chased Howie along a muddy path above the runoff of the dam. She was soaked. The water in the river below was brown and turbulent. Its gushing sounds rose above the sound of the rain, which was pouring. Howie ran into the forest. Rita followed, running as fast as she could. In the background she heard car doors slamming and voices. Before she realized what had happened she ran head-on into Howie, who had jumped out from behind a tree. The force of her impact surprised them both. She knocked him backward, and he grabbed her at the same time she grabbed him. They both dropped off the path and down the muddy hill, heading for the rushing brown water. At the last moment, her free hand caught a young sapling. Again the impact caught them both off guard. She lost hold of him completely. He caught her right foot, but she could tell he didn't have a firm grip. As his fingers began to give, she thought she could see fear in his eyes. "He was going to kill me," Howie said, out of breath.

"Who?" She knew in her heart that he was about to mutter Chad Whitaker's name, but at the same moment, Howie was sucked into the brown water. A couple of times, his head resurfaced, but then he vanished completely.

27

In the basement of a Madison church, Rita found a group of men and women loitering around a table, upon which was a coffeepot, foam cups, and a couple trays of cookies. Near the table was a circle of chairs. She spotted Mike and went to him. He smiled broadly and kissed her. "I was beginning to think you weren't going to make it," he said. She told him she had gone to the new house to shower and change clothes. He told her she looked beautiful and introduced her to the others. She could tell he was nervous. He laughed and said, "This has become the story of my life—hanging around basements of churches and soaking up coffee." The others laughed. They seemed more comfortable than he was, as if they had more experience.

The one called Holles asked the loitering people if they would take their coffee and cookies to their chairs. He was a tall, lanky man, who had a slight curvature of the spine that caused his upper torso to bend forward slightly. Everyone sat down. A smile on his face, Holles said, "I would like to welcome our newest member"—the others laughed at him, he even slightly giggled at himself—"and his wife, Rita." Several heads nodded. Holles continued, "This evening, I would like to start by opening a topic. How about the topic of powerlessness? Would anyone like to say anything?"

One man of Asian descent said he had experienced the feeling many times. He looked overweight and tired, like he hadn't had much sleep lately. He wore expensive clothes, but they were wrinkled. He said he had just gotten back from a trip to Las Vegas. His head was bowed so they couldn't see his shame. "It wasn't even for me. I'm so lucky at the tables that others want me to gamble for them. I made fifty thousand dollars for someone in the past two days. At first I thought it was all right. I rationalized that it wasn't me gambling because I wasn't losing my own money. Then last night, when I was exhausted and hanging over a table, I realized I was as much of a slave to gambling as I had ever been. I was powerless before that table." He drank some of his coffee.

Another man nodded. This was a balding man with a red face. He too was well dressed, only his clothes were starched and pressed. He looked like he might have gotten dressed up just for the meeting. He said that at one time or another he had lost everything in his world to gambling. "That includes a wife, several jobs, my health, a couple of homes, a few cars—you name it, I've lost it. The funny thing is, I thought I didn't need anything or anyone. In fact, there was a time when I said, to hell with it. I felt powerful because I was able to lose everything and not be personally touched. I now realize all of that didn't empower me, as I thought, but was an example of my own powerlessness when it came to gambling."

Mike smiled and said, "I'm sure glad I'm not a real loser like the rest of you bums." That brought a healthy round of laughter from everyone.

Smiling, Holles said, "That's a good way to describe all of us. As compulsive gamblers, we're all losers."

"Seriously," Mike continued, "before I met Rita, I had been a loser all my life." He looked at Rita. "Something I never told you, and I want to be honest now"—he was staring at her—"is that the reason I lost my first wife is because of my gambling. I destroyed our relationship and everything we had. Then I went for years, living in my own little world, powerless to a disease I thought I could regulate myself." His eyes shifted to the circle of people who were watching him. "I even entered my relationship with Rita thinking that I could control it all. I was helpless in the end." He looked at Rita again. "Without an incredible, beautiful person like you, I would have lost everything again, and would have been the biggest loser that ever lived."

The evening in the basement of the church was like that, touching.

In the car afterward he looked over at her and said, "Thank you for being here tonight."

She studied him. "You're really trying to beat this, aren't you?" she said.

"Like I said, I never thought I'd end up living in the basement of a church."

From what he had told her, all of his Gamblers Anonymous meetings were in the basements of churches.

He smacked his lips. "Are you hungry?" he asked.

"Starved."

"Let's pick up Greg and go someplace where we can get something to drink and have a good steak." He started the car and put it in gear.

Feeling guilty, she said, "I don't need anything to drink."

"Oh, yes, we're at least going to make a toast to your promotion as the chief criminal investigator for the state of Wisconsin."

Since the appointment had been made, she had been commuting back and forth between Milwaukee and Madison. They had found a new home and had been spending the weekends in it. The rest of the time, they were living in Milwaukee so that Greg and Mike could finish the academic year. She said, "Fine," then, "Mike, I'm concerned about Greg."

He must have known what she was thinking about because he said, "We're not taking him out of school. It's not like he has to start another school in the middle of the semester."

"No, it's not that. I'm worried about him losing his friends."

"I don't mean to sound rude, but it's not like he has many friends right now."

"He has friends," she insisted.

"Sure, he has acquaintances. People like him. He's turning into a likable young man. But he's also someone who's had a lot of trauma in his life, especially in recent years. I think he's withdrawn; perhaps he's even become a bit introverted. He doesn't want to get hurt again. Who does?"

Rita quietly said, "That's why I think maybe I should take him to a psychiatrist or a psychologist."

They were driving under the streetlights, which cast yellow images into the car. The yellow lights flashed on and off, as if somehow controlled by the dividers in the pavement.

"Believe me, I've been around kids his age a lot of years, and there's no need to panic. I say the change of environment is going to do him good. Before you know it, he'll have left the past behind and have a whole new set of friends. This is a good place to live."

She looked at him, flashing in and out of the shadows. "You think so?"

Her anxiety was relieved the moment they arrived at their new home and got out of the car. The home sat in a quiet residential neighborhood on the northwest side of Madison. It was a large wood house that sat back in the trees of almost two acres of snow. Yellow floodlights illuminated the lot. Suddenly, out of nowhere, a snowball hit her. She heard Greg giggling. Charging, she followed the sounds. Next thing she knew, she heard another voice giggling. She spotted Greg trying to make a getaway. She lunged through the air, nabbing him as he tried to escape from her. He went down in the snow. A boy she hadn't seen before stood over her and Greg. He said, "I wish my mom was as cool as your mom."

Greg introduced him. He was Alex Barnes. Greg said, "Can he have supper with us? I mean, can we order something like pizza and have it delivered?"

Alex was a skinny, blond-haired kid. He said, "They deliver pizza here. We order it every Friday night."

Mike appeared. Greg introduced him too. Mike asked, "Alex, is that all right with your mother and father?"

The two boys went to check.

Mike helped Rita up out of the snow. He said, "See what I mean? Do you feel better now?"

She didn't say. They walked to the house that was still barren of furniture. It was much larger than their Delafield house, much larger than anyplace she had ever lived. It was a good night. She and Mike made love. Yes, she was feeling better. And thinking too. She was still feeling good the next morning when she woke up in the predawn gray. Sometime during the night the answer had come to her. She thought she knew how Al Hoeveler had gained control of Whitaker. She dressed, went through the empty house to the kitchen, and made a pot of coffee, from which she filled an insulated cup, one that she normally carried in the car with her when she now drove back and forth between Milwaukee and Madison. She wrote out a note for Mike and Greg, then left the house.

In a rural area outside of Delafield, she found Chad Whitaker's home. It sat out of sight on a road marked as "Private Residence: No Trespassers." A mansion hidden in the trees.

A kindly woman in her sixties answered the door. She was dressed in a sweater and slacks, and was very formal in how she talked about Chad Whitaker.

Rita waited in the marble foyer while the older woman went in search of him. Then she returned to get Rita.

Whitaker was in the indoor pool and didn't bother to get out. Instead he treaded water and made small talk until the older woman was out of earshot.

Once the servant was gone, he said, "I'm sorry to hear about how things have been going in the CID." He didn't sound sorry. "This has been a sad time for all of you."

She replied, "And I'm sorry about Howie."

His hands and feet moved comfortably in the water, keeping him afloat. "A bad apple."

"I was alone with him when he died," she said.

"So I heard."

"Not much gets past you, does it?"

He smiled smugly. "You might say I've built my business by keeping informed."

"Speaking of business, in my business we have something that the courts take very seriously. It's called a dying confession. It's when someone is at the point of death and makes a confession."

Whitaker swam to the side of the pool and held on. "I know what it is. What's your point?"

"My point is, Howie made a dying confession to me."

"You'll never get away with this. I'll have a team of lawyers after you within the hour."

"Fine, but things will turn real ugly for you before it's all over."

"What do you want?"

She shrugged. "I'm a practical person. I know how a lengthy investigation can tie up resources, and in the end we may have managed to do little more than ruin your name."

"I'm listening."

"You closed up and left the state once. I want you to do it again. In return, I'll close my investigation."

"I won't be pushed around."

"Fine, but I won't wait very long."

He laughed at her.

She turned and left. But she didn't go home. Didn't want to right away. Instead, she drove to St. Luke's Hospital and visited the child abuse wing. Though she was depressed, visiting with the children in the wing made her feel like she was doing something productive. She helped feed one of the children lunch. She chatted with the hospital staff for a while, then set out for Madison.

Though it took only an hour to get back, it seemed like a long time. Why had she done such a stupid thing—confronting Chad Whitaker? she asked herself. She felt dirty and cheap. Depressed. Her head was throbbing again.

At home, Greg was excited. Everyone had been calling, he told her. Where had she been? Vince had called. Charlie had called. "Don't worry," Mike said. "I taped it for you."

He started the videotape. There was Chad Whitaker, announcing his decision to abandon the Milwaukee super-hospital project.

Rita took a deep breath. When she did so, she experienced an unmistakable feeling of regret. She was suddenly sorry she hadn't made the stakes higher. She glanced at Mike. Their eyes made contact for just a moment. He seemed to have seen something in her eyes, something that frightened him. He looked away.